High Hopes Tavern

Ken Nunn

Copyright © 2012 Ken Nunn

Library of Congress Control Number: 2012944550

All rights reserved.

ISBN-13: 978-1-938766-01-5

DEDICATION

This book is dedicated to my brother, Harry, my father, Arthur and my mother, Leona.
They have gone to Heaven, but are alive and well in my heart.
They left me a heritage of hope, for which I am grateful every day.

CONTENTS

	Acknowledgments	i
1	The Missing Piece	1
2	Girls' Day At The Beach	12
3	"When Do I Start?"	20
4	Meeting The Grande Dame	24
5	Recollections	32
6	Hand-Me-Down Dreams	35
7	The Sail Sale	38
8	Schmoozing The Cruising	43
9	New Kid On The Block	48
10	An Unwelcome Letter	52
11	New Friends	55
12	A Potential Problem	70
13	Caught Off Guard	75
14	"Papa, What's This Letter All About?"	82
15	They Might Come To Blows, Papa!	88
16	Two Ladies And A Princess	98

17	Action Plan	104
18	Family Time	112
19	"May I Help You With Your Strap?"	115
20	Emotions	121
21	Could It Be?	126
22	Something To Consider	135
23	Fire!	139
24	Sam…It's Me, Gary!	148
25	A Changing Tide	153
26	The Truth	157
27	Clarice And Daniel, This Is Kevin Preston	166
28	Betrayed	177
29	We've Got A Deal	183
30	Dollars and Lots Of Change…All In One Night	192
31	Lucky…It's Clarice Calling	197
32	A Lesson For The Preacher	202
33	The Inspector Is Here To See You…	208
34	The Grand Re-Opening	215
35	Lauding Lauderdale	220
36	Call Her First	226

37	An Elderly Customer	239
38	A Dream Fulfilled	244
	About The Author	251

ACKNOWLEDGMENTS

Jay Gordon

I am deeply appreciative to Jay Gordon for all he has done to assist me in realizing my dream to write a novel. He told me it wouldn't be easy -- and was he right. He taught me to read, read, read. I learned plot development, how to create characters, how to sharpen my punctuation skills, and far too many additional literary aspects to list here.

Jay continued to work with me on editing my book, ignoring my temper tantrums when we didn't always agree. He taught me so many things about writing. The one that stands out the most and I'm confident every author will agree, "writing a book is easy, editing is a… well, I'll be nice…tedious!

Thank you for everything, Jay.

Stephanie Chatten

To my friend and publishing advisor, Stephanie Chatten of Emerald Chasm Entertainment.

Your artistic talents and publishing skills were invaluable.

Rob Fountain

Thank you for your technical support and listening to me scream when my computer decided to die.

To the professionals and friends who offered advice and encouragement. Debts of gratitude are also owed to the venues used to create the imagery of the fictional High Hopes Tavern.

Many Fort Lauderdale companies were mentioned as homage for their quality of service and products, not for any remuneration.

Princess Cruise Line © is a ™ of Princess Cruise Line Ltd. ©

CHAPTER 1

THE MISSING PIECE

The high energy crowd at the High Hopes Tavern converged around the half-dozen TV sets as the onscreen action reached a crescendo. It was a religious fervor reminiscent of their ancestors around an intense wood fire. Except they gnawed on chicken wings rather than bison bones. Men perched on barstools with a splintering of rowdy women unfurling nearby like birds on a telephone wire. Some gathered in the main bar for a few minutes and left, replaced by others, drawn to the excitement on the oversized TV sets. A few stood with their hands grasping the shoulder of a loved one. Others clasped their hands behind their heads.

A few stood with a hand making an occasional stroke around the shoulder or down the back of an agreeable companion of the opposite sex. They all gawked in near silence as the Miami Dolphins quarterback dropped back to pass. Two receivers darted down the field. Undaunted by two mammoth pass rushers, the quarterback lofted the football fifty yards down the field. No one breathed; everything became slow motion. Groans erupted from the 'Fins' faithful as the ball spiraled past the receiver's outstretched hands. A handful of Buffalo Bills fans cheered and shared high fives. Normal sounds resumed in the bar.

The High Hopes Tavern is not a sports bar, so the TV sets served only for viewing purposes. Management would not allow the distracting sound of televisions to interfere with the ambiance of an upscale tavern. The game's momentum shifted. Roars of celebration and boos of dismay, continued loud and boisterous in response to each play.

To some, football is an archaic means of transferring aggression suggestive of the Roman gladiators. For football fanatics, whose Sunday afternoon ritual is cemented in the broadcast of the local National Football League game, the action on the field was understandable. They gloated on the advantage of the TV close-ups, not available in the stadium. The closed captions for the hearing impaired, skimming across the bottom of the screen, lagged behind the action, confirming what they saw but could not hear. They were viewing high definition muscular bodies on a high definition TV, which captured the attention of the women at the bar.

Nancy Larkin, "Lucky" to her friends, heard the fuss as she reached her favorite watering hole. If she preferred quiet, she could have stayed at the Palms Bar in the hotel where she worked. It was a greater allure to be with boisterous men in a den of high excitement. She thought, *There may be a few women inside, but the numbers are in my favor. It's about time a little more estrogen seeped into that pool of testosterone.*

She paused a moment before leaving the blistering Fort Lauderdale sunshine for the cool, dim interior of the High Hopes Tavern. She smiled and thought, *A reasonable person might wonder why a front desk agent at a high end hotel would leave work to decompress at a neighborhood tavern with a bunch of locals.* She threw back her shoulders, affixed her most charming smile, and ventured inside.

Who was ever happy being reasonable? she thought. Judging from the high noise level, Mr. Right could be here tonight. Even Mr. Right *Now*.

Lucky is a Dolphins fan and blended comfortably with the crowd. The room grew silent as the kicker took two swift steps forward. He kicked the ball toward the distant U-shaped goal post. Seconds later the referees lifted their arms, signaling a field goal and three points. The Miami Dolphins tied the game with four seconds left.

The locals, some dressed in Miami Dolphins logoed shirts and hats, cheered and high fived each other. A sprinkling of boos erupted from the Buffalo visitors, who were in town to soak up Fort Lauderdale's winter sun. Their Bills had let them down.

The information about going into overtime jogged across the bottom of the TV screens. The noise level returned to normal decibels as the fans broke loose from the TVs to get refills.

"Hey, Antonio. The Dolphins just tied the game. Can you turn the sound on for the overtime?"

Antonio handed the remote control to one of the locals. "It's my head if Mario walks in anytime soon. You know he doesn't want the sound on."

"We'll take the blame, Antonio."

A coin toss always decides which team will receive the ball first. Overtime is scheduled for fifteen minutes; however, the game is over once one of the two teams scores.

The heat in September usually favors the hometown Miami Dolphins. "Gentlemen, this is heads, the other side, tails," the referee explained showing each team captain a shiny coin. "Buffalo, you're the visiting team, it's your call."

"Heads," the Buffalo Bills team captain yelled. The coin flipped several times in the air, before it dropped on the beaten-down grass trampled by players who jiggled the cylinder on the scales dangerously close to the three hundred pound mark.

"Heads it is. Buffalo will get the ball first," the referee indicated which team would defend which goal.

Lucky nudged her way toward Pete and Antonio as they smiled from where they stood sentry behind the bar. Antonio, her favorite of the two, slid a cocktail napkin in front of her. He leaned across the bar and kissed her on the cheek.

"Your usual, Lucky?"

"Sure, after a long day, why not? My feet are killing me and the sun is scorching. You would think, after all these years of living in Fort Lauderdale, I would be accustomed to sweltering."

"Lucky, I feel the same way, but don't we enjoy those warm temperatures when our neighbors up north are freezing?"

The faithful gathered at the screens again after the obligatory commercials expounding the virtues of everything from car insurance to fast-food chains.

The MetLife blimp provided an aerial view of the stadium where sports fans were treated to unfolding views of the ocean, the palm trees, and high-rise condominiums off in the distance. The blimp flew around lazy clouds and panned the aggressively blue ocean waters characteristic of South Florida. The camera then zoomed back to the field.

Lucky rejoined her fellow fans.

Players from each side stood along the sidelines, shedding the towels protecting their heads from the heat. They awaited the ensuing kickoff. The huge fans set up at each side of the benches to cool the players whirled at full speed.

The Miami kicker walloped the ball. The Buffalo kick return specialist caught it on the five yard line.

"I'm running this sucker back all the way," he shouted with confidence to his teammates blocking in front of him.

He hotfooted toward the ten yard line, the twenty, the thirty. He dodged and twisted four more yards before two sweaty hands tackled him to the ground. Buffalo would begin their drive for a score from an advantageous spot on the field.

On the first down, the Bills quarterback threw a perfect spiraling dart to their wide receiver. He was tackled, but not before gaining an additional twenty yards.

The Miami fans screamed. "Defense," followed by two pounding slaps on the seats in front of them. "Defense, defense!" They continued encouraging the 'Fins to dig in and get the ball back.

The TV camera crew panned the stadium, stopping at two shirtless males holding a big, "D" next to a huge replica of a fence. Many fans from both teams sported painted faces with their team logo and colors. The weather in South Florida always drew a respectable number of supporters from the opposing team, especially those from cooler climes.

Another first down and ten for the Bills! The quarterback faded back to pass. In an instant he heard the loud grunts of the lineman and thundering clicking cleats. He lowered his head and skirted one pass rusher but was quickly smothered by two other Dolphin defenders. The screams of, "Defense, defense!" grew even louder. The Miami faithful at the tavern joined in.

After huddling, both teams lined up. The Bills

quarterback dropped back to pass. A Miami player tipped the ascending ball, propelling it farther into the air. It was caught by a surprised, but alert, Dolphin player. He clutched the ball with both arms and galloped toward the Buffalo goal, accompanied by a phalanx of three other Dolphin defenders. Without a Buffalo player close by, the crowd danced with their feet and hands in a jumble of bear hugs as the Dolphin player crossed the goal line.

The referee signaled a touchdown!

The play-by-play commentator yelled, "What a game. The Miami Dolphins' will win this game 26-20 after coming back from a fourth quarter deficit. We now take you to Dallas for the four o'clock game between the New York Giants and the Dallas Cowboys."

"Wow, what a thriller," Lucky said to Antonio. "To win the season opener is like getting on a roller coaster. Any season comes with lots of ups and downs. At the end of the ride you're either glad it's over--or you continue to the playoffs. *Maybe* even the Super Bowl!"

She overheard an obviously gay customer jokingly ask his more sports minded buddy if the Super Bowl was a large chafing dish. Lucky almost spit out her wine laughing.

Antonio returned, "Another glass of wine, Lucky?"

"A Dolphin victory deserves as much."

She stared at him as he leaned back to pull a bottle of Sterling Chardonnay from the cooler. Lucky thought, *I would certainly welcome a little illegal use of his hands.* She wondered, *Maybe I'm not his type.*

A generous pour was the norm, which Lucky especially appreciated today.

At age forty, Antonio Castellanos' smooth, tanned Brazilian skin and well-built frame always lured Lucky into carnal thoughts. His body smelled of coconut bath oil. She sifted through her dainty purse to retrieve a lipstick. With a hunter's instinct she applied a generous coat of her signature *Crimson Red*. "George Clooney, if you're in town--

this could be your lucky night!"

After the game, the crowd dwindled. Only the regulars and a handful of visitors remained. With the same hustle and precision of a grounds crew at the stadium, busboys gathered up the used glasses and reset the tables for later arriving guests. Lucky settled into her favorite seat, which allowed an unobstructed view of the cabin cruisers, yachts, and sailboats motoring along the celebrated Intracoastal.

"You know, Antonio, sometimes my life feels like a giant puzzle. All the parts are in place, except the big piece of blue sky still in the box. For me, the missing chunk to complete the puzzle is a man who cares about me -- as much as I care about him. Gee Antonio, are you a piece of blue sky for some lucky girl, or are you still looking for your own piece of blue sky?"

"It's a puzzlement," he responded. "Uh-oh, Yul Brenner beat me to that remark in, 'The King and I."

"Look at the couple on the other side of the bar. They seem to be making sweet music. I can't help staring at them. You can tell they care for each other." She was pensive for a moment before continuing. "I'm happy for them, but I can't help wondering when it's going to be *my turn.*"

Luckys' excitement over the Dolphins victory began to fade. She became riveted by a kaleidoscope of melancholy memories that deepened as she focused on the couple in the shadows. Across the room, the woman loosened the top two buttons of the gentleman's shirt and tickled tiny circles in his silky chest. He lifted her hands and nibbled her fingers.

Lucky looked back at Antonio.

"I'm thirty-eight. In my previous life as a flight attendant, I traveled all over the world. Most people only dream of places I've visited. London, Paris, Rome, Australia, Asia, and my personal favorite, Shannon. Sure, it's exciting, but most pleasures in life are better when they are shared."

"You will be happy someday, Lucky. Trust me, you *will* be. With your looks and how well you've taken care of yourself, you're ahead of the game. You're the kind of woman other women like and men are comfortable with."

"Thank you, Antonio. I struggle to maintain my appearance, but it's worth the effort."

"You know I'll do anything I can to help you find happiness. The crowd is picking up again. I better keep my eyes on the rest of the bar. You know Mario. He gets antsy when customers wait too long for a refill."

Mario emerged from his mini-office. He mumbled to himself as he made his way behind the bar for a quick exchange of animated conversation with Antonio. He left Antonio with a pleasant smile and a hint of laughter as he walked from behind the bar to slip onto the seat next to Lucky.

"What's up, gorgeous?"

"Not much, Mario. It was a grueling day -- between the heat and standing on my feet for hours. The best news: The 'Fins won in overtime."

Mario gestured to Antonio, "When Lucky's ready, she deserves a refill on the house."

"Thanks, handsome, you're very kind." She reached over to squeeze his hand.

She took a moment to savor Mario's good looks. Six foot one, with a full head of well-groomed wavy salt-and-pepper hair, a good match with his olive skin. He wore a crisp white shirt, and pressed slacks, along with spit polished shoes. A hint of *Givenchy Gentlemen* cologne added a touch of masculine elegance. At sixty-eight, he was a catch for women who preferred a mature man.

"So, Mario, how's the emphysema? I'm sure this heat doesn't help."

"Yeah, sometimes it makes me cranky. It could just be an excuse for bad behavior. Wouldn't any man looking at such a beautiful lady be short of breath?"

"Every time I listen to you, I place another dollar in my

savings jar for a trip to Italy."

"Before I blush, let me change the subject and ask how Samantha's doing"

"She's on her way here for a drink. She sounded stressed when she called.

"Well whatever's bothering her, I'm sure a refreshing cocktail should alter her mood. I need to get back to the office; Melanie is due any minute."

Lucky raised her glass with a nod and wink. "Thanks again for the drink."

"Here's my beautiful daughter now, I'll catch ya later. Look out for Antonio. Don't let him seduce you. A beautiful lady isn't safe in this place."

What makes you think I won't seduce him?" she laughed.

He joined Melanie in the office as she skimmed the daily lunch receipts. He winced at her ensemble of a flowery sun dress, oversized sandals, and her sunglasses at rest above her forehead.

He resisted the impulse to comment on her quirky outfit. With a hopeful tone he asked, "Any busier today"?

"No, we weren't too busy, Papa." She brushed her long raven hair back from her face and secured it with a clip. Remember, we're coming to the end of summer but the snowbirds are still at their northern nests. Business is always quieter without our winter time residents."

"I can't wait until they come back," Mario sighed. "You have something most girls in their twenties don't, a controlling interest in a tavern. I can't afford to be too reserved about our reserves."

"Papa, at the risk of repeating myself, I am not interested in taking over the business. I'll soon earn my degree in Interior Design. Why study so hard at what I want to do -- and make a U-turn?"

He kissed Melanie's forehead and whispered, "We can talk about this later, *cara mia*? Time to get back out front and greet our customers."

He joined Lucky and Samantha at the bar. "Hi Sam, I was just asking Lucky about you. How was your day at work? Care to share with Papa?"

Lucky chimed in, "Tell him Sam. Perhaps Mario can help."

"Ah, Mario, the problem is my job -- as usual. I thought I was going to make reasonable money at the Peacock's Feather. I expected someday I would be a manager of the restaurant. So far, I sense a dead end."

Mario gestured to Antonio to signal Sam's arrival. He hustled to where the three of them sat.

"Hey, Sam," Antonio said with a smile." A pleasure to see you again, sweetheart. Ya drinkin' today?"

"Just a Diet Coke, thanks."

"Put it on my tab," Mario motioned to Antonio.

"Thanks Mario. Hmm, perhaps I should order a beer or something stiffer--something more likely to drain the pain of my day at work."

"You're welcome to a free upgrade if you'd like something more potent."

"I better not, but thanks, Mario."

"On another note, I've heard you're an excellent worker, Sam."

"My boss tells me I am. The customers I wait on treat me well. I'm disappointed by the lack of opportunity to advance. I want to learn the management side of the business as well as wait tables. I mentioned this upfront during my interview with him. He seems to have conveniently forgotten."

"Would you be interested in working here if there were an opening, Sam?"

"Are you kidding? In a heartbeat. I think we're a good fit, Mario. Does this mean you need a waitress?"

"Well, yes, but I'm also looking for someone who can host once the busy season starts. Three nights of the week you would wait tables; two nights, you would be the hostess."

"Okay, Mario, should I play hard to get or just ask, 'when do I start?'"

"Let's discuss this in private. How's tomorrow afternoon at four-thirty?"

"Sure thing. I'm off and I'll be here!"

"Gotta run, ladies. Until tomorrow, Sam."

Lucky patted Sam on the shoulder, "Things are certainly looking up for you. You're a perfect fit for this job."

"I always thought you were suited to be a flight attendant. I never understood why you left a glamorous job at the airline. I thought you enjoyed what you were doing."

"The industry changed. After a while the traveling got to me. I couldn't stand being cramped any longer in a giant bus with wings. There's no fun in bouncing around the sky at 35,000 feet."

"Well, now you're settled on the ground, and we're both off tomorrow. Why don't we plan a day at the beach?"

"I like the idea, Sam. Maybe I can snare one of those macho puppies who seem to *live* at the beach. Lord knows, when it comes to the sport of romance, I haven't scored.

CHAPTER 2

GIRLS' DAY AT THE BEACH

The ladies arrived at the beach early and well ahead of the visitors and residents who would come later. They had selected a spot when a well-tanned, sandy-haired young man strolled toward them.

"Beautiful young ladies such as yourselves should be seated in chairs with an umbrella for shade, rather than lying on a sandy beach blanket. The cost is seven dollars for the whole day," he said with a seductive grin.

"You're not too shabby looking yourself, honey. The compliment and fair price landed you a rental."

He began his performance. They watched his flexing muscles in silent pleasure. He plunged the umbrella pole into the sand and swayed it to secure it in place. By the time he brought the chairs, they were both taking short breaths. They sent him on his way with a generous tip and began to spread their large beach blanket. They claimed more space than necessary on the soft white sand. The salty ocean air signaled the satisfaction of a day of freedom from work.

Sam asked, "Aren't we the decadent girls today?

"At last, *we* get to relax. The eye candy ain't bad either," Lucky giggled.

"Yeah, where's the waitress with my drink?"

As she sank into the chair, Sam pulled off her T-shirt, to expose a skimpy, but fashionable blue and white two-piece bathing suit. Lucky wore a more sedate one piece version, also blue.

They settled in and began the ritual of slathering sunscreen on themselves and each other.

"Gee, Lucky, you must go to the beach a lot more than I do. Your bottle of sunscreen is so much bigger than mine."

"Sad to say, Sam, my body is a bit larger too."

The smoke from a nearby barbecue pit began to fade, but the smell of charcoal lingered as a man brushed sauce on a selection of meats.

A small cabin cruiser, its engines off, bobbed several yards beyond the designated swimming zone. A potbellied, shirtless man fished off the bow as his lady companion dove into the water. She swam a few yards and stopped to tread water. Minutes later she returned to grab the ladder on the side of the boat to pull herself back on deck.

More sun-worshipers began to fill up the beach. A short distance away, two teams of young men gathered to play volleyball. Lucky and Sam could catch bits of testosterone-fueled chatter. Even more enjoyable was their narcissistic posing. The ladies enjoyed the beach ballet of muscle motion.

"How long y' think before one of them reaches too high and loses his trunks?" Sam asked.

"I don't relish the idea of spending the night in jail, so I'm not going to pull them down myself." Lucky said with a wink.

"Let's hit the water and keep ourselves from behind the wire mesh of a police car."

They kicked off their flip-flops and hopped toward the surf, shrieking as their feet skimmed the hot sand.

Sam leaned toward Lucky as they treaded water.

"You know I get together with Mario today about the job at High Hopes Tavern. Even though he's a friend, I'm nervous. Any helpful hints?"

"Don't be nervous, he's a sweetheart. I've known him for a long time, Sam. He expects his employees to be loyal, on time, and caring about customer service. He also thinks it's important for them to work as a team. Customers pick up on stuff like that."

They swished around the water and chatted before they were distracted by the warble of a siren. An emergency vehicle with lights flashing came into view as it slowed down on A1A. A second emergency vehicle slowed and parked behind it.

"I wonder what's going on?"

Lucky and Sam swam toward the beach. Once they could stand in the water, they were pushed along by a series of waves until they reached the waters' edge.

A small number of spectators gathered on the beach. Paramedics jogged toward a lone lifeguard. They carried a stretcher and other medical equipment to assist a man who had been rescued from the sea.

Lucky and Sam hurried to join the growing throng of onlookers lured by the action.

The paramedics hustled, methodically pumping

seawater out of the victim's stomach. Lucky squirmed and chomped on her fingernails, not missing a finger. Oh please, God, let this man live. *My mother*, she thought to herself. Lucky's emotions flipped from hope to remembrance. Her mind filled with flashbacks. She envisioned her mother. Just four years ago she was hooked up to paraphernalia like this. She watched the man sprawled on the beach. *Come on mister, come on*, she prayed in silence.

"Are you okay, Lucky?"

"Yeah, I had a flashback of my mother's last heart attack. I can still hear the siren blaring. Motorists scrambled, allowing the emergency truck to pass them as we raced to the hospital. I remember sitting next to the paramedic. He had attached an IV bag to her arm, and an oxygen mask covered most of her face. I couldn't even get a clear look at my dying mother."

"I'm so sorry, Lucky. That must have been a traumatic experience."

"Yes, it was". She was admitted to the Coronary Care Unit. I sat next to her bed, holding her hand. The only sound was from the dreadful machinery tracing her heartbeat and her shallow breathing. Her eyes were closed and she appeared to be at peace. I still remember my last words to her just before she slipped away, *Mom, oh mom, I will miss you so much*. She died eight hours after being admitted.

Lucky wiped her eyes and came back to the present as the man coughed and groaned. The paramedics quickly placed a portable oxygen mask over his nose and mouth. They pushed the man back onto the sand as he opened his eyes and struggled to get up.

"Hold on, fella," a paramedic said. "Sir, we need to take you to the hospital."

"Oh my God, I almost drowned," the man muttered as he shifted to a more comfortable position.

Lucky gazed at the white-haired man in his sixties. "He

looks familiar to me. I think I've seen him at High Hopes Tavern."

"Shit, Lucky, you're right," she whispered. "Isn't he the guy who is about fifteen years and a thousand miles behind the local fashion? She thought for a moment and added. "Of course, "O" magazine hasn't featured my wardrobe yet either."

The lifeguard knelt by the victims side as the paramedics prepared to transport him to the hospital. "You're going to be just fine, sir," another paramedic said in a comforting voice. Shouts of support replaced whispers of concern.

The crowd burst into applause. Several of the volleyball players saluted the rescuers with two fingered whistles.

Lucky moved closer to Sam. "Would you mind if I followed the rescue truck to the hospital?"

"Why would you want to do that?"

"I think he might need someone to talk to."

"Sure, if you think it would help. I'm going to stay here until I leave to meet Mario. I don't get many days at the beach, so I want to enjoy every minute."

Lucky slipped a sundress over her bathing suit. She gathered her things and jogged toward the paramedics carrying the stretcher. They balanced the stretcher as they moved along the uneven sand. Another paramedic, carrying a medical bag, followed a few feet behind. She caught up with him.

"Sir, sir?"

"Yes ma'am, what can I do for you?"

"I'm not a relative of the gentleman you saved, but I've seen him at my neighborhood tavern. I'd like to follow you to the hospital in case he needs someone to talk to. I know I would."

"That's kind of you, ma'am. We're taking him to Holy Cross. I'm pretty sure he'll be there overnight."

She soon fell behind the rescue truck since it only slowed at red light intersections while she had to stop for several. As she parked in the visitors' lot, the paramedics came out of the emergency room. She hurried to thank them.

"You guys were such heroes today."

"Thank *you*, ma'am. We're trained to perform. Saving lives is what we aim to do."

Lucky approached the nurses' station a few steps beyond the entrance. "May I visit the gentleman who was just rescued from the beach?"

"You must mean Mr. Kent. The doctor is examining him now. He will be in room 214 later. You can get a visitor's pass at the main entrance."

Lucky picked up her pass but waited a bit to give him time to settle in. She approached the door and thought to herself, Gee, I'm about to visit a man I've never met. She hesitated before knocking.

"Mr. Kent… Mr. Kent?"

"Yes…yes?"

She peeked inside.

"You don't know me. My name is Nancy Larkin. I was on the beach today when you were rescued."

"Yes, Nancy, please come on in. I'm a little hard of hearing so please speak up."

Lucky offered her hand. "You must be exhausted and shaken from your ordeal."

"Yes, you're right. Have we met?"

"No not really. Mr. Kent, to my friends, I'm "Lucky," so please feel free."

"Well, my name is Daniel Dooley Kent, and I go by Mr. Kent." She was surprised by his insistence on formality.

"Mr. Kent, I've seen you at the High Hopes Tavern and thought you might like a visitor after all the excitement today."

"You do look familiar, Lucky. Yes, definitely a close call. I'm grateful to be alive. How sweet of you to come. I've never experienced a sense of welcome at the High

Hopes Tavern. Your visit is a unexpected pleasure.

"You *do* make quite a presence at the tavern, Mr. Kent."

"Yes, Lucky, my wardrobe may be somewhat outdated and unconventional for the area, but I don't believe in changing to please others. Despite the heat, I'm comfortable in my blue blazer ensemble."

"The monogrammed cuffs on your shirts and your pressed slacks are impressive. The fancy shoes add distinction to your blue blazer. Definitely, an ensemble."

"I suppose it's okay to keep my narrow mustache as a trademark?" he asked playfully.

Lucky continued in that mood. "I suppose the elegant walking cane is part of the uniform?"

"Ah yes. My famous hand carved black cane with the silver lion's head. Let's keep this our secret but it's not needed for support. Just my little bit of showmanship. I guess my style doesn't quite fit in at the tavern."

"Where are you from, Mr. Kent?"

"Okay, now that we're becoming friends, let's forego the 'Mr. Kent."

"Thank you, Daniel."

"I was born in Boston, where I lived until I retired eight years ago. Most of my ancestors were educators. I followed suit, becoming an English professor at Harvard. My investments and pension are good to me. After retiring, I decided to relocate to Fort Lauderdale. No more shoveling snow and freezing winter temperatures for me. You don't have to shovel the sunshine! I still maintain a small place outside Boston, which I rent to a deserving young couple."

"What do you do, Lucky?'

"I was a flight attendant for almost fifteen years. Now I am a front desk clerk at the Crystal Sands Hotel on the beach."

"Why did you decide to stop being a flight attendant, Lucky?"

"The airline business changed a lot. I grew tired of the fast pace of travel. Speaking of a fast pace, I still have several errands to run. I should be getting on my way. I'm sure we'll talk again at the tavern."

"Sure thing, Lucky. That's something to which I look forward. I'm not much of a social person. You, though, have restored my hope that there are still some genuinely caring people waiting to be discovered."

Closing the door behind her, she glanced back, and was sure she saw a misting in his eyes.

CHAPTER 3

"WHEN DO I START?"

Built in the sixties, and a piece of vintage Fort Lauderdale architecture, the High Hopes Tavern sits directly on the Intracoastal on a slight incline overlooking the waterway. It slopes down a series of terraces and patios to the water's edge. The tavern's distinct logo, a silhouette of three stately sailing masts, stands alongside the tavern and shifts lazily with the breeze. The front, relatively modest, was outlined at the base by rocks retrieved from the sea following a hurricane years ago. Most of the exterior wood was recovered from dilapidated buildings along the Florida coast. Docked on the Intracoastal is a small cabin cruiser, included in the purchase price of the restaurant.

The relentless summer heat and the salt air from the nearby ocean have not spared the wooden frame from peeling and fading. Inside, the tavern's design is broken up into several spacious enclaves, each with a slightly different nautical theme. Most people gather at the long semi-circular bar, well positioned to give guests a splendid view of the passing sailboats and yachts.

Sam had selected a simply cut tropical dress for her interview. She popped a breath mint and swept into the High Hopes Tavern with a flourish.

It was late afternoon and quiet inside. A small group sat and chatted at the bar. Two couples were enjoying a burger and fries under the awning of the patio. The sun broke through the clouds after a quick passing thunderstorm. Mario sat alone at the other end of the bar carefully poring over invoices. Next to him was a glass of iced-tea with a straw and melted ice. He shook his head, not pleased.

"Excuse me, Mario, I'm early. Should I wait at a table until you're ready?"

"No, no Sam, I could use a break from this depressing paperwork anyway. I like that you're early. Would you care for something to drink?"

"Will I need a drink to get through this interview?" she asked with a smile.

"No, Sam. Not at all."

"Then I'll wait until after we're done."

"I'm impressed by your business approach. The professional way you're dressed also gets extra points. You can put away the notepad. I've known you long enough to believe you'll be a good fit. Let's talk about salary before I forget. I'll start you at eight dollars an hour, plus *all* of your tips. Please keep that detail to yourself. As a hostess you'll earn more. We can negotiate that later."

"You're starting rate is generous, Mario. May I still call you Mario, since I'm going to be an employee?"

"Yes, of course, all my employees do. The off season is the best time to join the team. Being in the restaurant business I'm sure you're aware a couple of months from now it will be hectic with the return of the snowbirds. Those folks who escape the northern winters sure make a difference. You're hired, Sam. I am curious, though, why the High Hopes Tavern? How were we lucky enough to get you?"

"Even if you're not single like me, everyone needs friends. Most people have a favorite place to gather and socialize. The High Hopes Tavern is always welcoming. It's a comfortable getaway where we share problems or celebrate, whichever is appropriate to the occasion. We serve as an automatic alarm system for each other. When someone doesn't show up for happy hour, we check to be sure they're okay. Anyone who sits alone chooses to. Everyone here is treated like a VIP. Did I answer your question?"

With a tear in his eye, he hugged Sam. "Come on... let me take you behind the scene."

They meandered toward the compact kitchen, stopping so Mario could point out things of interest. Charles and Al, two of the four chefs, were prepping the evening's fare. Mario introduced Sam, and explained the operation. They ended up back at the bar.

"I would expect you'll want to give two weeks' notice at the restaurant, Sam."

"Yes, of course, it's customary. A smart person never burns bridges. On the other hand, if they get upset and fire me, I could start here earlier, right?"

"Absolutely, let me know once you've worked out the details."

"Great, now--- about that drink..."

Mario grinned. "I'd like one as well. So, what's your pleasure?"

"I'll take a margarita please with salt. No beer for me today, it's a special day."

Antonio stopped washing glasses and walked toward them. "What will it be, boss?"

"I just hired Sam as a waitress and part-time hostess. She'll have a margarita, and I'll take my usual. And pour yourself one to congratulate Sam."

"Hey, you wrote the rules. No drinking behind the bar. Want to get me fired?"

"I wrote them in *pencil*, Antonio."

"Thanks, but I'll take a rain check, Mario. Welcome, Sam. You look absolutely stunning today. I'll work my magic, and two perfect drinks will appear before your eyes in no time."

She enjoyed Antonio's wizardry and his graceful movements.

Antonio returned with their drinks. "Here you are, guys. A flawless margarita for a flawless lady," He turned to Mario. "A tasteful drink for a tasteful gentleman." They both saluted Antonio-- and then each other before taking the first sip of their drinks.

"All hands on deck," Mario said.

"I'm sure it's going to be smooth sailing, Sam replied."

If only she had been right.

CHAPTER 4

MEETING THE GRANDE DAME

A few blocks from the High Hopes Tavern Lucky swerved to avoid hitting a wayward beagle. She pulled to the curb to rest her head on the steering wheel and gulped for air.

Okay, she thought. *This calls for a glass of wine. What a stroke of luck for my nerves, High Hopes Tavern is only a few blocks away.*

Still shaken, she hurried inside and felt an immediate

sense of relief.

"Hey, Lucky," Sam shouted. "We're over here."

Lucky dodged and twisted between the after-work revelers and stopped only to exchange brief remarks. Seconds later, she reach Sam and Mario.

Mario stood to give Lucky a hug. "Please, take my seat. I want to make a call from the office. You and Sam can enjoy some girl time. If you're still around, I'll see you later."

A chilled glass of Sterling Chardonnay appeared in front of Lucky.

"Your usual, Lucky."

"Thanks, Antonio." She puckered her lips to create the sound of a kiss.

Antonio nodded and grinned as he moved to serve a customer next to them.

"I *need* this chardonnay, Sam. I barely missed making some body's pet beagle a hood ornament. He darted in front of me. For one glorious moment he must have thought he was a greyhound. I jammed on my brakes so hard I nearly needed a change in pantyhose."

"Are you sure you're okay?"

Antonio overheard them. He leaned back in their direction and teased, "Stand up and turn around-- I'll check for stains."

"Don't runway models get seventy-five dollars an hour? A clever bartender might insist nothing's wrong with me that another glass of chardonnay won't fix. You decide."

She returned her attention to Sam. "How did things go with Mario?"

"He saved me from shopping since I already own some black skirts and white blouses."

It took Lucky a moment. "Congratulations! The next drink's on me."

"Hey, if you're buying, I'm drinking. Speaking of people with better luck than they anticipated, how's what's-his-name, the guy who almost drowned?"

"He'll be fine, thanks to the lifeguard and the Emergency Medical Technicians. His name is Daniel Dooley Kent. Don't ya just love it? Turns out, he's a retired English professor from Boston. Taught at *Hahvahd*." She thought for a moment and added, "There's something about him I like."

"You mean sexually?"

"No, Sam-- just in a friendly, quaint manner."

"Was he ever married?"

"I never asked. Why?'

"I'm just curious. With the way he dresses, I thought he could be gay."

"Never asked him that either, but we did talk about his attire. He sort of reminds me of myself in a way. He's well-traveled, successful, but yet is not a happy person. Look at me, all my life I've tried to make someone else happy, only to always end up alone. Did I ever tell you about my first relationship?"

"No. But I've always thought I should learn more ancient history."

Lucky slowly ran a finger around the rim of her wine glass as she collected her thoughts. I could always say, "You're cruisin' for a bruisin' but that might reveal my age. The shocking part is we met at church."

Sam pretended to clutch her heart in alarm, "You... at a church function?"

"Why not, I go to church. We were at a Saturday night social. Billy walked over and asked me to dance. Later, he asked me to dinner the next week."

"So...what happened?"

"Well, I went to dinner with him and enjoyed it more than I expected. We got together for a while. I was sure I was falling in love."

"Billy didn't care that you flew and were out of town quite a lot?"

"He didn't have a problem with that? He was cursed with two problems of his own-- alcoholic and bi-polar. So many times he promised me he would stop drinking, but didn't. When he got drunk, his behavior was both pathetic and disgusting. The alcoholic rants sometimes led to violence. I vowed the first time a person hit me would be the last. The bi-polar illness can be controlled with medication. The alcohol problem got to be so bad, I had no choice but to leave him since he wouldn't go to AA. Sam, he broke my heart."

"Whatever happened to him?"

"I have no idea. He might be dead for all I know. Why does first love have to be so stupid?"

"I don't know. This is the first time you've opened up to me. I sense Billy wasn't your last heartbreak."

"You're right. Before I started coming here, I frequented a bar called, *Water's Edge*. I met a guy there named Mike. The more we learned about each other, the more I liked him. He was so handsome and caring. He had begun seeing another girl, but she worked long hours. Mike told me he was not so sure it would work with her. I still wanted to keep my distance since I can fall in love in a heartbeat. The last thing I wanted to do was get hurt again."

"Are you one of those girls who has a *wash-and-wear* wedding gown tucked away in the trunk of her car?"

"Sam, how did you guess? That's why God invented polyester. That's not to say the ripple of a manly muscle wouldn't make me swoon.

They looked at each other and began to laugh.

Lucky continued, "I was in the bar one evening when Mike walked in. He sat down next to me and ordered his usual gin and tonic without his usual enthusiasm. He confided in me that he had broken up with his girlfriend the night before. My emotions ranged from sorrow for him to jubilation for me. I thought now *I* get a chance."

"I think I can predict where we're going with this, Lucky."

"Yeah, we began to date and within three months,

rented an apartment together. We even took a trip to Niagara Falls. About eight months later he came home from a doctor's appointment with bad news. Turns out he had cancer that was spreading throughout his body. He died about a year later. His death affected me so much. I was overwhelmed. I went to counseling for four months. I still think of him." She wiped a tear from her eye. "We were committed to each other."

Lucky took a photo of him from her wallet. "This was Mike."

"He was handsome. I'm sorry for your loss, Lucky."

"Thanks, Sam, your friendship is an important part of my life. To be truthful, one of my greatest fears is that the best times of my life may be in the past. I bet *you're* having better luck in the romance department."

"*Puhleeze*. My love life would have to reach up to touch the bottom, Sam replied." I've got a few notches in my belt. I still prefer younger men, which probably makes me a bit naïve. I dated one guy for six months or so."

"I thought you might be a chicken hawk."

"No, twenty-five and up is fine."

Why did you break up? What's he doing now?"

"Seven years in prison for armed robbery of a liquor store."

"Good Lord, Sam, maybe the good guys are only on television."

They began to collect their things to leave.

Mario returned to the bar. "Ah, you two are still here. Good, I can use the money." He rubbed his hands together, pretending to be greedy.

"We were getting ready to leave, Mario. Seems to be a good-sized crowd tonight."

"Not bad, not bad, but hey, can you both stay for at least one more? Clarice Thompson called to make a dinner reservation. She should be here in about fifteen minutes."

"Clarice Thompson, you mean the elderly Southern lady who always wears a brimmed hat?"

"That's her, two Grey Goose dry martinis before dinner, and she's off to her usual table."

"I'm not one to argue with martinis, but I need to go …"

"Please, Lucky, I want Sam to meet her since she's going to be working here. It could help for you to make friends with her too. Drinks are on me."

"Okay, Mario, as usual, you win! No more than one, and I'm leaving."

"You, Sam?"

"Sure, Mario, when Lucky mentioned the lady who always wears a brimmed hat, I remembered seeing her before. I guess the time has come to meet the legendary Clarice Thompson. First, I'm going to grab a cigarette. I'll be right back."

Once outside she leaned on the wooden fence to enjoy the fresh breeze and watch a variety of boats sail by. Sometimes people on a boat would wave. She always waved back. The calm waters of the Intracoastal provided a comforting serenity. Sam's New Year's resolution to stop smoking was an annual event. By February she uttered the familiar promise, *I'll quit next year.*

Sam had seen Clarice in the tavern before, but had never exchanged pleasantries. They both hailed from the South, yet exhibited contrasting versions of Southern heritage. Only as a favor to Mario would she stay behind tonight. A lone ashtray sat on a nearby table where she patted out her cigarette. She took a deep breath and headed inside.

The early evening sunlight brightened the inside each time the door to the tavern opened. The brightness intensified as Clarice arrived and lingered for her grand entrance.

Mario walked toward her, "Ah, Clarice how *are* you this fine evening? You look stunning as usual." He pecked each cheek.

"I'm *mahhvelous.*' How stunning to be seen. Being a

Southern lady, I have a certain image to maintain. When I know I will be seen by such a wildly handsome man -- and of course, I'm referring to you -- my standards rise even higher."

"Ah, Clarice, you're the only person who can make a guy with olive skin blush. Come, a cocktail is in order. I'd like you to meet our new waitress, Samantha Burnside. She'll be joining my team soon. She's around here somewhere."

The air-conditioner was set at high chill. Clarice still refreshed herself with an ornate fan as she glided toward the bar.

Lucky stood speaking to a young couple she had checked in at the hotel earlier in the day. Clarice's entrance caught her attention. She leaned toward Antonio and whispered, "Gee, I didn't realize fans were *de rigueur* until after sundown."

They both stared at the fan. One side portrayed an image of Christ praying in Gethsemane, the other featured an ad for a local funeral parlor. Clarice's favorite area is at the end of the bar facing the waterfall. She considers this her amen corner. When she's in the tavern, her favorite seat somehow becomes available. Mario ordered her usual, and excused himself to find Lucky and Sam.

Clarice wore a chic outfit consisting of a tailored lavender suit with a blue silk blouse. A string of pearls draped her neck. The lighting accented an oversized diamond on the hand holding the fan. She wore a wide-brimmed hat, blue to match her heels, belt and handbag. She placed her elegant sun glasses into their case and methodically returned them to her purse.

A former actress, Clarice's career had reached the heights of the dinner theatre circuit. For all her Southern charm and social status, her hairstyle remains in the Johnson era of the late sixties.

Mario found Sam. They greeted customers as they slowly made their way to the amen corner, where Clarice savored her first martini. Sam was beginning to feel relaxed. She walked toward Clarice and offered her hand. "If Mama could see me now -- a poor girl from outside Charleston gets to meet a lady of quality from Savannah. I've been looking forward to this honor. May I introduce myself, Miss Clarice?"

"Of course, you must be Samantha Burnside. We're going to pals, I'm sure."

It could happen. Or not.

CHAPTER 5

RECOLLECTIONS

Lucky walked into to her small, but elegantly furnished, beachfront apartment. Her taste in decorating hinted she was well-travelled. Every room was accented with handicrafts and *objets d'art* gathered from her travels around the world. Each was thoughtfully placed to create a theme and serve as mementos of the time spent in each destination.

She was feeling a bit tipsy, but not at all guilty, about extending her stay at the tavern. Lucky was proud to have helped Sam get the job. As she showered, she heard the rhythmic Latin tone from her cell phone.

With a soapy hand she fumbled for it.

"One minute, please."

She quickly rinsed her body, grabbed a towel, and pressed the speaker button.

"Hi, Lucky. I called to be sure you got home alright."

Yes, I think I'm in one piece, but I'm still checking."

"Hey, thanks for the tips about Mario yesterday. He's interesting. Now I know him even better. I find his Italian flair a little sexy. It's a shame he's a little beyond my age range, but I am looking forward to working with him."

"That's what friends are for, right?" she asked.

"Well, yeah, that-- and borrowing a sexy blouse and pair of shoes now and then. You didn't get to meet Clarice. We looked around and didn't see you."

Two guests from the hotel spotted me. I wanted to welcome them to High Hopes. I'm sure I'll meet Clarice soon. She's a regular for drinks and dinner. I've also been told she can be quite demanding after fortifying herself with a few Grey Goose martinis. I don't want to misjudge her," she continued, as she slipped into a black silk bathrobe.

"Yes, prejudging can get a girl in trouble. Hey, I gotta run. Let's talk tomorrow."

"Sure thing, Sam. Maybe you'll wake up and find Mr. Wonderful on the other pillow."

"No one's been close to my pillow since a cheapskate tooth fairy left me two bits."

She flipped her phone closed, giggled to herself and thought, *How silly to take a shower. Now I'm wide awake.* She poured a glass of Sterling Chardonnay and headed to the bedroom where she sifted through her scattered pile of DVDs. Her fingers stopped at the familiar comfort of *Sleepless In Seattle*.

How pathetic, how many times have I seen this? She popped the DVD into the player and sprawled back into the pile of pillows on her bed.

As she watched the sad man on the screen, she became distracted by recollections of her own romantic disappointments.

The sadness continued to gnaw at her and grew more hurtful as she recalled the brief time she dated Francisco. He was another failed attempt at romance she hadn't mention to Sam. She met him at the High Hopes Tavern while he was visiting from San Juan. He was only in town for a long weekend.

Lucky took some time off so they could spend their days touring the sights of Fort Lauderdale. They dined out each evening, usually at one of the more secluded restaurants. Even more satisfying was the pause in bleak, lonely nights of sleeping alone. She would awaken to feel Francisco's strong arm around her waist. She took comfort, even for a brief time, knowing half of her bed was occupied. She flew to San Juan for long weekends for the next two months.

Shortly after her last visit, Francisco called with a suspicious number of reasons why the relationship wouldn't work.

She dabbed away tears while viewing a scene where Walter, Annie's fiancée, meets his future in-laws at a Christmas Eve dinner. At that point, her memories of Francisco displaced any possibility to focus on the film. She had vivid recollections of the first time she met his friends. She kept trying to focus.

I'm not going to cry again, she thought. *Focus, focus, focus.*

She continued to view the film long enough to enjoy the happy ending.

It's time to reevaluate my desires, she thought to herself. *I must appreciate what I have and stop fretting over what I want.*

As she slipped the DVD back into its sleeve, she continued to let a lesson of the film sink in. *Fantasies can be comforting, but they do not fill the other side of the bed. Hey, there's a reason, why bedding comes with two pillows.*

CHAPTER 6

HAND-ME-DOWN DREAMS

It was half an hour after the bar closed. Antonio completed his end of the shift survey of the liquor on hand, noting what Mario would need to order later in the day. He grabbed a cigarette from his shirt pocket. *Time to count my tips.*

He set a cup with a small amount of water on the bar to hold his cigarette ashes. *When am I going to quit this stupid habit?* he thought, as he separated the bills by denomination. His cell phone rang. *At this time of night only my honey would be calling.*

Antonio took a drag on his cigarette and answered the call. "Hi baby, how are you? I appreciate your patience, sweetie. "I'm counting my tips, but the pile isn't too high tonight. I'll be on my way shortly."

He listened a moment as he continued to count. "If there's some roast beef left, a sandwich would be a nice welcome. Maybe with some swiss-cheese with mustard and a pickle? Wait -- after four years, why am I telling you how I like my sandwich? You are the same lover I left at home this morning, right?"

Antonio heard laughter through the phone. "I guess you were wondering the same thing, babe. Thanks for making the sandwich and don't forget some potato salad and a cold one."

He returned the laughter. "What, I'm not dessert enough for you?" Hey, I gotta run, it sounds like Melanie and Mario are arguing in the office. See you soon. Love ya." Antonio closed his phone.

The voice level dropped as he knocked on the door to say goodnight.

He smiled at Melanie. "I didn't think you were going to stop by tonight."

"I wish I'd stayed home. Papa and I are exploring some differences. I'm sure I sounded kind of cranky. I promise I'll be more cheerful tomorrow."

As he left, the shouting resumed almost before the door closed. *Here we go again*, he thought. *She doesn't want ownership in the place, yet she argues with Mario about his business decisions. It's not my concern. I'm headed home to my honey.*

The uproar continued. "Why would you even think of hiring another waitress during the slow season, Papa?"

"Sam has a hell of a lot of experience. She hates the job she's in. She's a real catch, Melanie. Besides, when did you begin to take an interest in the place?"

"When you make too many risky decisions, papa. I understand how much this place means to you. It's still a business. Times are still tough and people are not drinking and dining out like they used to."

"Melanie, when you take over, you can make the hiring decisions. Until then, I will. So you know, I'm also looking for a part-time bartender to help Antonio. He's registering for his final semester at culinary school and needs more time off."

"I've told you several times, I don't want to take over the business. Papa, you've reminded me before that grandma and grandpa grew up poor in Italy. At times, food was scarce. I can't imagine how you maintained the strength to grow vegetables and learn how to cook so you could feed the family."

"My dream, Melanie, was to open a winery or restaurant."

"And I respect your dream. You made enormous sacrifices in your life to provide for us." She reached over and gently touched his hand. "We will always be grateful for that, papa. By providing for us, you enriched our ability to achieve our own potential. It's only because of you I don't need to settle for hand-me-down dreams."

CHAPTER 7

THE SAIL SALE

Summer afternoon thunderstorms are as common in South Florida as "early bird" dinners. At times the rain can be torrential and the lightning fearful. They generally pass quickly, occasionally leaving a radiant rainbow as an apology for any inconvenience. This day was no different. Sam sought shelter underneath the awning of a travel agency. The sound of the rain pelting the pavement grew louder. She stepped back closer to the office window to avoid getting soaked. A brightly colored sign enticed, "Have We Got A Sail For You!"

The rain continued forcefully. Small pockets of puddles began to assemble close to the curb. *What the hell*, she thought, *I might as well dry off and see what the prices are."*

The travel agent set aside her paperwork and greeted Sam. "How may I help you with some travel plans,

Miss...?" The agent paused to hear her last name.

"Burnside, Samantha Burnside. My friends call me Sam. I saw your cruise poster in the window."

"I'm glad you came in, Sam. I'm Eileen Golden." She offered her hand.

"I'm just curious how much cruises cost. I've never been on one, but always thought it might be fun."

"Were you thinking of the Caribbean -- or perhaps a trip through the Panama Canal? We can help you plan travel anywhere in the world."

"I'm not sure. I was hoping you could help fill in those blanks for me."

When would you like to sail?"

"I don't know for sure. I'm starting a new job in a few weeks. The challenge is to squeeze in a few days vacation before starting a new job. There's also the question of whether my friend can join me."

Eileen selected several brochures from a rack behind her. She spread an array on her desk in front of Sam. The Caribbean brochure caught her attention. Sam was immediately attracted to the sense of relaxation portrayed by a tanned couple caressing in a hammock under a palm tree. Eileen pointed out the choices for a seven day Caribbean adventure.

By the time Sam left the agency the streets were beginning to dry. *It would be nice to escape the rainy afternoons for a week.* As she drove, Sam considered ways to excite Lucky about the cruise. Equally important, she wondered, *How can I get time off from a job I haven't started?*

A call to Lucky's cell phone went directly to voicemail, but she returned the call a few minutes later.

"Hey Sam, it's me. Sorry for not returning your call sooner. The Gap had shorts on sale so I stopped to buy some. I was trying to squeeze a couple of extra pounds into a pair when you called. What's up?"

Lucky rolled her eyes. "You have a special idea for where I can wear the new shorts and you want me to meet you at High Hopes at seven thirty. You do this often, Sam. You throw me a tidbit to get me excited and then reel me in like a fish." "Yes," she laughed, "Seven-thirty it is."

Lucky wondered what Sam was planning now. *One thing for sure with Sam, I'm never bored.*

Sam arrived at the High Hopes Tavern a few minutes early. As the sun ricocheted off the Intracoastal she squinted to see if Lucky had arrived.

Mario spotted her. "Hey, Sam, how's my favorite new employee? Have you resigned from your other job yet?"

"Sure did, Mario."

"And?"

"I'll know tomorrow if I need to work my final two weeks."

"Just let me know."

"Mario, would it be okay if I need an extra week before I start?"

"Sure. We're still in the off season. You got big plans?"

"I hope so. I'm meeting Lucky here any minute now. I'm going to try to talk her into a cruise."

"You're certainly living in the right city for that!"

Fragments of the happy hour crowd remained when Lucky arrived. She took an extra moment to appreciate Raul, one of the more comely waiters. His snug pants telegraphed a readiness to please. She felt a tap on her shoulder as she reached the bar.

"You're right on time as usual. Are those your new shorts, Lucky?"

"Yeah, it was time to treat myself."

They hugged each other and Sam thought, *Hmmm, time to treat herself.*

"Speaking of which, let me talk to Mario about getting us a table for dinner. My treat."

"Pete was refreshing their wine glasses as Sam returned. "Mario is such a sweetheart. We've got a table at eight."

"Are those travel brochures in your bag?"

"Yes, but for more fun right now, let's cruise the men

for a while. Look at all these cute macho puppies."

"Yeah, and I'm lovin' 'em all."

They sat like a pair of lighthouses scanning the shore. They sipped their drinks and swiveled their heads, commenting on every man without either a wedding ring or the telltale puffy band of flesh where one had been.

Lucky's head stopped to focus on one guy. He posed there in his ensemble of traditional blue blazer, khaki pants, white shirt with monogrammed French cuffs, and brown alligator loafers. He had an open collar today. His trimmed mustache might have included a few strokes of an eyebrow pencil. His usual pocket handkerchief was tucked neatly in place. He leaned on his cane, adorned at the top with the lion's head motif.

"Sam, there's Daniel.

"Who?"

Daniel Dooley Kent, the man rescued from the ocean on Tuesday. He appears to be doing well. I should go and say hello."

"To be honest, he could be a character in a B movie from the early 50's. I'll come and get you when our table is ready, Lucky. Maybe I can get an autograph."

He smiled as Lucky approached. "Daniel, remember me, Lucky Larkin? How are you?

"Of course, Lucky, I'm pleased that you're here. I'm doing well, thank you."

"May I buy you a drink, Daniel? I'm having dinner with my girlfriend Samantha but I have some time before our table is ready."

"How gracious, Lucky, I gladly accept. As you can tell, I'm sailing solo."

The bar was getting busier. Pete was doing his best to pump out the drinks. Mario stepped behind the bar and began to assist. *If it's this busy on Thursday*, he thought, *I really do need another bartender.* Mario quickly spotted Lucky with a twenty in her hand.

"What would you like, Daniel," she asked.

"Bourbon on the rocks with a twist of lemon is my usual drink of choice."

She remembered he was a former Harvard English professor. She still stifled a giggle at his, "usual drink of choice" remark.

Mario overheard and responded, "Comin' right up!"

He handed Daniel his drink. "You're something of a celebrity. Lucky mentioned your beach emergency. You're lucky to be alive." Mario extended his hand. "I'm Mario Bellasari. They tell me I'm the owner of this place, but the bank may disagree. We have a tradition at High Hopes Tavern to welcome new friends with a complimentary drink."

"Thank you. Your generosity is appreciated, Mario."

"I've got to run, but Lucky is the expert in taking care of our distinguished guests."

"Yes, I'm beginning to realize that more every day."

In all the times he'd been in the High Hope Tavern, this was the first that anyone had spoken to Daniel. Somewhat shy, he kept to himself. It had always been just a quick nod or hello from someone close to where he sat. Tonight was different. He stood with Lucky, to share a drink, some conversation, and an occasional laugh.

Lucky spoke up. "That's Sam waving. I guess our table is ready."

"Go and enjoy your dinner. I'll catch you again soon. Thank you, Lucky--you're most gracious."

His eyes followed her affectionately as she and Sam fell in behind the Maitre d'.

Lucky turned back and noted that he was tapping his foot to the beat of the music.

CHAPTER 8

SCHMOOZING THE CRUISING

The enclave just beyond the bar featured comforting pastel blues and greens. Indirect lighting of complementary shades created added subtle hues. The soft lighting from above accented the original maritime oil paintings, with dark wood frames. Overhead paddle fans matched the rhythm of the leisurely dining service.

The Maitre d' led Lucky and Sam to a table for two. He selected a quiet corner between an elaborate waterfall and an aquarium of multi-colored tropical fish.

"Ladies, I've seated you at Raul's table, away from the hubbub. Bon Appétit." Lucky and Sam settled in to enjoy the ambiance of the murmurs of those around them, the jazz band, and the wine.

Raul greeted them with a smile as soon as they sat down. "Hello Ladies, your wine glasses are almost empty. May I freshen them for you while you decide what's most appealing on the menu?"

Lucky thought, *I'm glad I haven't had too much wine, or I'd tell him what he can start me off with.* She giggled to herself wondering, *Who gets to wake up next to him every morning?* "I've only had one glass. Let's be adventurous and order another?"

Sam quickly nodded her approval.

"I understand you're both enjoying Sterling Chardonnay," he said.

"You understand correctly, Raul."

Sam leaned closer to him and said, "My name is Sam Burnside. Mario recently hired me. I start to work here next week."

Raul winked. "I'll be sure to compliment him on his excellent taste."

As Raul headed for the bar, Sam fanned herself with the oversized menu.

Whew, what a butt! I'm already starting to fantasize about being closer to him, possibly something a little more intimate. He's so gorgeous, what if he's gay.

"Now that we've dispensed with the hot flashes, let's see what you've brought to show me."

"Ya know, Lucky, we live in the cruise capital of the world, and I'm still waiting for my ship to sail. I was trapped underneath the awning of a travel agency during today's thunderstorm. A poster in the window made me curious about what a cruise would cost. I learned that rates are the lowest they've been in years." Sam slid a brochure next to Lucky's wineglass. "Can you believe these prices for a seven-day Caribbean cruise? I want to go, and I want you to come with me."

"Sam, you're about to start a new job."

"I already spoke to Mario. He's gonna let me start a week later."

Lucky turned the pages of the brochure while Sam filled in the details Eileen had given her earlier. They leaned closer and talked more about the possible adventure. Sam watched her carefully and sensed she was becoming excited by the idea.

Raul arrived with their chardonnay. "Are you ready to order, ladies?"

"Almost. Can you give us a few more minutes? I'm working a cruise conspiracy here."

"Just signal when you're ready. Pretty ladies always get my attention."

"Lucky, let your mind wander for a minute. A week in the Caribbean. The sun. Sitting by the pool sipping drinks with those silly little umbrellas. The food and entertainment. Did I mention the single guys?"

"I must admit, I do like the thought of taking a cruise, Sam. I hope I can get the time off. You're talking two weeks from now which is narrowing in on the tourist season. Are you sure the ship is not full?"

"Yes, I already checked. Oh, I forgot one minor detail. I need to tell the travel agent, "yea" or "nay," by tomorrow."

"Tomorrow?"

"Yes, only two Veranda cabins remain available. If we want one, we must confirm our plans by 5:00 P.M. tomorrow."

While they paused to let everything sink in, Raul returned to the table. "Ladies, would you like to hear tonight's specials or are your minds already set on something from the menu?"

"I'm not sure I can handle anything more special than you. You better be careful or we'll drag you on this cruise with us."

"Don't temp me, I can be packed by the time you finish dinner!"

After they ordered their entrée, Sam hoisted her glass. "Time to rock the boat."

"You're always thinking of exciting things to do."

Lucky wished she could share Sam's joy of life, her sense of being open to new adventures. She, on the other hand, was often preoccupied by the fear of being two years shy of forty and still alone. *Perhaps I do need this cruise*, she thought.

As Raul set the heaping plates of shrimp scampi in front of them, Sam's eyes wandered to his shirtsleeves. Each was folded back far enough to expose a patch of manly black hair. His classic Hispanic features gave her a shudder of pleasure.

"Isn't that your friend Clarice at the bar?"

Sam turned her head toward the amen corner. Clarice was decorously sipping a Grey Goose martini.

"That's her. Such a classy lady, and so interesting. She still dresses to please herself. No conforming to the more casual, T-shirt and jeans local costume for her."

"Yeah, Sam, just like Daniel Dooley Kent." Lucky turned and looked around the bar. "I think he's still here somewhere."

"Isn't that something," Sam laughed, "The whimsical Daniel Dooley Kent and the esteemed Southern belle, Clarice Thompson, here at the same hour. Do you think they know each other?"

"I'm not sure, but Daniel mentioned he didn't speak to many people here at the tavern. Somehow a former professor being shy is unimaginable. He is, though. It's unlikely they've met."

Sam chuckled, "Maybe it's time for an intervention."

"Yeah, you're right, Sam. I get the feeling they're both quite well off. Yet both choose to sit here alone. Everyone needs the warmth of companionship."

"You really are lonely, aren't you, Lucky."

"Yes, I am. I've had one failed relationship with Billy and also lived with Mike, who passed away. I was *especially* hurt by a guy from San Juan. I never told you that story. Each hurt in a different way. I've dated here and there, but I still live behind a foolish mask of hope, pretending there really is someone out there for me. With Mike, I knew he loved me, as much as I loved him. I'm sure there is someone else out there for me, but I'm afraid."

"Of what, Lucky?"

"Sam, letting romance back into your life is like planning a trip to a place you haven't been in years. Memory recalls the scenery and the weather that sends you racing to the beach, but forgets the hassles with the miserable hotel, the questionable food, and the intolerable noise. Maybe it's how our brains cope with conflicting recollections, but it sure can be misleading. There's comfort in just staying home, where there are no surprises."

"You do want someone in your life again, right?"

"Yes... very much. Sam, I believe knowing who we are is never easy. We try to navigate our lives without surrendering to the snarling monsters of memories at every intersection. No matter how unpleasant our past is, at least there are no surprises in what we've already endured. We hold on to what we remember, because something different for the future might be even worse. So, we remain trapped. Most of us are lost without any reliable signpost to a safe place."

Sam's face became as stern as a schoolteacher during detention. "Well, Lucky, you either choose to stay on the merry-go-round, or leave the park. Those horses keep on dancing whether you're there or not."

CHAPTER 9

NEW KID ON THE BLOCK

"Come in," Mario said, responding to a hard knock on the office door. A good-looking young man entered. "What can I do for you, son?"

"Mr. Bellasari, my name is Robbie Alston. I read your ad in the paper for a part-time bartender."

Robbie glanced around the disheveled office while Mario quickly removed papers and books from a chair to clear a place for Robbie to sit.

Mario reached into the equally messy desk and tore an application from a pad and handed it to Robbie. "I'm sorry for the disarray, but if it weren't for my daughter coming in occasionally, the office would look even worse. Here, please fill this out and let me know when you're finished. Take your time. As you can see, I've got a ton of paperwork."

"Thank you, sir."

Mario discreetly examined his appearance. He saw a man in his mid-twenties with blond hair and blue eyes. His swimmer's build suggested he had the necessary strength to lift heavy cartons of liquor. Mario appreciated that he was polite and well dressed. He realized, unless Robbie blew the interview, he would hire him.

Robbie quickly completed the application. "I'm not quite sure of the phone number for one of my references," he said as he returned the application to Mario. "I'll verify the number later today and call you."

Mario scanned both sides of the application.

"So, Robbie, tell me a little about yourself, your experience as a bartender and anything else you think I should know."

"I'm still in college. I have an AA Degree and I'm working on my BA in Science with a minor in Chemistry. I've supported myself with work as a waiter or bartender. I prefer to tend bar.

"So, you've been in the business for a long time?"

"About four years."

"I'm sure you can handle customers who have had too much to drink?"

"Yes, I can. I cut them off as politely as possible, usually with a big smile. If I need to, I always throw in a line about my concern for their safety and I don't want them to end up with a DUI."

"Should I decide to hire you, when could you start?"

"How about thirty minutes from now, Mr. Bellasari? Lend me a tie, and I'm ready to start."

"I prefer for my team to call me Mario. I like your spunk, Robbie. Let me check a few references, and I'll call you tomorrow."

"Thanks. I'll wait for your call."

Mario returned to the bar. "How was your day off, Antonio?"

"I just worked around the house. Dwight was at his office. "Did I miss anything here?"

"Well, I just interviewed a guy named Robbie Alston. Does his name sound familiar?"

"No, not to me. Why, are you looking to replace me, Mario?"

"You know you're here for the long haul, Antonio. You did ask for more time off for your culinary courses. I want to be sure I can schedule bartenders around your classes. Hiring is a roll of the dice, but Robbie interviewed well and I've got a good feeling about him. He also has prior experience. I thought perhaps some of the other bartenders around town may have mentioned his name."

"You're always so thoughtful. Thanks for planning ahead."

"He would only be part-time for now. I think I'll start him tomorrow."

"Sure, fine with me. I'll be here to show him our setup."

Mario walked briskly back to his office. *That went well.*

Robbie was sprawled across his couch, half asleep, with nothing on but his faded jeans. A gold cross on a chain dangled toward his left armpit. The top buttons of his jeans were open, revealing a patch of his Florida Gator briefs. His eyebrows moved to the rhythm of his sleep. An opened pizza box dominated the table. All that remained was an orphan piece of crust with nothing but teeth marks.

The breeze from the balcony flirted with the gauzy curtains behind the couch. The cell phone ring was jarring. He sat up, stretched, yawned, and answered the call.

"Yes, this is Robbie Alston. Who's calling," he asked

with a groggy voice, and then listened.

"Oh Mario, I'm sorry. I was napping." He sat up and rubbed his eyes.

"Hey, that's great. What time do you want me there? I'll be there tomorrow at three thirty sharp. Thanks!"

"Oh and Robbie, please wear a white shirt, black pants with black shoes."

"That's fine, I've got them all. I'll be in tomorrow, sir. Thank you again!"

He pumped his right arm in triumph. *It's time to celebrate. A couple of drinks and gettin' laid will do the trick.* First, a leisurely bath. He turned the knob to create a steady stream. When the water was halfway up the tub, he lit candles at the edge of the tub. He submerged into the steaming water. Soft blues music from ceiling speakers set the tone for a lengthy bath.

His hand slid down for a little tug. *No*, he thought. *I better save it for the real thing.*

Half an hour later he emerged from the tub with a towel wrapped around his waist to savor his image in the mirror. He caressed each candle before wetting his fingers to douse the flame. He smiled as the flame sizzled and stopped.

He grinned as he locked the door behind him. "Now for a little of the dark side."

CHAPTER 10

AN UNWELCOME LETTER

Mario reviewed Robbie's completed paperwork. "Everything appears to be in order, Robbie. Let's go meet Antonio. He'll show you our setup and answer any questions."

Antonio finished cutting the last lemon. He scooped up the slices and crammed them into a large plastic container. He then adjusted the music volume and was waiting for his first customer as Mario and Robbie walked toward the bar.

He sized up Robbie as the two men approached.

"Antonio, meet Robbie Alston, our new part-time bartender."

"Robbie, this is Antonio, he's my main man here at the bar."

"I'm really pleased you're here so I can take some time off to finish my classes."

"He's in your capable hands, Antonio."

"Stick close to me tonight, Robbie. You'll be the apprentice to the Magician of Mixology."

"Hey old timer, I have animal magic. Ask any of the ladies where I've worked."

"Is that my cue to growl?

Mario headed toward the office and heard Melanie unlock the office door. "Good afternoon, papa," she whispered, kissing her father's forehead. "How ya doin'?"

"Ah, Melanie, the love of my life. Your papa's doing well. I'm supposed to be opening the mail, but perhaps you can give me a reason to put it off.

"What if I told you I think I aced my exam today?"

"That's my girl."

"Or, more important than my academic excellence, who's the cute new guy behind the bar?

"Remember? I told you we might be getting a new part-time bartender. I know *you* didn't think it was a necessary expense."

"Yes, papa, but he's so cute. My business opinion may be altered. Let me go introduce myself to the newbie. He *should* know the daughter of the owner, right?"

"I'm glad your business sense is still intact," Mario said with a hint of sarcasm.

He blew her a kiss as he entered the office. An envelope on the top of the pile caught his attention. It had the return address for the bank that held the mortgage on the tavern. He ripped the envelope open. *What the hell do they want now!*

Mario stiffened. He had overlooked an item at the time

of signing. A balloon payment of twenty five thousand dollars is due in ninety days. *Melanie will shit if she learns about this . Calm down, Mario. There has to be a solution. I've got ninety days to figure something out...and I'd better.*

He placed the letter in the pocket of his briefcase and scurried toward the bar. As he got closer to Melanie, he was surprised to see Robbie's hands cupped over hers.

"Chivas and water please, Robbie,"

Robbie reached for the bottle of Chivas and grabbed a glass. "He's interesting, papa," she whispered.

"His hands squeezing yours, what's that all about?"

"It's all about somebody besides you who thinks I'm beautiful." She leaned forward and fluttered her eyelashes at triple speed.

Robbie served Mario his drink. I'll leave you two to talk. Two young ladies just sat down."

"I think he'll be fine. He's very attentive, papa."

Mario and Melanie talked and laughed for a few minutes before he took his last swig of scotch. "Gotta go, my love. I'll be back later."

As he left, he looked back at Robbie. He was leaning close to the two ladies with a hand resting on each of them.

I hope he doesn't overplay those hands.

CHAPTER 11

NEW FRIENDS

Clarice felt a gentle and much needed breeze as she sunned herself next to the pool with her eyes closed. She languidly trailed her fingers in the water while listening to a memorable selection of Tony Bennett tunes on her iPod. Moments later, she opened one eye and leaned over to check the time on her diamond studded watch. It was 5:30 P.M. She gathered her belongings and sauntered to her bedroom to prepare for her Saturday night ritual. She would arrive at High Hopes Tavern promptly at 7:00 for her two martinis, followed by dinner at 8:15.

For her evening attire she had selected an ensemble of a light blue pants suit, dark blue shoes, a simple gold necklace and a white belt, rimmed hat, and white gloves. Her gloves were draped over her simple, but elegant handbag that rested on her bed.

Two cars waited ahead of her for the valet at the tavern. Clarice crept closer as the other drivers exited. She knew all the valet staff and tipped them generously.

Her turn came quicker than expected."Ah, Miss Clarice. Welcome home."

She stepped from her car and handed Richie a twenty dollar bill.

"I'll tuck your Mercedes in the spot I save for you."

A gentleman leaving the tavern held the door open for her as Clarice made her entrance.

Phillip, the Maitre d', kissed her hand. "With the radiance of Clarice we can dim the lights in the dining room." With an extravagant bow, he asked. "How is the divine Miss C?"

"Nevah bettuh, Phillip, nevah bettuh. " She strolled to her stool at the amen corner.

Robbie approached Clarice. He wore a tailored white linen shirt which flattered his slender frame. The top two buttons were open to showcase his trimmed chest hairs. "Good evening, ma'am. What's your pleasure?"

"You're a new face, young man. At what propitious moment did you make your debut?"

"This is my second night, ma'am. I hope I'm not out of line if I say you create a spectacular image."

"I accept all compliments, my dear, especially from handsome young men. I'd like my usual, which is a dry Grey Goose martini, straight up, with two olives, please."

Robbie smiled at her seductively as he stirred her martini.

"Tell me if I've made it to your satisfaction, ma'am."

Clarice took a sip and nodded, "Perfect. What do your friends call you?"

"Robbie, ma'am."

"I'm Clarice Thompson and you pour a soothing martini, Robbie."

She slipped him a five dollar bill. "This is for you. Put the drink on my tab."

He took both her hands and stroked them. "Thank you, Mrs. Thompson."

"It's *Ms*. Thompson. I prefer you call me, Clarice. She scanned his body deliberately. "I'm sure you'll do very well here."

"Like you, Miss Clarice, I graciously accept all compliments."

A little ambitious with the hand stroking, but perhaps I'm guilty of a forgiving nature, she thought.

Before leaving home, Clarice had prepped for the evening with a chilled glass of champagne. She began to sense a comforting buzz after a few sips of her first martini. The aroma from the kitchen reminded her she was navigating on a nearly empty stomach. She tapped her foot to the beat of the trio and allowed her memories to converge from her performance days in the dinner theater and the good times in Savannah.

As she surrendered to the setting, a man jostled between her and another customer. With a twenty dollar bill in his hand, he stood waiting his turn to order. "I'm sorry ma'am. I'll be out of your way in a moment. The place is crowded tonight, isn't it?

"Yes. Can I make more room for you?" Clarice replied quickly shifting slightly away from him.

"A bourbon on the rocks with a twist," he said to Antonio. "I apologize, ma'am. Daniel got his drink and slowly inched his way through the crowd before taking up a position in the corner.

"Who is that man; he's somewhat familiar?" Clarice asked Antonio.

"I believe Lucky Larkin told me his last name is Kent. I don't recall meeting him."

"Lucky Larkin… she's Samantha's friend, right?"

"Yup, been friends for years."

"Samantha and I have met, but I haven't made Lucky's acquaintance as of yet."

"I expect they'll be in later. This *is* a Saturday night.

Lucky's usually searching for Mr. Right. Many of us hope she finds him soon. She deserves happiness."

Clarice sat savoring each sip of her martini. Her husband had left her for a younger woman. She again caught herself reminiscing about the good times with him. Even in a room filled with people, by her second martini, Clarice was alone. *Am I becoming invisible?* She chose to talk to fewer people, which could be part of the cause for becoming obsolete.

"Excuse me, is this seat taken?" Daniel asked, pointing to an open stool.

"I believe the person sitting there was just escorted to his table for dinner." Clarice was amused by his attire, but being a Southern belle, kept her observations to herself. She also knew she was not exactly *in* when it came to dictates of South Florida fashions.

"May I?"

"Certainly."

He placed his cane on the back of the stool and sat down. Clarice was relieved by the unexpected sincerity in his voice. He wore a Navy blue sports jacket, white shirt, complete with an ascot. She could tell his tan pants and dark brown alligator shoes were expensive. Clarice noted that, like most other older men, he seemed to use hair dye as if it were marinade. His trim mustache was dyed to match his hair.

"My name is Clarice Thompson. Before you ask about mah accent, I'm from Savannah. And you are?"

"I'm Daniel Dooley Kent. My pleasure to meet you, Clarice Thompson," he said, extending his hand. "I'm also a transplant, as it seems most everyone is in Fort Lauderdale. I'm originally from Boston."

"Well, that explains a lot."

"What do you mean by that, Clarice? Oh, I apologize, may I call you Clarice?"

"Yes, as long as I may call you Daniel."

"I think I can make an exception for a lady as lovely

and elegant as you. So, Clarice, what explains a lot to you?"

"The way you dress. I find your attire somewhat unusual for this climate. You're clothes are different from the usual shorts and beach shirt most men wear here. On you it's quite impressive."

"Why thank you, Clarice. But the same applies to you. I've seen you here before and always found you dressed impeccably. You maintain that distinctive Southern appearance which I find so charming."

"Mr Kent, I *am* a work of fiction, and this, gesturing toward herself with a flourish, is the final draft!"

Clarice was intrigued. Perhaps she had misjudged him. Her original perceptions were of him being self- centered and aloof. She now amended her thoughts to consider he could just be shy. She liked him.

Sam tapped her shoulder. "Good evening, Clarice."

"Sam, you're looking captivating."

"Thank you, Clarice. Whom may I ask is this gentleman?"

"Sam, allow me to introduce Daniel Dooley Kent."

"The pleasure is mine, Mr. Kent. I believe you know my friend Lucky."

"Oh yes, of course, of course. Is she here tonight?"

"Yes, she's around somewhere."

"My dinner reservation is for 8:15, Sam," Clarice said raising her martini glass. "I would be honored if you and Lucky would join me for dinner."

"The pleasure would be ours."

"Daniel, would you join us as well?"

"How thoughtful, I'd be delighted."

"Excellent. I believe this special occasion calls for patio dining. It provides a casual, yet tropical atmosphere for us to get to know each other."

Clarice excused herself and headed for the Maitre d' station. Daniel's eyes followed her.

"Hi, Daniel," Lucky said, seeming to startle him with a peck on the cheek. "I see you've met Samantha."

"Yes. She's quite charming, like you."

"Lucky, Clarice asked if we would join her for dinner, along with Daniel. I accepted for the both of us. I hope that's okay with you."

"Sure, fine with me," she responded with a slight hint of reluctance while sipping her wine.

Clarice returned to her amen corner. "Why you must be Lucky Larkin." Sam has said enchanting things about you. I'm Clarice Thompson."

"Clarice, you're every bit as lovely as Sam described." Lucky shook her hand.

Clarice lifted herself onto her stool and raised her martini. "To new friends."

"To new friends," the others repeated, lifting their glasses.

The four sat for a while enjoying their cocktails and conversation. As the time of their reservation arrived Phillip approached. "Miss Clarice, you're table is ready. Follow me please."

"Shall we, everyone?" Clarice asked. She placed her trademark fan in her purse and picked up her glass to enjoy the last sip.

Phillip took Clarice by the arm and led the way with Lucky, Sam, and Daniel keeping the pace behind.

"Phillip, you know I enjoy the security of a man's arm holding mine. You did switch my reservation to a patio table, correct Phillip?"

"Of course, Miss Clarice. Need you ask?"

"My dear Phillip, one should always *inquire* rather than *assume*! Clarice thanked him with a ten dollar tip after he pulled her chair out for her.

"Miss Clarice, your Southern accent is so mesmerizing. I'm always pleased to seat you."

"Thank you, Phillip."

"Daniel, would you do me the honor of sitting next to me?"

"Certainly, Miss Clarice."

As they settled, they quietly appreciated the view. The shades of evening combined a mixture of blue and green tropical lights shining on the palm trees. They co-mingled beautifully with the brighter lights from the tavern's interior restaurant and bar area only feet away. The splendor of the moon shining on the Intracoastal was a gift, a present from above.

Sam's eyes widened. She smiled and cleared her throat, tapping Lucky on the thigh as Raul approached the table with menus. His neatly pressed tuxedo pants and shirt caught everyone's attention.

"Good evening, my name is Raul. Would anyone like another cocktail before dinner?"

"A liquid refreshment is always in order, Raul. My drink is a dry Grey Goose martini, straight up, with two olives."

"You must be Clarice Thompson. I'm honored."

"Just how did you know who I am, Raul? Am I the only lady here who drinks dry Grey Goose martinis?"

"No Miss Clarice, but you are easily the most elegant. Antonio and Pete always speak highly of you. I asked Phillip if I could possibly serve your table this evening."

"Darlin', if your service matches your charm, this will be an especially delightful dinner."

Daniel Dooley Kent spoke up. "Bourbon on the rocks with a twist for me, Raul." Lucky ordered a glass of Sterling Chardonnay, Sam decided on a Heineken.

As Raul left the table, Sam quickly shared her thoughts. "He certainly is a hunk. Working here will definitely be more interesting.

❧

Lucky's thoughts turned inward. *I've been thinking all day about the need for a man in my life, yet here I sit at dinner with strangers. Clarice and Daniel certainly look financially secure, and I'm a hotel front desk agent. How am I ever going to find someone? I wish Sam had asked me before accepting the dinner offer.*

Clarice began the conversation by turning toward

Samantha and Lucky. "Mario tells me you girls are going on a cruise."

"Yes, Clarice, we're leaving a week from tomorrow," Lucky said, perking up.

"Good for you, girls." Daniel added, "I've never taken a cruise. My friends tell me only good things about them."

"We chose a Veranda stateroom, Miss Clarice. What a thrill it's going to be to smell the salt ocean air while leaning on the railing."

"I'm sure it will be comfortable, Lucky. Hailing from the South, to me a veranda is a veranda when it surrounds a Southern mansion with fluted columns and servants loitering on the lawn." With a sip of her martini, she added, "when it's on a cruise ship darlin', it's a balcony." she smiled.

Sam studied Raul as he served another table their entrées. "Lucky is my best friend, she said, and I love her dearly, but oh baby, would I love to be sharing the balcony with Raul."

"Hell, Sam, I love you too," Lucky grinned. "Waking up next to a man wearing nothing more than his underwear would be my preference as well."

Lifting her martini, Clarice took a sip. Tell me, Lucky, why there would be a need for the underwear?"

"I like the way she thinks." Lucky said.

With everyone's menu set aside, Clarice motioned to Raul. "I think we're ready to order.

He scribbled down their selections and headed for the kitchen.

"I'd like to learn something about each of you, Clarice said. Daniel, let's begin with you. I heard you've met Lucky before this evening. Mario mentioned something about an incident while swimming, I believe?"

"Yes, old men with a heart condition should learn to exercise a bit less vigorously. That, my dears, is all too boring. You're probably more interested in how I came to live in Fort Lauderdale. As I grew older, I needed more excitement than you can get teaching at Harvard. I come from a family of educators and my area of interest was English. I taught there for 34 years before retiring six years ago. I moved to Fort Lauderdale and never looked back."

"Very impressive, Daniel."

"Thank you, Clarice."

Sam commented to Clarice and Lucky, "a retired English professor, from *Hahvard* no less, I guess we better watch how and what we say," she said with a hint of humor in her voice.

"Oh please, be who you are. I'm just thrilled to make new acquaintances this evening."

Clarice nodded. "Yes, and besides, Sam, I am well past the age where anyone should presume to tell me what to think or say. I have earned the right to be propelled by my own engine!"

Raul reappeared. "How is everyone doing with their drinks?"

"I'll take another beer please, Raul"

"Certainly, Samantha, anyone else care for another?"

"I'm good", said Daniel. "Me too", Lucky added.

"No more for me, Raul," Clarice quipped. "Any more right now and I'll be flying."

"Is that my cue, Clarice?"

"Your cue? Why would you say that, Lucky?"

"Your comment about flying. For close to sixteen years I was a flight attendant. I grew tired of the business. I didn't enjoy being away from home most of the time. People would scream at you because a computer glitch accidentally assigned the same seat to two people. Things like that. After a while, the so-called glamour is gone. My love life is non-existent. I am looking to get married and settle down after many hurtful attempts at a long-term relationship."

"I always thought being a flight attendant would be so exciting." Daniel interjected.

"Yes, but like I said, the glamour and excitement

fades."

Lucky wanted to move on.

Raul quietly served his guests.

"My word, look at the size of the yacht approaching." Clarice said, gesturing.

The engines on the behemoth purred as it glided by. The fortunate couples on board waved, as they hoisted champagne, as if to say, *look at me*. The group waved back at the passengers on the mega yacht.

"What a life," Lucky muttered.

Once the yacht sailed out of view, Clarice continued the conversation.

"I am not ashamed to tell you I am now seventy years old. My former husband and I were in show business. That's if you call the dinner theatre show business. We were part of the Miami Beach social and political scene which was a special time in my life. However, a few years ago, my husband left me for a younger lady. She was someone I mentored in show business."

"In my youth I danced with wild abandon on naked feet. In recent years I've moved on to pantyhose and sensible shoes…not a pretty migration. Of course, the wild abandon is still there. For now. I also find the Grey Goose Vodka to be a great lubricant for avoiding self-pity."

"You must enjoy so many wonderful memories, Miss Clarice," Sam said with a bit of envy.

"My mind is a lost-and-found of memories, all jumbled up and mostly of no real value. Then, magically, perhaps when I need it most, I stumble across a forgotten treasure and feel the echoes of the pleasure it once brought. At those times I savor the spirit of hope it now promises. Oh my goodness, is it me, or are those clouds over yonder making faces at me? See what happens when you encourage the musings of an old woman! You inspire her to be maudlin, which is not my style at all."

Lucky adjusted the napkin on her lap and leaned forward. "Juicy gossip serves as a substitute for maudlin anytime. What do you ladies think about the new bartender, Robbie?"

"Definitely cute, but a little too touchy-feely for me, Sam responded."

Clarice pretended distain, "*Au contraire*, I like his spunk."

"My dear Clarice, I'll be as touchy and spunky as you desire, when presented with the opportunity," Daniel said.

Clarice paused just a moment. "Somehow I feel confident in that, my dear Daniel."

"Ah, I hear a sound," said Samantha. "Like cards spinning and hitting nails, getting slower and slower and finally stopping. The card stopped at a picture of me. I guess it's my turn at the Wheel of My Life Game." Here goes. I was born in South Carolina, just outside of Charleston. I moved to Fort Lauderdale shortly after my only brother was murdered four years ago. He worked in an auto repair shop and was killed during an attempted hold-up." No one at the table spoke. Their eyes were fixed on Sam's face. She continued.

"My father, who is in his mid sixties, is a strict Baptist Minister. Because I don't buy into his religious teachings, we don't speak. I don't like organized religion, and only went to church because my father commanded me to go. My mother passed away three years ago. I believe she died from a broken heart brought on by my brother's death. His killer is still on the loose."

"I tend to like romance and, like Lucky, I've been hurt before. Just three months ago, the man I was dating showed up with another young lady at the restaurant where I work. I find that women give sex to get affection, and men give affection to get sex. That's a little about me, Samantha Burnside."

No one spoke for a moment before Daniel Dooley Kent cleared his throat.

"Sam, I am so sorry about your brother. I hope the police will soon find the person who killed him, and that he will be brought to justice."

"I appreciate your thoughts, Daniel. I hope so too. With a handkerchief pulled from the purse at her feet, she dabbed her eyes. Well, I didn't mean to put a damper on things, but we were sharing some of our life stories, as if we were family, right?"

"Yes, we were," Clarice added. "I'm also sorry for your loss; however, I do admire your courage for being forthright, Samantha." And, she continued. "I am one of those people who say that the family you choose is closer than the family you inherited. Look at any discussion of social heritage -- it all comes together as some definition of family."

After taking a sip, Daniel placed his water glass on the table. "All of us of a certain age remember when family life took place mostly around a kitchen table. Millions of people have lived without ever dining away from home, except on left-overs taken from home. Look at us now. Many of us take most of our meals away from home. Most of us are away from our blood family, which is spread around thousands of miles -- here and in foreign countries."

There was a momentary lull. "So, what do we do?" Clarice asked, sharing a little eye contact with everyone at the table. "We carefully select and groom an ideal family for this time in our life. Think about how many of us take many of our meals in this room. Or, when we travel, we dine out, which is itself often a major reason for travel."

With regained composure, Sam piped in. "I have cousins whose names I don't even remember. I know more about the people I see here each week than I do those in the family I was born into. What an honor to be chosen as family! Why, and my father would love this, it's almost biblical -- being among the chosen few."

"You're so right," Daniel added. "Now, would everyone like some dessert or a nightcap?"

No one wanted dessert, but they decided to return to

the bar for one final drink.

"Raul, we'll take our check please."

"It's been paid already, Miss Clarice."

"By whom?"

"I can't say, Miss Clarice, only that tonight you are the guests."

"And were *you* well compensated, Raul?"

"Yes, exceptionally well. Thank you for asking."

Sam leaned toward Lucky and lowered her voice, "I'd like to give Raul *my* personal thanks."

"You *do* like this guy don't you, Sam?"

Daniel winked and nodded at Raul as they stood up to leave their table. He whispered his thanks for not spilling the beans.

He is a kind and generous man. Buying everyone's dinner was his way of showing how much he appreciated his new friends. Clarice caught the wink and nod, which convinced her she was correct in her assumption. Daniel was the generous soul.

The crowd had dwindled. Antonio positioned four cocktail napkins on the bar as Clarice and her party approached.

"Another martini, Miss Clarice?"

"No thanks, Antonio. I'd prefer a Gran Marnier, straight up please."

"Ladies?"

"I'll do the same," said Sam.

"Lucky?" Antonio asked. "Make that three, she added.

Daniel ordered a Diet Coke. He pulled a fifty dollar bill from his wallet and handed it to Antonio.

"That's twenty three dollars even, Mr. Kent."

"Please, call me Daniel."

Antonio went to the register, rung up the amount and took the correct change from the register.

"Here you go, Daniel." Antonio placed the change in his hand as he counted.

Daniel handed him eight dollars. "This is for you."

By now, Lucky and Sam also figured out that Daniel had paid for dinner. They sat enjoying intermittent conversation while listening to the trio.

Shortly after, Lucky stood up. "I thank you all, especially you Daniel, for the dinner and the company. I think I'm going to wander around the bar once before leaving for the evening."

"Ah, one final search for Mr. Right?" Clarice asked.

"Yes, my fingers are crossed."

Sam had the feeling that Daniel might like some time alone with Clarice. She echoed Lucky's sentiment about wanting to try to find that special someone.

"Mind if I join you, Lucky?"

"No, come on."

They again thanked Clarice and Daniel for their company.

"We must do this again soon," Daniel said, pulling his stool closer to Clarice.

"Daniel, it's unusual that I've not seen Mario here tonight. Did you?"

"Come to think of it, I haven't either."

Clarice gestured for Antonio.

"Antonio, we've not seen Mario tonight, is everything alright?"

"Ah, um, um, yeah, everything is alright."

"Antonio, I'm reading something else into your *ah, um, ums*, Now you're talking to Miss Clarice, darlin'."

"Promise you won't tell anyone, Miss Clarice and Mr. Daniel?"

"We promise."

"He's in the hospital for some tests. Earlier today he was in the office and his emphysema acted up on him. He had some difficulty breathing, and I noticed a blush tint to his skin. I called Melanie and she drove him to the hospital."

"Antonio, you could have told us."

"No Miss Clarice, both he and Melanie do not want

anyone to know. He should be out of the hospital late tomorrow."

Daniel and Clarice agreed to honor Mario's wishes and not mention anything about this to anyone. They chatted for another half hour and decided it was time to leave.

"Daniel Dooley Kent, you helped create a magical evening," she said making sure to use his complete name. "The only way I can thank you for your hospitality is to return the favor. Would you accept an invitation to join me for dinner next Saturday?"

"I accept your invitation; however, there is no need for you to pay."

The moon was full as they left the High Hopes Tavern. Daniel and Clarice exchanged phone numbers and shook hands, leaving the possibility of a peck on the cheek for next week.

They both handed their valet ticket to the attendant. Clarice's car was the first to arrive. They shook hands one more time and Clarice drove off, giving Daniel one final wave.

The attendant opened the door to Daniel's shiny Lexus. "How was your evening, sir?"

"It was one of the best in a long time." He thanked the attendant and handed him a generous tip.

Clarice's car radio was always tuned to her favorite easy listening station. She drove home with mixed emotions, partially brought on by the afterglow of three Grey Goose martinis and a Gran Marnier. She had met a wonderful man, someone she always thought of as strange.

Clearly, she was bothered by Sam's troublesome past. Clarice liked Sam, but didn't see that Southern charm so normal for girls reared in the South.

Clarice found Mario's health issue even more disturbing. There was something about her and Mario that no one else knew. Not even Melanie.

CHAPTER 12

A POTENTIAL PROBLEM

Mario enjoyed the lingering fragrance from the yellow roses he held on his lap as a volunteer wheeled him out of the hospital. A snag in the paperwork delayed his departure, but he was happy to leave. He had shared his room with a pleasant man, but nothing compared to the fresh air and warmth of the Fort Lauderdale sunshine. Melanie was ready to drive him home and seemed relieved when her father was finally released. Her class would begin at three o'clock and she didn't want to be late.

In addition to the pills he was already taking for his emphysema, his doctor prescribed one additional antibiotic. Mario recalled the doctor's instructions that he must work fewer hours.

Once home, Mario sat on his couch, thumbing through the Sports section of the Sun-Sentinel. The evening news had just come on. A Chivas and water sat on the end table by his sofa. He took a sip and then reopened the paper and read an article exalting another Dolphins comeback victory.

He had only been out of the hospital for about five hours but was already getting fidgety. *Should I go to the tavern or stay home and relax?* He decided to go to the tavern but promised himself he would stay no more than two hours ... or so.

"Hey Mario, what are you doing here?"

"I was getting bored on my couch. And I need to check on you" he said with a grin. "Honestly, Antonio I don't know what I would do without you. How's everything going?"

"Fine, but I do want to talk to you about Robbie."

"Is there a problem?"

"Potentially" he whispered. "But let's talk later. I'm just finishing the nightly inventory."

"Sure. I'm not staying too long."

I wonder what that's all about, Mario thought. *Damn it. No matter what is going on, I cannot allow myself to be stressed...period!*

He spotted Lucky and Sam just as they were getting up from their table.

"How are two of my all-time favorites," he asked, kissing each on the cheek.

"We're doing marvelous. Shit, Mario, to be more exact, we're excited as hell. You remember we're leaving a week from tomorrow on our cruise, don't you?"

"Yes, I do. I was just watching the news earlier. A possible tropical storm may be headed our way. Let's hope she veers in another direction."

Sam looked fearful. Mario liked to kid around, but this was not a laughing matter to her.

"What tropical storm?"

"The news reports said something is brewing way out in the Atlantic. I'm sure it's nothing to fret about. You know how the weather people like their drama, especially during hurricane season. I didn't mean to frighten you.

"Not only that Sam, cruise line captains have years of experience sailing the seas. They certainly make plans to sail around a storm. Let's not create a problem if one doesn't exist," said Lucky.

"Come on ladies,' I'll buy you a drink."

"Not tonight, Mario. Thanks for the offer, but I've got to get to bed." Sam wished everyone a pleasant evening and left.

Lucky felt Sam may have been a little annoyed by his tropical storm prediction since nothing about a storm was mentioned on the station she listened to. Sam's temper can explode at times. If she was pissed it would be better for Mario not to see that side of her.

"I'm going to say goodnight too. I'm working tomorrow and it's getting late." Lucky gave Mario a hug and walked around the bar close to Antonio. She stretched her arms.

"I'm not leaving without a hug." Antonio came from behind the bar.

She squeezed his upper back. "Good night you sexy hunk of humanity."

"Good night, Lucky. Thanks for the 'sexy hunk of humanity,' comment. You made my night."

"I said it because you are."

"Did you tell Mario you're working tomorrow?" She was still clutching Antonio and had little intention of letting go right away.

"Yes. I'm working an early shift. Why?

"Well, I'm off tomorrow and I'm going to the beach. I

thought you might want to stop by."

For a brief moment her mind wandered. She envisioned her and Antonio on a large blanket underneath a beach umbrella. The gentle rippling of low tide waves not far off. Taking a chance, she might nuzzle next to him and place her head on his well-defined chest.

"Ah Lucky, I need Antonio to close the place shortly. Can I have him back?"

"Oh, and stop such a spectacular fantasy in midstream?"

As she reached the door, she puckered her lips and blew Antonio one last kiss.

"Coming to the beach tomorrow?" he shouted.

"Maybe I'll swing by once I get out of work."

Getting into her car she thought to herself, *What a lie. Shit yes, I'll be at the beach.*

"Mario, there's only four customers left. I'll keep my eye on them if they need another, but I *do* want to talk about Robbie."

"Yeah, so what's up? Where is he by the way?"

"He left before Pete did. Pete was scheduled off at nine, but Robbie asked if he could leave early. He said he had somewhere to be."

"I'm surprised by his lack of initiative, Antonio. He only joined us a couple o' weeks ago."

"That's not all Mario. He's touchy with the customers. He likes to stroke their hands while he's talking to them. I know it makes some of them uncomfortable."

"I'll keep my eye on him, Antonio. But one thing is for sure, we don't need a sexual harassment suit. I promised myself I wouldn't stay too long tonight and broke that promise. I have to head home and get some rest. Make sure the place is locked up tight."

"I always do. Take care of yourself. I'm glad you're doing better."

"Thanks, Antonio. Enjoy your day off tomorrow."

It was another typically tropical Fort Lauderdale

evening. Mario enjoyed living on the beach, and the ride home always made him appreciate how fortunate he was. Still, he thinks about what his life as a winery owner might have been like as well. His wife Louisa still lives on in his heart. Meanwhile, he was comforted by a breezy night and the necklace of palm trees reaching for hugs along the drive.

The day had been long and tiring and he was eager to pour one last Chivas and water and settle in front of the TV

He was troubled by Antonio's comments about Robbie. Mario wondered if he lost when he rolled the dice and decided to hire him. He woke up at two thirty in the morning. The TV was showing an old fifties movie. He turned it off, went to his bedroom, and crawled into bed thinking, *How can I rein in the stallion without losing some of the mares?*

CHAPTER 13

CAUGHT OFF GUARD

It was a glorious Sunday. By mid-morning the temperature was already a scorching seventy-seven degrees and climbing. The weather forecasters were projecting a high of eighty-eight, with clear sunny skies. In Fort Lauderdale, the chance of afternoon thunderstorms can never be ruled out.

Antonio could count on one hand the number of times he'd been to the beach on a Sunday. Between working all night and going to school all day, time at the beach was a rare treat. Having Dwight, his partner of almost four years with him, made the occasion even more pleasurable. When they do go to the beach, they opt for the section popular with other gay men.

Antonio and Dwight own a quaint two bedroom, two bath home in Poinsettia Heights, an upscale section of Fort Lauderdale. The back of the house features hibiscus plants, birds of paradise, and a variety of palm trees. An inground pool enhances the tropical atmosphere. When they socialize they prefer to have friends join them for dinner at their home. So far, no one at the High Hopes Tavern has met Dwight, or is aware he exists.

"How's this spot, Dwight?"

"Anywhere is fine with me, honey."

Antonio spread an oversized blanket on the sand, while Dwight opened two blue and white beach chairs. He placed them side by side on a color coordinated blanket. They shared the duty of piecing together a large beach umbrella, which they embedded into the sand. A radio and a cooler with soda, juice and sandwiches fit snuggly between the two chairs. To prevent the blanket from blowing away, they placed a solitary sandal on each corner.

Antonio stood on the blanket and removed his shorts exposing a black Speedo. His low body fat made the skimpy attire suitable. Dwight, still handsome at age fifty eight, kept himself in shape by regular visits to the gym. He wore the more traditional -type bathing suit. Removing their T-shirts, they slapped generous amounts of sunscreen on each other and headed for the water. As they reached the waters' edge, Dwight grabbed Antonio from behind. He lifted him up and tossed him into the warm ocean.

"Hey honey, remember, paybacks are hell."

"Well count on me to be on my guard, my dear."

They swam side by side, reaching a depth where treading water was the only option to keep from sinking. An occasional playful hug accompanied by sensual eye contact enhanced their affection for each other.

"Hey Dwight, I didn't tell you, but Lucky, one of my good friends from the tavern, might stop by to say hello. She works at the Crystal Sands Hotel."

"Oh. My dear, how does she know where to find you?"

"I told her I would be going to the beach today. I said I usually enjoy the area off Sebastian Street."

"Antonio, we like our privacy, I hope she's, well, accepting of us."

"This *will* be a test for sure. There's a possibility she may not show up. Lucky would like a lot more from me than I'm capable of giving. She needs to learn about us sometime."

"I couldn't agree more, Antonio. *I* certainly understand why she *would* want more. The fault is all yours for being so devilishly handsome."

"Touché, Dwight!"

Antonio pulled Dwight underwater. He grasped his head firmly and kissed him twice. He then took one finger and pointed to his own eye, then his heart, and then pointed at Dwight. They emerged from below the water, hugged one more time and began to swim toward the shore.

"Dry me off please, Antonio."

"Sure, anything for my sweetheart."

"You're aware this additional class I've signed up for will keep us away from each other another two hours each week. The good news is I'll graduate sooner."

"That makes the investment in time worthwhile. What class are you taking?"

"Restaurant Management and Marketing."

"Sounds interesting to me. I will always support you, my handsome lover and chef."

A cheery voice interrupted their conversation. Antonio turned his head to see Lucky hopping from foot to foot to cool her feet. She wore a black two-piece bathing suit, covered by a sheer white sundress.

"Hi, Lucky, please sit on the blanket. Better yet, take my chair if you want."

"No thanks, Antonio, I'll just spread my beach towel on the sand."

Lucky couldn't help but notice a handsome, but graying older man lying next to Antonio.

"Lucky, I'd like you to meet my partner, Dwight. Dwight, this is Lucky Larkin."

She looked perplexed as she shook his hand. For a moment she wondered if she had heard Antonio correctly. More importantly, she hoped for a better explanation of the term partner. Did Antonio have a side business?

It's a pleasure, Lucky."

"I'm pleased to meet you as well, Dwight. Your name is so interesting."

"I was born during the Dwight D. Eisenhower presidency. My mother named me in his honor. Though I didn't feel obligated to go bald...or have an alleged affair with my driver."

History was one of her favorite subjects in school, so she understood the humor in his comment. She liked Dwight already.

"So how was work today?" Antonio asked.

"Not too busy but I'm glad to be off. You know Samantha and I leave next Sunday on our cruise."

"Yes, bet you can't wait. Dwight and I want to take a cruise soon."

During her flight attendant training she learned how to deal with surprise situations. She had worked with gay men at the airline and thought her gaydar worked well. Today, she was totally caught off guard.

"Dwight stood up and dusted some sand off his bathing suit. "I think I'll go for a swim now."

"Go and enjoy. I want to talk to Lucky anyway."

Lucky waited a moment before she moved into Dwight's chair. Antonio shifted the ice, looking for a bottle of juice.

"Care for a juice, or Diet Coke?"

"No thanks, I'm fine."

"Lucky, Dwight and I have lived as a couple for four years now. We choose to keep our relationship private."

"Where did you meet?"

"That's a funny story. At least we think so. Five years ago on a Saturday afternoon, we both were at the cleaners picking up our clothes. The counter person waiting on Dwight placed his clothes on the same rack as mine while we paid. We gave each other a glance and a smile. To this day we don't know if we were both so nervous or what, but when we left the cleaners, I had his clothes and he had mine. The cleaning ticket had his name and phone number. I called to ask him how we were going to exchange the clothes. Dwight drove to my place. We began dating and moved in with each other a year later. The rest is history."

"Dwight is extremely handsome, and extremely lucky I might add. Do you guys have an open relationship?"

"I wasn't even good at sharing crayons in kindergarten; I certainly wouldn't want to share a partner."

"That's good."

"Now for the big question. How do you feel about our relationship?"

"It's not up to me to approve or disapprove. It's up to me to be understanding and continue our friendship." Antonio was relieved. She took his hand and held it tightly.

"Antonio, many gay men and women lose their friends when they *come out* to them. I believe that's wrong. I always hoped for more from you. I now understand that will never happen. For me to give up your friendship would be foolish. And if I did, well then perhaps I wasn't a friend at all."

"What a special person you are, Lucky. Most people always ask, "When did you decide to be gay? My answer to them is a question. When did you decide to be straight?"

"I'm sure your response throws them off course."

"Usually."

Lucky stood up and removed her outer dress, dabbed on some sunscreen and motioned to Antonio. "Come on, let's go join that man of yours. The water looks refreshing."

Dwight faced the horizon as Lucky swam toward him. Antonio dove in and headed away from Dwight, unnoticed as well. Lucky finally reached Dwight, and, acting as a decoy, began some small talk. He shrieked as Antonio grabbed him by his legs from underneath the sea.

"You scared the crap out of me, Antonio. I thought a large fish or something was biting me."

"I told you paybacks are hell, my dear. Gotcha, didn't I?"

Antonio wanted to hold Dwight in his arms as they treaded water, but decided against it. He could tell Lucky was disappointed learning of his relationship. There was no reason to elevate her pain.

They stayed in the ocean for another fifteen minutes. They spoke about work and friends, before Lucky said it was time for her to leave. They all swam for a short distance before standing to let the waves swat their behinds, thrusting them toward the beach. Still soaked, Antonio and Dwight sat in their beach chairs. Lucky dried herself off before pulling her outer dress over the wet bathing suit.

"It's time for me to get going. Dwight, I'm sure we'll see each again soon. She gave him a peck on the cheek and leaned over to Antonio and did the same. "See you at the tavern."

Lucky walked slowly from the beach, staring at the crowd of mostly handsome, well-built guys. *On a scale of one to ten, with ten being the highest, especially for his age, Dwight is definitely an eleven*, she thought.

At the car she performed her usual summer ritual. She turned the air-conditioner on full blast, opened all the vents and stepped outside while the car cooled down. She looked up at the bright sky and watched as a banner plane flew by, then looked down at the street. She shook her head. *Will I ever find someone for me?*

During the drive home, she was swept by an array of emotions. "I promise" she said out loud, "If anyone finds out about Antonio and Dwight, it won't be from my lips." Lucky also vowed to keep looking for her own special guy. To do this, she may have to reveal a closely kept secret of her own.

CHAPTER 14

"PAPA, WHAT'S THIS LETTER ALL ABOUT?"

"Maybe you can come to visit me next Christmas, Grandpa Mario. I miss you. Okay, here's my mom again."

Mario had tears in his eyes as Melanie's sister Connie returned to the phone.

"We all miss you, Dad. Perhaps we can visit you in Florida, next year. Rusty wants to take Jason fishing in the Keys. He's working a lot of overtime to save for a trip.

He's such a great guy and a good husband."

Connie could hear him sniffling. "I'll let you go now. I know you always attend the 5:00 P.M., Wednesday mass. We'll speak again next week, Dad. Big hugs and kisses to everyone."

He ended the call and noticed Melanie had joined the bookkeeper. She was in the office to review the payroll with him. She glanced into Mario's attaché case and picked up the opened envelope from the mortgage company.

"Papa, what's this letter from the mortgage company all about?"

"Oh, a reminder, something about the mortgage," he said softly. "I'll handle it."

She walked over to his side. "What do you mean, just a reminder letter?"

"Melanie, I thought you didn't care much about the business," he whispered.

She lowered her voice. "I don't, Papa. Your secrecy is a mystery though."

"Melanie, you're my daughter. I don't hold any secrets between us. I will say though you confuse me sometimes. You tell me you don't want to own the business, but you also want to be made aware of everything I'm doing."

"Papa, you misunderstand me. I want to help you with the business in every way while you're the owner. I just don't want to inherit the business."

"My dear, I've worked hard to make this your business. My dream is for you to own the tavern when I pass on. I don't understand why you treat it like nothing."

"Because, Papa, you're right. The dream is *yours*...not mine. My dream is to be a successful interior decorator. Why not share my dream with me? Perhaps Antonio is a good candidate to be the owner."

"We'll see, Melanie. Perhaps he is."

"So what's this reminder letter about, Papa?"

"Let's step outside, dear."

They left the office and stood in the hallway. Their

voices became hushed.

"Melanie. The letter is a reminder of a twenty five thousand dollar balloon payment due in ninety days."

"Damn you, Papa, why didn't you tell me?"

"Why worry you?"

"We need to find a way to make the payment, that's why. Our employees depend on us, Papa. We certainly can't default on our loan."

"I've been in worse situations. Things always work out, Melanie. No need to worry."

"That's not easy, Papa. We talked about the need to soon do some painting and refurbishing inside the restaurant."

"Yes, I know. Like I said, everything will all work out."

"I'm leaving now for a while. After Mass I need to run some errands, then I'll be back."

"I'm furious with you," she said hugging him. "But please drive safely, Papa."

Melanie returned to the office wondering how they would ever afford to make the payment. Like Mario, she realized the need to believe everything would work out.

She left the office and walked to the bar area to greet the team setting up for the evening. Melanie respected all of them and made sure she complimented each of them.

The large oak grandfather clock in his living room bellowed six times. Daniel sat in a wingback chair, absorbed in a British murder mystery. The pleasant aroma of cherry tobacco consumed the area as smoke drifted from a pipe he had specially made in Germany. He exploited the same apparel individuality at home that he did in public. A pair of black slacks, a blue velvet smoking jacket and white silk ascot adorned his lanky frame. His mustache, neatly trimmed and waxed, added to his *Hollywood* appearance.

He reached to answer the phone.

HIGH HOPES TAVERN

"Good evening, Clarice. I'm so pleased to receive a call from such a beautiful lady. He set his pipe in a nearby ashtray. "You're welcome for the compliment. He listened intently. "Yes, I do understand the distance from beauty to grotesque is mercilessly brief. However, it would appear you've witnessed its reversal with as few as two martinis."

Clarice's tone hinted she preferred not to stay at home this evening. "May I safely assume you're inviting me to join you for a cocktail later? Shall we meet at High Hopes Tavern in an hour, Miss Clarice?"

He picked up his pipe and lit it again, "Perfect. So you're not afraid if gossip begins to spread if we're seen together again so soon?"

Daniel tilted his head upward and grinned. "Very well stated, my dear. I'm pleased you don't feel any compulsion to exhume your buried fears for the amusement of others. Then I shall be at the tavern in an hour."

Daniel hung up the phone, exhilarated. He could hear the faint sound of children playing in the nearby park. Their joyous voices brought back fond memories of his time in the Northeast. He had enjoyed living in Boston. The summers there were especially cheerful. He could still visualize the grandeur of his small, but exquisitely maintained garden. He recalled the fragrance of his red and yellow roses. Now he lived in Fort Lauderdale and enjoyed retirement more every day.

He prepared himself for the evening and left the house with sufficient time to meet Clarice. The traffic lights played in his favor and he arrived earlier than expected, before Clarice.

"Good evening, Antonio. My usual bourbon on the rocks with a twist, please. Would you also prepare a dry Grey Goose martini for Miss Clarice? I expect her momentarily."

"I'll make her dry martini the minute she walks through the door, Mr. Kent. I will pour it as she takes her seat."

"Antonio, please call me Daniel."

He handed him a twenty and a five. "Please take out enough for both drinks and keep the change."

"You're extremely generous...Daniel"

Good service warrants a respectable gratuity, Antonio."

Shortly after he took a seat, Clarice arrived. Daniel found her grace compelling. Clarice didn't walk into the tavern... she glided. He stood to greet her.

He felt a slight tremble. Antonio delivered on his promise and poured Clarice a dry Grey Goose martini garnished with green olives.

"This is on Daniel, Miss Clarice."

"Thank you, Daniel, and thank you, Antonio."

"I must ask you, is the High Hopes Tavern your favorite place, Miss Clarice?"

"It certainly is, my dear. Oh, occasionally I keep myself under house arrest so I don't kill a parade of morons. But this is where I like to be when I venture out."

"I'm enjoying my evenings at High Hopes as well. Due to sweet people like you, Lucky, Samantha, and everyone else I've recently met. I was quite lonely before we all became acquainted."

"We're glad to get to know you as well. Speaking of Lucky and Samantha, I've not seen them lately."

"No, not since we all had dinner. I guess they're preparing for their cruise. They leave this Sunday."

"I'm sure they're as excited to be going on a cruise as I am to be with you tonight. May I add you look ravishing."

"Thank you, Daniel. You're such a handsome devil yourself. I should also add, distinctive."

The bar was beginning to bustle. Antonio worked one section of the bar while Robbie worked the other. The two only spoke to each other when necessary. For an unusually warm September evening, even Mario sensed the chill.

Mario greeted his other customers before joining Clarice and Daniel.

"Ah, it's two of my favorites. You both look your usual best."

"Mario. You're always such a gentleman."

"I try to be. You've not yet had your dinner…correct?" Mario asked.

"Darlin' this is only my first of two martinis. You know my routine."

"What about you Daniel?"

"No, not as of yet."

With only eighty some odd days left, Mario had to devise a way to make his balloon payment. Perhaps Clarice and Daniel, two successful people, might provide some ideas. Mario had never discussed the tavern's marketing or finances with any customer. He had faced difficult situations before but never *this* urgent. It was worth a shot.

"Please, be my guests. I need some advice on a monetary issue and your wisdom will come in handy. I'll be right back."

Mario walked to the Maitre d's station and blocked out table thirty-two. He made it clear to Phillip he was not to be disturbed. Their conversation would be serious business.

CHAPTER 15

THEY MIGHT COME TO BLOWS, PAPA!

Dwight stretched his arms before rubbing his sleepy eyes. The aroma of sizzling sausages was a welcome sign that Antonio was awake and preparing breakfast. He is a talented cook and soon to be chef.

Dwight wrapped his bathrobe around himself and strolled into their stylish kitchen.

"Good morning, handsome," he said with a smile and a peck on the cheek.

"Mornin', Dwight. I hope I didn't wake you."
"You didn't...the smell of sausages did."
"Are you hungry?"
"Yeah, for everything," Dwight said with a grin.
"Do you want your eggs over easy?"
"Yes, just like you, my dear." Dwight nuzzled his face into Antonio's neck, slowing to massage his back.

"Ah, Antonio...that's the Leo in you. So sentimental. I love it... and I love you!"

"Okay, Dwight which is the dominant force, lust or hunger?"

Dwight kept his eyes on Antonio. "I'm not gonna settle for anything less than both."

"Shall we surrender to hunger first?
"You're the boss, Antonio."

After they satisfied both appetites, Dwight asked. "What time are you leaving for work, Antonio?"

"3:00 P.M. I want to leave a few minutes early and buy a, *Bon Voyage* card for Lucky and Samantha. They're leaving on their cruise tomorrow.

"Who's Samantha?"

"Lucky's friend. She's coming to work for us at High Hopes Tavern. The cruise is her last hurrah before she starts her new position."

"Are Lucky and Samantha..." Before Dwight could finish his question, Antonio assured him their relationship was nothing more than a strong friendship. "Lucky is eager to find the man of her dreams. It's such a shame. She's a happy person, but still lonely. She's had tragic endings to her past relationships. One guy died and the other was an alcoholic. Her last jilted her a few months after they began seeing each other.

Jeez, Sweetie, what rotten luck."

"She's such a deserving person. I find her interesting. Lucky shared with me a deep desire to get married, but at the same time, I sense a resistance to commitment. I'm sure she'll find her love."

Dwight leaned over and hugged Antonio. "I hope she does, I know *I* did."

It was a day of chores. Together, they washed both cars. Antonio cut the grass while Dwight vacuumed and dusted the main rooms of their home. To the two other gay couples in their neighborhood, they were only slightly updated replicas of, "Ozzie and Harriet of 50's TV fame."

"Dwight, why don't you stop by the tavern tonight for a drink after your meeting? What's the name of the group you joined?"

"The *Prime Timers*. Our primary focus is social activities for us *more mature* gay *guys*. Our Fort Lauderdale chapter has about two hundred men. To be sure I keep my man happy I *will* stop by the tavern after the meeting. Remember though, I'm a private type of guy when it comes to straight bars."

"You're such a sweetheart. There's no reason to be heterophobic, Dwight. Mario wants to meet you."

"He's aware of our relationship, isn't he?"

"Could I keep something as special as you a secret?"

❧

Today would be Sam's last day at the Peacock's Feather. Several of her regular customers gave her a *Best Wishes* card. Some even included a monetary token of appreciation.

Before she left, Stan surprised her with a bonus check for one hundred dollars. She believed her decision to leave was the right decision for her. Still, tears flowed as she closed the door behind her for the final time as an employee.

Tomorrow she would be leaving on her first cruise. She and Lucky planned to celebrate tonight, at High Hopes Tavern.

Lucky tried to take a nap after work. The excitement of selecting her clothes for the cruise, packing, and going out tonight made it virtually impossible. She reached to grab her cell phone to answer an incoming call.

"Hi, Sam, are you as excited as I am?"

"You bet your sweet ass I am. This is your second cruise, but my first. Do you have me on the speaker again? You know I hate that."

"Yes, I'm beginning to pack my suitcase. You're going to have the time of your life. I hope the ship is full of single men."

"All I need is one, Lucky."

"Yup, just one special man. I've been on love's waiting list too long."

"What time do you want to meet tonight, Lucky?"

"How 'bout if I pick you up at 7:30?"

"That's a deal. I'll be ready. See ya later."

❧

Lucky listened to Carly Simon's, *Moonlight Serenade* CD. She joined in, a few notes off-key, when her favorite, *I've Got You Under My Skin*, played. She placed a few additional items in her suitcase and headed for the shower. She turned on the water, and couldn't help but think how wonderful the cruise was going to be. She was in a euphoric mood. The thought of a carefree week in the Caribbean sun was just what she needed. A short time later, she was ready to go.

Sam stood outside her place as Lucky pulled up.

"Taxi?" she laughed.

Sam got in and gave Lucky a quick peck on the cheek. "Girl, I am so ready for this cruise."

"Me to. But right now, it's a Saturday night in Fort Lauderdale. Let's get wild."

They talked about the cruise as they drove to the tavern.

"Don't forget your passport, Sam. The cruise line can't board you without one."

"Lucky, what's our plan if one of us is in the stateroom with a guest and needs privacy?"

"Simple. If the, *Do Not Disturb* sign is on the door knob, continue past the door." A few minutes later they arrived. "Well, here we are. Tonight the High Hopes Tavern, tomorrow the *Emerald Princess*."

"Look, Lucky. The legendary Miss Clarice and Daniel Dooley Kent are heading into the tavern, arm in arm."

"I'm not surprised. I think Daniel likes Clarice. Rumor is they were seen here earlier this week as well."

The sky was ominous and the rumbling of thunder clouds made a compelling case for Lucky to valet park. She grabbed an oversized umbrella from the back seat. As they reached the protection of the tavern's awning, huge raindrops pelted the street.

"*Bon Voyage*," shouted their friends as they entered. Mario wore a blue captain's hat, complete with a gold anchor, reminiscent of the Skipper on *Gilligan's Island*. A colorful array of balloons decorated their seats.

"I want this to be the best vacation for each of you. And Sam, the weather is supposed to be balmy all next week with no threats of a storm."

Mario motioned to Pete, "Give these young ladies a goodbye drink on the house."

"So nothing's brewing out there in the Atlantic?"

"Nope, nothing at all," Mario said. "I was just busting your chops."

Lucky turned around to respond to a tap on her shoulder. Clarice and Daniel stood in back of them.

"Good evening, ladies," Clarice said.

"Hello Miss Clarice, Daniel.

"Darlin', I'm interested to learn more about your cruise. Which ship is it, and where are you going?"

"We're sailing on the, *Emerald Princess*, to the Eastern Caribbean. She's a beauty from what the travel agent told me. There are pools, a spa, too many bars to count, a nine-hole putting course, a casino, theatre, restaurants galore, and I hope a lot of men.

"Ah, the Eastern Caribbean route. I believe you'll be

cruising to St. Maarten, St Thomas, Grand Turk and the Bahamas, correct?"

"Yes, how did you know?"

"My husband and I took numerous cruises. Before he left me for another woman, of course. Not to suggest she was a tramp, but she's had so many men that a repetition of names has begun. As a matter of fact, my former husband is her third Calvin!"

A long and intense crackling sound followed by a rumble of thunder provided a glow from the lightning. A second cadence of thunder followed.

Clarice's significantly enhanced eye lashes blinked rapidly above her martini. "Oooh, she must be listening,"

Daniel caught two men point at him and laugh. He didn't mind that customers starred at his outlandish attire. He was smitten with Clarice, and held a special place in his heart for Lucky. If it wasn't for her, he would still be standing alone, with the good times passing him by.

"Do you ladies need a ride to the port tomorrow?"

"I've arranged a ride already, but do appreciate your offer."

Sam set her wine down on the bar and shook her head. "Lucky thinks of everything. I'm so excited, I never thought about how we were getting to the ship."

Clarice noticed her table being prepared for her arrival. She stood up, took a sip of her drink, and nudged Daniel.

"I think our table is almost ready, my dear."

Daniel had a habit of lifting his right eyebrow and tilting his head to indicate his indignation. He held out his arm to escort Clarice to their table, Phillip quickly comprehended Daniel's annoyance.

"Miss Clarice, I'll lead you to your table. However, Mr. Kent will hold your arm this evening."

As he seated the couple, Daniel whispered to Phillip, "I appreciate your sharp observation and I thank you. He smiled and handed him a tip.

The fact that Clarice Thompson and Daniel Dooley

Kent dined again in private was not lost on the regulars. Gossip goes with the territory. Some glanced at the table where they sat and commented to each other. There could be no better indication their dining together would be fodder for further gossip.

Excited about tomorrow, Lucky and Sam sat and enjoyed their wine.

"What's Melanie doing here on a Saturday night?" Lucky asked. "She's usually on a date or with her college girlfriends."

'I can't say, but here she comes."

Lucky enjoyed Melanie's company, but was surprised to see her. "Melanie, what's up? How are you doing with your classes?"

"Excellent. Thank you, Lucky." Melanie turned toward Sam. "You must be Samantha Burnside, our new addition."

"Yes, my pleasure, Melanie." She shook her hand. "I've seen you here many times but we've never met."

"The same here Samantha. Welcome aboard."

Melanie took Sam by the hand. "I'm curious though. How did you manipulate a vacation before even starting?" she joked.

"Your dad's generosity of course, but I think you could have used me tonight. This place is hoppin'. The place is so busy you've even got Robbie, the bartender, waiting tables."

"Yeah, my papa asked him to switch duties tonight."

Melanie liked Robbie. He was young, attractive, and single. As far as she knew, he liked ladies. She also recalled her father's warning to be fair, but alert, to any possible touchy hand tactics.

Time slipped by. At 10:30, Lucky and Sam were still in the tavern.

Mario took a seat close to the door. "Are Sam and Lucky still here?"

"I think so, yeah, they're coming our way now."

"Speaking of the devils," Mario stood up to give each a hug.

"We're angels, Mario, not devils. At least until we board the ship tomorrow. Then, all bets are off."

"Care for a nightcap, ladies?"

"Not for me, Mario. I'm the driver, so this is my last," Lucky replied.

"Oh my God," Samantha said, pausing after each word. After taking a deep breath, she repeated. "Oh-My-God. Is he a slice of heaven?"

Dwight's aura exuded a confident masculinity. His well-toned body erased any possibility of a wrinkle on his Armani shirt. Anyone could tell he bought his trousers from an upscale men's clothier. He wore expensive shoes and was well-groomed. He wore a simple but expensive gold watch.

Antonio played it cool as Dwight sat down on one of the few open stools. He slipped him a casual wink and slid a cocktail napkin in front of him.

"How's the man of my dreams?" he said softly.

"Nervous, but glad to be here."

Antonio knew very well what Dwight drinks. To avoid any gossip he elevated his voice.

"What can I get you to drink, sir?"

"I'll have a Manhattan straight up, please."

Mario's gut told him the man who derailed Sam from leaving was Antonio's partner. Sam coiled like a snake, ready to attack when a man she wanted to meet appeared. Lucky thought, *It's time to leave...now.*

"Let's go, Sam. Tomorrow's the big day."

"Give me a second, Lucky. I want to say hello to gorgeous over there."

"Ah come on. He's married I'm sure."

Mario knew Lucky and Antonio were close. Tonight, for the first time, he was sure Lucky was in tune about his private life. He had to rescue her from this predicament.

Mario looked at Sam emphatically. "If you're talking

about the man who Antonio is now serving, he's taken. I'm told the person he lives with can be very jealous."

"Well whoever she is, she's one extremely lucky lady."

There was no sound but the collective biting of tongues as Mario and Lucky pretended not to have heard.

"Ladies, I envy you. I wish I could join you on the cruise. Have a great time and send us a postcard if you can."

"Thanks, Mario. We will."

By 11:00, only a handful of customers remained in the dining area. The bar crowd had thinned, but a respectable number remained. Those who stayed were quite lively. Short of an all out run, Melanie headed toward Mario in a fast pace. She looked troubled.

"Papa, you need to get in the kitchen, quickly."

"What's the matter, Melanie?"

"Robbie and Michael are having an argument. I think they might come to blows."

Mario arrived to witness the two clutching each others' shirts before two chefs separated them. Some broken dishes lay on the floor.

"What the hell is going on in here? You do understand any type of fighting is grounds for immediate dismissal don't you?"

Robbie breathed heavily. Sweat beaded his forehead.

"I was just picking up an order when Michael put his arm around me. He squeezed me tight and said, "customers are saying you're a shitty waiter and you're too touchy with the female customers."

Michael shook. "That's not true, Mario. He's crazy."

"I've never had two waiters fight in this place. I won't tolerate it…period. Now I want the both of you to go out and serve your remaining customers as if nothing happened. I'll see you both in my office Monday morning at 9:00 A.M., sharp. Is that clear?"

Robbie tucked his shirt back in his pants and straightened his tie, leaving the kitchen first.

"Mario, I would never lie to you. I never said anything to Robbie, but I did have to defend myself when he almost hit me."

"We'll discuss what happened Monday morning, Michael. You've been here a long time and never had a problem. It will all work out."

"I'm a professional, Mario. I'll let my work ethic overshadow what just occurred."

"Works for me, Michael. Between you and me, Robbie hasn't exactly ingratiated himself with the staff here."

Right after his shift, Robbie left the tavern, mumbling to himself. Some of the staff believed he left for good. They were right. But they certainly would hear of him again.

CHAPTER 16

TWO LADIES AND A PRINCESS

Samantha fanned her hands in the air to dry her freshly polished nails. She paced the floor, but stopped to raise the blinds and peer at the street below looking for Lucky's car. Her baggage was lined up by the door. She felt the excitement grow as she examined the pre-printed Princess luggage tags.

The plan was for Lucky to pick her up by noon in order to be at the ship by 1:00. Sam looked out the window again. She was startled to see a waiting black stretch limousine. A uniformed chauffeur escorted Lucky to Sam's door and knocked.

"Lucky, is that you?"

"Sure is, and our ride is here."

Sam gasped as she opened the door.

Lucky stepped in and gave her a big hug.

The chauffeur smiled at her. "Good afternoon, ma'am. My name is William and I'll be your driver today. Is this all your luggage?"

"Yes, William." Sam regained her composure. "Lucky...you really know how to surprise a girl."

"I told you I'd arranged for a ride. The limo is my treat."

At Lucky's request, William took the scenic route along the beach to the port. Eight cruise ships came into view as the limo glided over the bridge on the Seventeenth Street Causeway. Sam quickly recognized the Princess logo on the ship's smokestack. She pointed out the ship and patted Lucky's hand. "The Emerald Princess is enormous!"

"Here we are, Sam. The adventure begins today."

All of their senses were on high alert. What may have seemed mundane to the sophisticated travelers around them was pure excitement to them as they quickly passed through the official formalities to enter the port.

As they emerged from the limo, a cheerful stevedore greeted the ladies and asked them for their travel documents. After a quick glance he retrieved the luggage from the trunk. Lucky and Sam walked around to the back of the limo.

While Sam gave a generous tip to the stevedore, Lucky slipped a twenty dollar bill into William's hand. "Thank you, we hope to see you next week."

They stopped to absorb the overwhelming scene pier side. Sam was in disbelief. She watched the process to board twenty-five hundred passengers and provisions for them and a crew of a thousand. It was impressive and flowed easier than when she served a full house at the Peacock's Feather Restaurant.

An elderly man and his wife stood in front of them. He turned and smiled at Lucky and Sam. "Is this your first cruise, ladies?"

"Her first, my second. Hi, my name is Nancy Larkin, but my friends call me, *Lucky*."

"I'm Samantha Burnside, or Sam for short."

"This will be our forty first cruise. You'll enjoy it immensely. I'm Ralph Becker and this is my wife Florence. It's a pleasure to meet you both."

"Your forty first cruise? Jeez, that's astounding. Here I am thinking my second is a big deal."

"Perhaps we'll meet you ladies on board. Let us buy you a drink to celebrate your cruise."

"Ralph, we're not even on the ship yet and you already want to flirt with pretty girls" she added playfully.

Before long they were passing through security and on the escalator leading to the check-in counter. Within minutes they boarded the ship.

A smartly dressed member of the ship's staff stood at the entrance. "Good afternoon, ladies. Welcome aboard the Emerald Princess. What is your stateroom number?"

"C427," Lucky replied.

"Your stateroom is on the Caribe Deck, one flight above. You can take the elevator up one deck or use the stairs. Your luggage will soon arrive outside your stateroom door."

Sam was mesmerized. "Breathtaking... absolutely incredible," Sam said swiveling her head to take in the grandeur of the Emerald Princess Atrium. Silent glass elevators whisked jubilant vacationers from the reception area to the top of the ship. Below, a pianist played soothing music.

Reluctantly, they left the scene and headed for their stateroom. On the wall adjacent to their door was a gold card holder. Printed in bold, italic letters, was, Miss Samantha Burnside, Miss Nancy "Lucky" Larkin.

"Here we are, Lucky."

Sam put her boarding card into the lock and swung the door open. "Now, *this* is luxury. Can you believe that balcony, Lucky?" Sam bounced on one of the two beds, checking for buoyancy. "This is comfort. I can't friggin' believe how elegant this room is, but I'm sure I *can* handle a week of this, *or more*."

A letter from the ship's Captain and Officers welcomed them aboard. The *Princess Patter* daily newsletter outlined available activities as well as their location. To assist guests, the ship's deck plan was printed on the reverse side.

Lucky removed a card attached to a bottle of red wine waiting on the coffee table. "It says, 'Bon Voyage,' from, Mario and Melanie."

"They're the best, aren't they?" Sam said. "Lucky, this is beyond anything imaginable. And...we haven't even left port yet!"

"Come on, Sam. Let's get lunch and find out where everything is. Did I mention to be on the lookout for single men?"

"Only thirty times since you showed me the brochure two weeks ago. Sam grinned. So where do we go for lunch?"

Lucky pointed to a twenty four hour dining venue, Horizon Court listed in the *Princess Patter*. "This restaurant is upstairs on the Lido deck, close to the pools. Care to show off your body after lunch? I can hold in my belly if you can hold in yours."

"You bet your sweet ass I can, although I might turn blue first."

Deck fifteen was alive with revelers. A trio in Caribbean style shirts serenaded passengers with Calypso rhythms. Others navigated fully-loaded food trays from Horizon Court to poolside lounge chairs. Some guests were already reclined in the bubbling hot tub, even though the South Florida sun had reached eight-two degrees by noon.

Sam's eyes bulged. "All this food – so beautifully presented. Somebody took the time to carve faces into the side of the watermelons. One of them seems familiar. I wonder if I dated him."

"Let's hope we both find guys livelier than these. Although you have to give them credit for oversized smiles

— in spite of the dental work they need."

Lucky spotted two people leaving a window table and raced to save it. She set her tray down and pointed to a plane taking off from the Fort Lauderdale/Hollywood International airport. "I'd be willing to say they're people on that plane who just got off this ship, Sam. I bet they wish they were still with us instead of headed home."

"Speaking of where I'd rather be, check out the arms on the guy over your right shoulder."

"Where, I don't ...Oh *yes*, Sam said, placing her right hand over her heart. Let me catch my breath."

"I *told* you. Imagine, this is only day one."

They ate their lunch, shifting for a better look at every man without a lady in tow. "Let's sit for another ten minutes to digest the strawberry shortcake, Sam. After that, let the manhunt begin. Surely there's a young hunky guy out there who needs some lotion on his back."

"Be sure to check for a wedding band before you make an offer," she laughed. "I'm sure the ship has a doctor. I doubt his service will be free if some angry wife beats the crap out of you."

"Come on -- time to hit the pool."

"Fine, but we have to be ready for the safety drill at 4:00 P.M. It's a hoot, Sam! Those short old ladies in orange life jackets remind me of driving by a pumpkin patch in October."

"Okay, as long as you don't expect me to be the scarecrow!"

There were numerous single lounge chairs, but no pairs. Sam might flirt with the best of them, but finding her way around the ship alone was not on her agenda. Not yet anyway.

"Hey, Lucky, one deck up...to the right. I see two vacant lounges."

A short race later they were breathless but satisfied. They sprawled on the lounge chairs and began to enjoy the scenery, including the vertical male variety.

The combination of three rum runners and the hot sun proved too much for Lucky. The evidence was what sounded suspiciously like a snore. Sam turned away from the railing where she had been watching the water below. "Lucky, Lucky, she said tapping her on the shoulder. It's 3:30. Don't we need to get ready for that drill thing?"

"Geez, Sam, I dozed off, didn't I? Yes, we need to go to the stateroom and get our lifejackets. Just give me a minute to wake up."

They opened their stateroom door to the fragrance of a dozen long-stemmed roses. Their names were printed on a card with a gold border.

"I wonder who sent them?"

Sam opened the card. "Enjoy your cruise, Clarice and Daniel."

"What a surprise," Lucky said.

They grabbed their lifejackets and glanced at the sign posted on the back of the door for directions to their muster station. Passengers filled the elevators, hallways, and stairways as they all headed to their assigned areas.

"Please line up with the taller people to the rear," directed a crew member with a clipboard in hand.

Lucky struggled with the strap of her lifejacket. A good looking young man approached with a smile. He untangled her strap and connected it properly into the plastic clip on the belt. Without a word, he returned to his place in line, two rows away.

"Who was that?"

"I have absolutely no idea, Sam, but somehow -- with seven days ahead of us -- finding out is definitely on my agenda."

CHAPTER 17

ACTION PLAN

At exactly 10 o'clock Monday morning Mario heard a knock on his office door. Michael stopped pacing when Mario opened the door but fumbled with his notes as he sat down. Even though Mario chatted with him, Michael was nervous as they waited for Robbie.

They waited. "Well Michael, I've got 10:30. I had a feeling he wouldn't show. I didn't witness what happened, but I can't imagine you instigated anything. Enjoy the rest of your day, we'll talk again later.

"So do you think Robbie quit?"

"I guess so. I just don't understand him. He had so much potential."

"I know *I'm* grateful for my job. I'll be here this afternoon when my shift starts at 5:00, or a little before."

As Michael left, the phone rang. Mario answered and waved good-bye.

"Darlin', Clarice callin'." Her Southern cadence still gave him a twitch.

"Yes, I know your voice, Clarice. How can one forget your lovely accent, not to mention, we did…well, you know."

Clarice knew where he was headed and interrupted him.

Mario continued. "Of course, I recall asking you and Daniel for some marketing recommendations." Mario tapped his forehead with four fingers. "Lunch tomorrow will be fine, but I don't want Daniel to go through the trouble of cooking. A generous offer my dear, but I thought we'd go out on the cabin cruiser. I like the privacy. I'll supply lunch from the tavern."

Clarice mentioned she probably would stop by for a cocktail this evening, but agreed to meet by the dock at 11:45 tomorrow morning."

"You're a doll, Clarice."

Mario leaned back with his hands behind his neck. He reflected on Clarice and Daniel's generosity of spirit and how this nurtured a sense of family.

Before long, the reality of the balloon payment intruded into his thoughts. Whatever ideas Clarice and Daniel had to offer needed to be in place soon. Drawing on the small amount in the business savings account would only delay the needed renovations.

Clarice was perched on her favorite stool at the amen corner by 7:00.

"Hello, Pete. Haven't seen you in a while. I'm confident

my martini will be as satisfying as always."

"You can be sure, Miss Clarice."

"Is Antonio here?"

"No, he took the night off. Some celebrity chef he admires is making a guest appearance at the culinary school."

"Oh, and where's Robbie tonight?"

"Gone...he's history, Miss Clarice. I'm not one for gossip, so let's just say he wasn't a good fit."

"I'm disappointed. I liked the young man. Is Mario in the house?"

"No Miss Clarice. He left already." Pete poured her martini. "He asked me to extend his apologies and said he would meet you tomorrow."

Mario finished his preparations as he waited on the cabin cruiser for the arrival of his guests. The boat bumped calmly against the rubber pilings secured to the moorings by heavy rope. He was calmed by the sound of the water lapping against the boat. Clarice and Daniel arrived just as he finished placing the napkins and silverware next to the fine china.

"Ah, Clarice. What a pleasure. You always appear so young and vibrant."

"Let me repeat my ancestors. I'm in pretty good shape for the shape I'm in."

"It's a shape that inspires us all. Welcome aboard." He reached for Clarice's hand to steady her.

"Hello, Daniel."

"Thank you for your invitation, Mario."

Mario gave them a quick tour of the craft before they settled in on the back deck.

"May I offer you a Grey Goose martini, Clarice?"

"Oh no, darlin'. I don't drink martinis before noon. " Stretching the word, *However*, into three syllables, she added, "I would recommend you keep the bottle handy.

Do you stock any Sterling onboard?"

"Certainly."

"Daniel, how about you? Your usual bourbon?"

"Perhaps later. A Diet Coke or whatever diet soda is onboard will be fine."

Mario poured a generous glass of Sterling for Clarice before placing a can of Diet Coke and a glass with ice next to Daniel. He poured himself a small Chivas scotch. Mario took a sip to calm himself before passing around a large plate with a selection of imported cheeses and vegetables."

"I thought we would enjoy our beverages first and talk business over lunch."

"Fine with me," Daniel replied.

Clarice reached for Daniel's hand. "I agree as well, darlin'."

The gesture kindled Mario's suspicion this was becoming more than a friendship. He chose not to comment. He had shared past intimacies with Clarice, a fact they obviously kept private. She wanted more in a relationship than he was willing to offer. They remained good friends.

They shared their thoughts on how quickly the summer passes, and how thankful they were for a season--so far--free of hurricanes.

"How about the Dolphins this week? Clarice added. "Another last minute victory." The men exchanged surprised looks. "You both look flabbergasted. I've been a Dolphin fan for years."

Mario jumped in, "Barring a lot of injuries, they could do better than I expected this season. Would you care to go to a game?"

"Sure...I imagine your friendships extend to those with enough influence to secure a box seat for us."

Mario blew her a kiss. "Anything to see you in a Dolphin's T-shirt."

Daniel lifted his glass. "Wouldn't that be a treat!"

Mario maneuvered the cabin cruiser away from the

dock and sailed leisurely up the Intracoastal, creating only a slight wake. He passed several inlets and finally entered the ocean pathway. Two miles out, he stopped the engines to let the craft troll, submitting to the ocean currents.

"Would anyone like another beverage before lunch?"

"I'll take another glass of chardonnay, darlin'."

"Nothing for me, water will be fine, said Daniel."

Mario poured another glass of chardonnay for Clarice. He brought hot lobster bisque, cold lobster salad, tossed green salad and other delicacies from the tavern's kitchen.

"I'm impressed," Clarice nodded.

"So, Mario, you asked us to provide you with some suggestions for marketing the High Hopes Tavern. Any particular reason you selected us?"

"Yes, two reasons. You're both professionals. You rank at the top of my list of friends. What I will share with you is understandably between us."

"Of course, precious."

"A twenty-five thousand dollar balloon payment on the tavern mortgage is due in less than ninety days. The summer business declined this year, and I need some ideas to generate more revenue. The need is urgent."

"Hmm, Mario. We thought something was amiss—with no idea what. We want to help"

"Thanks, Daniel."

Clarice added, "Daniel and I wondered if you would consider starting a happy hour. We suggest you begin at 4:00 in the afternoon until 8:00 in the evening. Lower your drink prices a dollar or two during those hours. You'll make up the difference in volume. This is a tradition in some places, and often successful."

"The idea has merit. I just don't know if starting a happy hour will bring in additional money fast enough?"

Daniel took a sip of his Diet Coke and set the glass down. "I am somewhat reluctant to suggest this, Mario, for fear you might imagine something that is not true," Daniel said nervously.

"Go ahead, I'm open to all ideas."

"Well, my suggestion is for you to advertise in the gay publications in town. Gay people here seem to have a substantial amount of disposable income, and they appreciate gourmet food."

"You are rather fastidious in your attire, but I find it admirable."

Clarice, never without her notable fan, swept it slowly back and forth, clearly amused by Mario's comment.

"Yes, he's somewhat fastidious, but an attentive person might notice a single wayward hair," she added with a slight chuckle.

"I can assure you I'm not gay, Mario."

"Personally, it wouldn't matter if you were." I maintain an open mind. This idea makes sense."

"My concern is the timing, Daniel. Mario needs the money soon."

"True, Clarice. Mario, what if I loan you the twenty-five thousand? My life was in a downward emotional spiral until I met Lucky. She made me feel welcome at the High Hopes Tavern. Then I met Clarice and every day gets better. I'm grateful to you and all your customers. This would be my thank you for the wonderful friends I now enjoy."

"Thank you, but no, absolutely not, Daniel. I must earn the money on my own. What a generous gesture, but one I cannot accept."

Clarice, startled by Daniel's financial offer, tapped her fingers on the table. "I think we're sitting on the solution, Mario."

"That certainly deserves an explanation, my dear."

"The boat--you need to sell the boat. It must be worth quite a bit more than the amount you need."

"I can't do that, Clarice. I use this boat to attract business. I've discussed weekly luncheon contracts with community and local organization leaders on this boat."

"Were the results positive, Mario?"

"Yes."

"Now for the big question. When did you last take someone out on the boat to obtain their business?" Daniel piped in.

"Close to a year ago."

"There's your answer, Mario. I think Clarice's idea has merit. Fewer than ninety days are left before the note is due. The process will take some time if you do decide to sell the boat."

Mario thought for a moment, "I'm not keen on the idea, but realistically it should be an option."

"Ah... another idea. The best method to increase your profit is to increase your revenue. What if you added different entertainment? You already pay a trio," Clarice added.

"Yes, you don't want to be just another place with karaoke, Daniel commented."

"I'm not following you, Clarice. Hiring entertainers is expensive and adds to the cost of doing business."

Clarice looked out to the sea and then back at both men. "Another way to gain additional customers is to have them entertain each other. Like sharing stories. Look at how much time we all spend sitting around talking about how we ended up in Fort Lauderdale and why we're still here? Wouldn't that be an original show? Many of your customers are excellent story tellers, some are musicians. Think of the synergy of talent"

"Clarice, you may just be on to something here. What do you think, Mario?"

I think that may just be the best idea yet."

"I'd be pleased to coordinate this effort for you," Clarice suggested. "I may even offer a name. How about, 'Lauding Lauderdale'?"

Daniel added, "You should promote this on your website too."

After another hour and much discussion Mario turned on the engines and turned the boat slowly toward the

Intracoastal, heading back to the dock. Daniel and Clarice leaned back into their chairs to let the salt air and sun caress their faces. Mario remained quiet as he steered the boat, preoccupied by the fear he may need to sell the boat.

After they docked, Clarice and Mario exchanged air kisses. Daniel and Mario shook hands.

At Daniel's place he and Clarice had another drink and reviewed their suggestions.

"So, interesting-- Mario thought I might be gay?"

"Well, now he knows you're not."

"Clarice, I wonder if perhaps we are at the point in our relationship where we should…advance to the next step."

Pausing, perhaps a bit too long, Clarice noted his growing discomfort. She stifled a giggle and concluded. "At this point a true Southern lady would clutch her bosom and pretend to swoon."

"I can hardly wait."

With the sway of a coquette, she took him by the hand and led him to the bedroom. "I have always depended on the wisdom that a man should be encouraged ... to be a man."

CHAPTER 18

FAMILY TIME

After an early evening nap Mario drove back to the restaurant deep in thought. He rehashed the suggestions Clarice and Daniel had offered. The borrowed money was now on borrowed time.

He entered the restaurant and sensed a smaller than usual dinner crowd. *I can't wait for the snowbirds to return*, he thought. He mingled with customers before pouring a Chivas and settling into a stool at the end of the bar.

"Hey Mario, mind if we join you," Michael asked?"

"Please, join me. Let me get you guys a drink."

Mario enjoyed sharing time with his employees who worked hard to make the business a success. He considered them to be family. He signaled to Antonio to give them a drink.

"What's up, guys?"

"Not too much, Mario. We had a small dinner crowd tonight."

"Yeah, apparently."

Raul seemed anxious, repeatedly folding a napkin on the bar.

"Something on your mind, Raul?"

"Yes, but nothing bad. I'd say it's more of a suggestion. I've mentioned to you I'm an artist. I work here full time because I can't make a living off my paintings. I have a question, Mario. Would you permit me and some of my artist friends to display one of our paintings on the walls here? Another sales site would help us. Of course you would get a commission on the sales."

"I would like to help you, but wouldn't the galleries be upset with me?"

"No, because each artist would be limited to one painting at a time. High Hopes would be a new venue for them. To make a purchase, the buyer would take the artist's card from the painting and the purchase would be made at the gallery."

"Your suggestion might attract a few more people who appreciate art. I sort of like the idea, Raul. I need to think it through, but I'll make a decision soon."

"Our goal is to expand the market for our artistic talents."

"Is art what brought you to Fort Lauderdale, Raul? Did you go to art school here?"

"Yes, I went to an excellent art college. The weather here is perfect."

"What brought you here, Michael? You're a transplant,

right?

"I came here on vacation with my parents. I like to fish and surf. I realized if I lived here I could do both all year-round."

An hour slipped by but Mario enjoyed getting closer to his team. Alvita, the first waitress he hired at High Hopes Tavern, sat down to fold her apron in the *Conch Shell* dining room.

"Alvita, come on. Enjoy a drink. Happy hour may be over, this is our family hour."

Mario was aware she was close to being eligible for Social Security, but she made good money in tips at the restaurant. He wasn't worried she would take retirement and leave. She took a seat next to Mario and the guys.

"We were just talking about why we live here. You were born here, right Alvita?"

"Yes, my family is from Jamaica, but I was born here." Buy me a few drinks and I just might get drunk and tell you what year."

"I don't think we store enough liquor in the bar to get you to divulge such information. I'll buy you one anyway."

The four of them shared a hearty laugh. Mario raised his glass.

Alvita took a sip of her drink and began. "My parents worked for the airlines in Kingston, my mom with Eastern and my dad with Pan Am. I've traveled a lot."

"On propeller planes I'm sure," Michael quipped.

"Don't be funny, Michael. I might come over there and whip your ass."

"Oooh, do you kiss your mama with that mouth?"

They enjoyed learning more about each other and talked until closing. As he lingered in the office he reflected on the conversation with his team. It was the final evidence he needed. Lauding Lauderdale would be a go. After all, whether people are new here or are simply looking for reasons to stay, their main motive will always be high hopes.

CHAPTER 19

"MAY I HELP YOU WITH YOUR STRAP?"

Lucky and Sam leaned over the railing of their balcony. As the ship maneuvered away from the dock, the water below churned, creating small, white waves. A sudden loud blast of the ship's horn startled them.

"What picture-perfect weather today, right, Lucky?"

"Yes, and we got our money's worth, Sam. The tour, the lunch, the time at the beach. On our next cruise, perhaps we can both enjoy such an adventure with a special guy. Too much to hope for?"

"Nope, I agree. So what's up for tonight, Lucky?

"Dinner is at 8:30, so I thought I'd first spend some time in the casino. So far, I can't seem to win with the male gender onboard. Perhaps my luck will be better at the slot machines."

"Okay by me, Lucky."

I'm going to take a shower and get dressed. Should I wait for you to get ready?"

"No, go ahead. I'm going to sit on the balcony and enjoy the salt air for a bit. I'll meet you at your usual place in the casino at 8:00."

The casino was an erratic scene of enticing sounds and color. Lucky enjoyed the whirring reels of the slot machines. The metallic sound of coins dropping into trays. The bing-bing-bing of the winners' machines. The colorful flashing lights. Her pulse quickened. To her, the casino is a place where hope triumphs reality.

At one of the craps tables, a gaggle of gamblers hovered around an elderly lady. Lucky recognized her as Florence from the check-in line at the pier. A sizable stack of chips in front of her, accompanied by cheers from the crowd around the table, sent a message. Florence was winning big money.

Lucky stood close by as Florence lectured all the gamblers at the table.

"I paid for this trip with my winnings from the last cruise, because I quit while I was ahead." She pulled a mound of chips toward her and dropped them in a bucket. "My body may be clumsy, but my brain is still nimble."

She turned to take her chips to the cashier's window and bumped into Lucky.

"Hi, Florence. I would say you had a winning day."

"Yes, Lucky, I did."

"Where's Ralph?"

"He's probably hustling some young female to buy him

a drink," she laughed.

"You accept his philandering?"

"He's harmless, and doesn't require a leash, but a muzzle might help. I allow him his fantasies. I've gotta run, Lucky. I'm at the same table every day. Join me."

"Sounds good. I'd like to learn. Perhaps with your help I can live up to my name."

"It will be my pleasure to provide some insight into the game. You're on your own with the luck part."

After a brief detour to cash in her chips, she headed for the bar in search of Ralph.

Lucky studied the action at the table. While she collected mental notes on some of the gamblers' strategies, she reached to casually adjust a shoulder strap.

A voice behind her whispered, "I see your straps are still giving you problems."

Caught off guard, she turned around. "Like everyone else these days, I'm sometimes *strapped for cash*. Otherwise, I do quite well," she responded.

"I haven't seen you since the lifeboat drill."

"How might you miss me? It's only me sailing with twenty seven hundred of my closest friends."

"Ah, but are they all as lovely as you?" He offered his hand. "My name is Karl Koerner."

"I'm Lucky Larkin."

"How lucky am I. May I buy you a cocktail?"

"Another time, Karl. I'm joining my girlfriend here at 8:00."

"What if I promised you a seat where you can see your friend when she arrives?"

"You're a persuasive guy, Karl." She struggled to keep her demeanor calm, but inside ached to reach over and stroke his cheek. She reminded herself she only met him a couple of sentences ago.

"Sure, I can make time for one drink,"

Karl led her toward two vacant seats closer to the casino entrance. "What would you like?"

"A glass of chardonnay, please. Sterling if it's available."
"Excellent choice."

A handsome bartender asked, "What's your pleasure, folks?" His name tag read "Tommy." He hailed from Indonesia.

"We'd like a glass of Sterling Chardonnay, and an Old Fashioned."

Lucky raised her eyebrows, "You like the potent stuff, don't you."

"Yeah...my dad drank them. I tried one, and after I hacked for the first ten minutes, I decided I liked them after all. They've been my favorite drink ever since."

"So, are you sailing alone, Karl?"

"No, I'm sailing with my partner.

"Do you mean partner as in business partner or gay-lover?" she asked.

"Partner as in co-worker. I'm curious though. Why can two girls meet for lunch and give each other a kiss on the cheek? They can dance together and no one pays any attention. Even going to the restroom together is not an issue. But two guys together are presumed to be gay. Unless they're at a sporting event or playing pool and scratching their crotches."

"I never gave that a thought. You're right, and I apologize if I made you uncomfortable."

"Would I invite you for a drink if I were, you know...gay?"

"You're right, of course."

"My partner's name is Gary. Two years ago his wife died of a heart attack. This cruise is his first social outing since. He'll be here shortly."

"I really feel stupid now. I'm so sorry to hear about his wife."

"Where does a Lucky girl live?"

"In Fort Lauderdale, not far from where we boarded the ship."

"From what I've seen before we boarded, it's a

beautiful city. Gary's flying home after the cruise. I'm hanging around for a few days before returning home. Perhaps you can show me around?"

"I could probably be persuaded." There was nothing tentative in her tone.

"What kind of work are you in?"

I'm a front desk agent at the Crystal Sands Hotel on the beach. The winter season is always hectic, but I enjoy my work. How about you?"

"Gary and I are detectives."

"Where?"

"Just outside Atlanta."

She became more attracted to him as the conversation continued.

He was tall and well-proportioned with dark brown eyes. He dressed and spoke well. They spoke a short while before Lucky spotted Sam.

"Sorry Karl, Samantha's coming through the door. Time to go."

"So soon? We still have a sip or two left in our glasses."

"I told Sam to meet me here at 8:00," she said gulping down the last of her wine.

"Any chance we can meet again tomorrow?"

"You're the detective. You figure it out. Here's a clue, though. I'm usually in the casino every night around this time."

"I usually don't like to play detective on vacation, Lucky. My specialty, though, just became 'Missing Persons.' I'll catch ya later."

Sam greeted her with a peck on the cheek. When Lucky chuckled she asked, "What's so funny?"

"Oh, just something Karl shared with me about when girls meet."

"Karl?"

"Yeah, remember the guy who adjusted my lifejacket strap?"

"That was him?"

"Sure was."

"Okay, details. I want all the details."

"There's not much to tell. We only had one drink, Sam. He's a detective from a city somewhere outside Atlanta. He's traveling with a colleague whose wife died a couple of years ago. We might run into each other tomorrow. That's if he's a good detective."

"What do you mean you *might*? Why didn't you set a time and place? When I walked in, you two were sitting at the bar. He's easy on the eyes. I was hoping to meet him. If I were you, I would have skipped dinner to get into his pants."

"Yes, I know. You're a little more reckless."

"Guilty as charged."

"For me, it's more than just the hunt. I'm searching for romance, not just sex. I'm thirty eight and single, with a biological clock ticking loud enough to burst an eardrum."

"I understand, Lucky. I also don't believe utopia exists."

"Me neither, but sometimes I feel like I'm sleepwalking through my life. I realize I'm old fashioned in many ways, but I still believe love is like music. There's a variety of rhythms, beats, high notes and low notes. Properly orchestrated, a sensational sound permeates the air."

"You mean the, 'to have and to hold, for better or for worse,' type of love?"

"Exactly. Is there still room in our culture for such a phenomenon?"

"Yes, but the gap is closing."

"I want more high notes in love than low notes."

"Well, Lucky. Maybe Karl can compose just that song. Perhaps *he's* your maestro."

"Hey, my love life has not been pitch-perfect. Maybe there's hope. "Many a good tune has been played on an old piano."

CHAPTER 20

EMOTIONS

The dinner table at the High Hopes Tavern usually occupied by Clarice Thompson alone now took on a new identity. Mario and the staff now called it the, *Thompson-Kent Love Corner*, for seldom did either dine without the other anymore.

Until she met Daniel, Clarice always judged herself by her past self- image, rather than the woman she had become. His attention helped update her self-image.

Daniel was still flamboyant in dress; Clarice still extolled her Southern charm. These qualities continued to attract the crowd's commentary, which amused them.

"Why your husband would even *think* about leaving you is a mystery to me."

"Over time things changed, Daniel. I guess the chemistry dissolved after a while."

"His loss! You can't *dictate* chemistry, can you?"

"Are you trying to tamper with my emotions, sir?"

"You divined my intention. Think of it instead as curiosity."

"Calvin and I shared a good life in the beginning. At least I thought so. To be active participants in the dinner theatre circuit presented its own challenges. We socialized with the elite of Miami Beach, which both excited and drained us. Calvin wanted to succeed as an actor. His mistake was to combine his ambition with greed and lust.

"A deadly mix for any business!

"His lust cost us our marriage. I don't claim to be innocent. I also have my own vices, but aging begins to erase the amount of time left to pursue them."

"Are you saying some confessions will follow?"

"No, but seventy begins the downside of life. You can take that as a warning."

"Is remarrying in the picture?"

"You wouldn't be inquiring about the two of us would you, Daniel?

"Yes," he paused. "I suppose I am."

"I believe the correct term for someone beyond the conventional age to marry, is spinster. A title I could cheerfully relinquish. I can't tell you how flattering I find this to be and also how appealing. At the time Calvin left me, it tainted my expectations of men. I would be more comfortable if we take this slowly.

Clarice being willing to consider remarrying was exhilarating to him. He suspected the rapid growth of his emotions to be well beyond a typical pace. He took her hand. "Shall we partake of another cocktail?"

She smiled. "Sure, but shall we move to the bar?"

"Certainly, my dear. At least now you are aware of my thoughts."

Clarice hesitated to reveal her feelings any further this evening. The drinks began to take an effect. She reached into her purse for her trademark fan and began its stately rhythm.

"Now, I don't see a staircase, but if one existed here at the tavern, I would stand at the top and pinch my cheeks for the added color before skipping down into your arms."

"Clarice, I never thought of myself as Rhett Butler -- but you do make a superb Scarlett O'Hara."

They stood up from their dinner table and clasped each other's hand before joining their friends for a last drink.

Antonio greeted them warmly. "Do I dare ask?"

Clarice replied. "I *do* wish to change the composition of my drink tonight, Antonio. Perhaps three olives rather than two."

"Yes, Miss Clarice," he said, smiling as he shook his head in amusement.

Daniel spoke up. "My usual please, Antonio."

"Right away, my friend."

A sizable crowd encircled the bar. Antonio shook the last drop into her martini glass.

"Here you go. A Grey Goose martini with *three* olives and Daniel's usual."

She smiled at Antonio and handed him a twenty dollar bill. "This is for you. You not only mix an incomparable martini, but you're also an attentive listener."

"Listening skills are covered during the first day of bartenders school,"

"Which day does the instructor cover being irresistibly handsome?"

"Ah, Miss Clarice. You exude such charm. Your energy is always inspiring."

"Why yes, darlin', in the spirit of full disclosure perhaps

I should admit my long held philosophy, 'If you rest, you rust."

"I can't image anyone has ever accused you of either resting or rusting." Daniel added. Now I have a surprise for you."

The trio returned from a break. As they took their places, Daniel whispered a request to the sax player. After the end of the song's intro he held the microphone up to his mouth and began to sing, "What I Did For Love" from the long- running musical, "A Chorus Line."

Daniel's tenor voice suddenly transitioned the room from loud festivity to a respectful hush. From his office Mario noticed a distinctly lower level of voices and laughter outside. He wondered what caused the change and left to satisfy his curiosity. The only sound from the bar was an occasional shared comment. Daniel was still singing.

Daniel's last note was greeted by vigorous applause, cheers, and whistles. He modestly acknowledged the recognition as he slowly made his way back to Clarice.

She kissed him as he reached her side. "What a voice! I find no end to your surprises."

Mario approached the couple. "Wow, Daniel, you were sensational!" He motioned for Antonio. "Give this man a drink on the house."

"Sure thing, Mario. Man you rocked the place, Daniel."

"I wouldn't go that far, Antonio, but I'm delighted you enjoyed my song."

"Enjoyed it… hell. Your singing talent was the best kept secret since W. Mark Felt admitted he was, Deep Throat, the famous Watergate informant." Clarice said with a slight slur.

"My voice is only part of what I care to share with you, Clarice."

"We need to take our time," she said."

"You're definitely worth waiting for," Clarice."

"Would it be a revelation if I told you Mario and I

enjoyed an intimate relationship a year or so ago?"

"Yes, it would be. As you said earlier, things change. Is Melanie aware?"

"Not unless Mario told her, but the past is the past."

Clarice took his hand. "Whatever the future holds, I want it to include you."

"To the future," he toasted.

"Yes, to the future."

CHAPTER 21

COULD IT BE?

This was their first glimpse of the Turks and Caicos. Sam and Lucky stood on the pier ready to board the tour bus. "We're just waiting for five more people," the young escort for the *Governors Beach Break* excursion announced.

Within minutes they boarded the bus and got settled. "I can't believe we have only today and tomorrow before we dock in Fort Lauderdale." Sam said.

"This cruise is even better than the first one. My stomach is filled everyday with gourmet food, but my sexual appetite is still dieting."

"Nothing yet with Karl?"

"No." Lucky responded as she slid the window down for some extra air. "You're not going to believe who's running toward the bus, Sam."

"Let me think, would it be Karl and his friend?"

"You're a winner, Miss Burnside. Step up and collect

your prize. The last few seats are only two rows in back of us. Sounds like our lucky day-- and theirs too!"

"Look at the arms on Karl's friend. Isn't it cute how that little bit of sideburn comes down one side of his chin and up to the other side." Sam resisted a leer as the two men boarded the bus.

"Hey, Karl's worth a little extra attention to," she reminded Sam.

The two latecomers boarded the bus and tangoed down the aisle without endangering arms and legs that spilled into the aisle.

"Lucky, what a surprise. And this must be Samantha. I caught a glimpse of you when Lucky and I were at the casino bar."

"You must be Karl, and your friend is?"

"Gary," he responded. "We finally get to meet."

Lucky pretended to be annoyed, "So you two are the reason we're leaving ten minutes late."

"Yup, halfway down the gangway I realized I left the tour coupons in the room," Karl said. "Sorry for that."

"But *worth* the wait, I'm sure," Sam replied. "Are those your muscles, Gary, or did you borrow them from the ship's fitness center trainer?"

They're a combination of genetics and hard work--on the job and at the gym."

The representative took a quick head count and nodded to the driver. He pulled the knob that swiveled the door to close. "Ladies and Gentlemen, welcome to the *Governor's Beach Break* tour. I'm Aimee and I'll be giving you a brief history of the sites along the way to Governor's Beach. Our driver today is Luis."

"You guys better grab those two seats soon," Lucky warned. "We'll catch you later."

The vivid shades of water and tall royal palm tree views so elegantly promised by the brochures began to appear outside the window.

"You can be sure they're going to ask us to join them

on the beach, Sam. What do you think?"

"What a silly question. It's time for a better look at those bodies."

"Remember, Sam, Gary may still be healing from emotional scars. Don't expect a fast assault. You're not a fleeing suspect."

"Sure, but it's time for an encore performance on this cruise."

"Do you mean, there's been a first and you're just getting around to telling me? Details girl."

"I met a guy at the pool earlier when you were taking one of your famous power naps. We spoke for a while and took a dip in the pool. He mentioned his stateroom number and said to stop by if I wanted a good time. I must admit, he was a rather dignified flirt and rated a 10 in bed. Why are you so shocked?"

"You're right. I should be accustomed to your antics by now. You certainly bring a whole new meaning to the term, Secret Service."

"You're sure nothing's going on with you and lover boy two rows back'?"

"Nothing...at least not yet."

"Maybe he's looking for an upgrade to the shore excursion." You said he's staying in Fort Lauderdale after the cruise. Any idea where?"

"Somewhere on the Seventeenth Street Causeway, I think."

"You're not sure, Lucky? Honey, if you want to get laid, these details should be at the top of your 'to do' list."

"Who said I wanted to get laid?"

"You didn't. The look of desperation on your face was a giveaway!"

The bus slowed and finally stopped in the beach parking lot. The other cruisers hurried off the bus. Lucky and Sam took their time to gather their beach bags so the men could catch up with them.

"Would you ladies like to spend some time together?"

"We could have been off this bus two minutes ago. Why do you think we stalled?"

Lucky took up a position next to Karl as she exited the bus. Sam walked next to Gary. They selected an isolated location on the nearly pristine beach underneath two umbrellas protecting them from the sun. Lucky and Sam rearranged the lounge chairs so they would face the guys.

"What's everyone drinkin'?" Gary asked.

"I'll take a chilled Heineken," Lucky replied.

"Me too," Gary said.

"Same for me. You're up Sam."

"Leave it to me to be the odd ball. I'll take a margarita with no salt."

"Three Heine's and a margarita without salt."

"You can't carry them all, Gary. I'll go with you." Sam and Gary headed toward the tiki hut bar.

"She's quite the flirt, isn't she?"

"Yes, she is Karl. I did tell her about Gary's loss and not to come on too strong."

"I'm sure he'll be okay. I'm more interested in us." He touched her back with a brief stroke.

Jovial, coconut suntan oiled people filled the seats at the tiki hut bar. Close by, a steel drum quartet, outfitted in colorful tropical shirts entertained beach goers with Caribbean rhythms. Couples danced in the sand, swaying their drinks as they bobbed, occasionally taking a sip.

Sam called to Gary with a wave of her camera and clicked as he responded.

"You sneak, you!"

"I still want one without a shirt."

The bartender greeted them. "Welcome, you're up guys."

Sam grabbed a quick peek at the little bird's nest of hair clustered above the V in his T-shirt as Gary ordered the drinks.

"Karl is staying in Fort Lauderdale for a few days after the cruise, right? Do you have to get back right away?"

"Yeah, he's got some vacation time, but I don't."

"Is he staying at the same hotel you were in before getting on the cruise?"

"Yes, the Embassy Suites on the Seventeenth Street Causeway."

"He won't be too far from where Lucky works."

The bartender placed the drinks in front of them. "Here, Sam. Take your margarita and Lucky's beer."

Karl spotted the two approaching and clutched his throat in an exaggerated gesture. "You got here just in time to save us from dying of thirst."

They squeezed under the umbrellas and swapped childhood stories. Lucky stood up and took a few steps toward the ocean. "Who's up for going in the water?"

Sam quickly added. "Gary's had a T-shirt on too long. Anything to see his chest."

Lucky and Karl hopped across the hot sand toward the shoreline. Gary took a moment to remove his T-shirt. As soon as he knew Sam was watching he struck a body building pose. "By special request," he said.

"A judge in the Olympics would be holding up a card with a giant '10' on it about now."

He snapped his beach towel toward Sam and chased her into the water. They swam to join Karl and Lucky.

"This is a special treat to see you girls without a lot of clothes. If you're planning on dressing up for formal night this evening, Gary and I have reservations at Sabatini's. Care to join us?"

"Sam, it's your call."

"Where do I sign up?"

"I guess the tuxedo rental paid off. Let's meet at the Crooners Lounge at 7 P.M. We can have a cocktail or two, then dinner at 8:00," said Karl.

Sam dangled one arm around Gary's neck while her hand roamed his chest. Lucky inched away from Karl.

"I'm heading back to the beach, guys."

Karl dipped his head under water and then wiped his

face. "I'll join you."

He held Lucky's hand as the ocean current nudged them gently toward the waters' edge. They grabbed towels and began to dry themselves off.

"Everything will be fine, Lucky."

"What do you mean?"

"I'm a detective. I can tell when something is disturbing someone. You're worried about Sam and Gary, aren't you?"

"I don't want anyone to get hurt. I've been through that kind of pain."

"I promise *I* will never hurt you."

"I'm pleasantly surprised by Sam's reaction to you both. She loves a man with a muscular body, but she has this thing about law enforcement guys."

"Why?"

"Four years ago, her baby brother was murdered in South Carolina. His killer was never found. She thinks the police have forgotten about the case."

"Arrests can be a tedious process unless someone confesses. Leads come slowly because people don't want to get involved. How was he murdered?"

"He worked in an auto repair shop and was shot to death during a robbery."

"Where in South Carolina was this?" Karl asked.

"In a small town near Charleston."

"You won't believe this. Gary got a tip on the hot line before we left on vacation. It eventually led to the arrest of a murder suspect. The incident took place around the time Sam's brother was murdered."

"Geez, Karl. Are you thinking what I'm thinking?"

"Yes. Sam might be swimming with the detective who caught her brother's killer."

"Something is now adding up. Sam and her father have feuded for years, but last week he called the restaurant where she worked. The manager told him she was out of town, but he would get a message to her. Sam didn't want to ruin her vacation mood and hasn't called him back."

"Are we thinking the same thing, Lucky?"

"The answer is yes if you're thinking he called about the arrest of a suspect."

"How do we handle this, Gary?"

"Gently. I'll bring Gary into the loop and we'll come up with a decision. Don't say anything to Sam for now."

"Sounds good."

Sam and Gary joined them under the umbrellas.

"A towel, boys and girls? Lucky asked.

"No thanks. I'll let the sun dry me off."

"Same here," Gary smiled. "I wish the shower in my gym was as warm as that ocean water. It can certainly relieve any tension."

"Somehow I think some tension is about to begin" Lucky whispered to Karl.

"Looks like you got some sun today."

"I think you're right, Karl. I hope I'm not too burned."

The four sat under the umbrellas learning more about each other. Soon, Lucky glanced at her watch. "We better start heading for the bus."

Sam stood up first. "So long, Governor's Beach." She said with a salute to the ocean.

A few vacationers on the tour slept on the way back to the ship. Others chatted quietly, occasionally snapping a picture through the window to capture the beauty of the island. The tour bus settled in between the yellow lines and stopped only yards from the ship. As Karl climbed the gangway he thought of a castle and how magically this Princess owned the waters she sailed. His thoughts quickly shifted to the more mundane concern of, *How will I share the news with Gary that he may have arrested the killer of Sam's brother?*

Lucky reminded the guys as they exited the elevator that they were to meet at the Crooner's Bar at 7:00.

"7:00 it is, ladies."

It was a short walk from the elevator to stateroom

D414. Karl noticed the ice bucket had been recently replenished. He grabbed a small bottle of bourbon from the mini-bar. "You want one, Gary?"

"No thanks."

"Gary, can we take a few minutes to talk about something I learned today?"

"I know... you think I'm falling for Sam, don't you?"

"How long you grieve Heather's passing and what you do is your business. This *is* about Samantha."

"Ouch... it's serious when you call her, Samantha. What's up?"

"The guy you arrested for murder just before we left for the cruise, what's the story on him?"

"No more than what I already told you."

"Sam's brother was murdered."

"Come on, Karl, you're shittin' me."

Before you swam to meet us, Lucky told me Sam is not impressed with the legal process. She usually doesn't like law enforcement officers. It goes back to her brother's murder."

"So you think the guy I arrested killed Sam's brother?"

"Could be."

"I'll tell Sam I think we may have him. That will be good news for her."

"No, Gary. We need to think about how to handle this. There is another piece to the puzzle. Lucky also told me that Sam and her father do not speak. He called her this week at work. The manager offered to get a message to her."

"So, did she call him?"

"No, Lucky told me she wanted to wait until the cruise was over."

What if he isn't the guy and it's just a bizarre coincidence?"

"Don't know, Gary. If we let her father tell her, it just might be the catalyst to repair their relationship. I don't think we should say anything to Sam. I don't want to interfere in any possible patch-up with her father. From what Lucky tells me, it's a tense situation."

"I agree. I'll dig into this when I get home to verify he is the guy."

"Makes sense. In the meantime, let's hope she calls her father. If the guy you arrested is guilty, you'll still be her hero. I'll tell Lucky everything is still *hush-hush* for now."

"That's the best idea."

"I'm sure we'll trade phone numbers when we dock Sunday."

"What the hell are you waiting for with Lucky? I've already got Sam's number."

"Seems like she has yours too. In more ways than one."

"Any chance you want to get lucky with Lucky? Let me know and the room's yours."

"It's funny Gary. I think I've made it clear, but she never responds. You'd think being a detective I'd figure this out quicker.

"A guy who wants to get laid should move faster."

"Finding out why someone doesn't want to have sex with me isn't exactly a police investigation, Gary."

"Yeah, but seven days on a cruise ship without having sex qualifies as a crime."

"So are you telling me that you're ready to move on again?"

"Perhaps."

CHAPTER 22

SOMETHING TO CONSIDER

Mario hurtled past the bar. "You're here early again, Antonio. Please stop by the office when you can.

"Sure, I'll be right behind you."

He continued to provision his bar in anticipation of a Friday-sized crowd. Antonio looked forward to the afternoon rituals of his regular customers and filled their drink orders on autopilot. He stalled his routine and headed for the chat with Mario.

"What's up, Mario. You're scaring the crap out of me."

Mario picked up some old newspapers from the chair next to his. Antonio sat down.

"No reason to be alarmed. We open in fifteen minutes so I'll make this quick."

"It's your dime, Mario."

"You know Melanie and her sister are my only children. I wanted at least one son. One as hardworking and talented as you."

"Thanks, you'd make a great dad."

"Soon you'll be finished with culinary school."

"Yeah, what a long haul."

"What are your plans for the future? Do you want to be your own boss, or do you want to continue to work for someone else?"

"I've neglected to consider my future, but the topic deserves more thought. Graduation is coming soon."

"Luck was with me when I found this place. You are an important part of the success of this tavern. My wife's insurance money provided the purchase deposit."

'Your employees are lucky too."

"I would like to share some of my good fortune. We still owe a small amount on the tavern. Melanie and I talked about what will happen to High Hopes after I stop working. I had a dream she eventually would own and operate the place. She's not interested.

"Yes, she's made it clear to me as well."

"Are you interested?"

"Jesus, Mario. You caught me off guard. Give me a minute to catch my breath. What an exciting proposition."

"I'm looking to the future. I want this tavern to continue to be a place where people come to relieve their tensions and build friendships. I'm sure some hotshot real estate firm would love to sell for me. I could place an ad in all the papers and business journals for a buyer. Another idea is to give a break to someone who deserves it. You're at the top of my list."

"I'm speechless." Antonio's eyes filled with tears. He stood up and embraced Mario. "I had no idea why you called me in here, but this is beyond anything I expected."

"If you're interested, the terms will be in your favor. You will need to make an investment of time and money."

"Is Melanie aware of your thoughts?"

"Yes. It was her idea."

"I will need to speak with Dwight about this. We share our income and expenses. We'll need to be sure this makes financial sense."

"That's understandable, Antonio. Please keep this conversation between us."

"Agreed."

"I trust you, and I trust Dwight."

"What's the next step?"

"Speak with Dwight and get his views. If you both agree, I'll begin to let you in on the finances of the tavern."

The door to the office opened and Melanie walked in.

"Am I disturbing you guys?"

"No. Antonio and I were sharing our ideas for his future."

She walked to her father and gave him a hug followed by a kiss on both cheeks.

"I'm next, Melanie."

"Antonio, as long as you've worked here, we've never hugged, let alone kissed."

"Surely it's not sexual harassment if we both agree."

"You're right, but only two kisses. You're too handsome for me. I might get a crush on you. Besides you're partnered." She kissed him coyly on both cheeks.

"Now go out and wow our customers, Antonio."

"It will be *especially* easy today."

Antonio closed the door behind them. They heard his whistle from the hallway to the bar.

"What did he think about your plans?"

"You mean our plan. I gave you all the credit."

"So what do you think, papa. Is he interested?"

Wasn't he whistling when he left?"

CHAPTER 23

FIRE!

"Hello," Mario said with a sleepy voice. He opened one eye and glared at the clock. It was 4:40 in the morning.

"Yes, this is Mr. Bellasari, and I do own the High Hopes Tavern."

"Officer Paul Owen Frederick, is that what you said your name is? I'm sorry. I'm not quite awake. What's going on, officer?"

The news jolted him awake. The intermittent beep of the police recording system was evident as he listened to the Officer Frederick tell him the tavern was on fire.

"Officer Frederick, you said the fire started in the kitchen?" Mario listened further before responding. "I'm on my way. Yes, I'll drive carefully."

Mario grabbed his clothes from the chair next to the bed. Trembling, he opened his cell phone and pressed the number one on the speed dial. He tried to compose himself before Melanie answered.

"Papa" displayed on her cell phone. A call from her father at this hour was a signal something was seriously wrong.

"Melanie, High Hopes is on fire. Meet me at the tavern as soon as you can."

She began to say something but Mario cut her off.

"Melanie, please, just put some clothes on and meet me. Yes, call Antonio-- but let's try not to panic, dear."

He picked up his keys and wallet and raced out the door.

Mario skated through the blinking red traffic lights. Within minutes, as he waited at a red light, he let his face fall into his hands and took a deep breath. *Thank God there are only three blocks to go.*

The pungent smell of smoke made his stomach twitch. He took the final turn to witness the flames chomping at the kitchen. The street was a chaos of fire trucks, police cars, and an ambulance, all strategically parked to combat the fire and maintain an orderly detour for motorists. A police aide was leaning against his vehicle as Mario approached.

"I'm Mario Bellasari. I own the tavern."

"I was told to expect you, sir, but I'll need some form of ID."

Mario fumbled with his billfold to retrieve his driver's license. After a quick glance at the license, the aide removed the barricade to let him pass through.

He parked as close as allowed to the damaged portion of the building. He got out of his car and took a few deep breaths as he wrestled with his emotions. This was a sight he had never allowed himself to imagine. He felt relief that the damage was limited to one section of the building.

He stopped the next passing firefighter. "Who's in charge here?"

"Chief Stone. That's him by the hook and ladder truck."

Mario stepped around all the fire hoses and other firefighting apparatus.

"Chief Stone, I'm the owner of High Hopes Tavern."

They shook hands. "Mr. Bellasari, the fire is under control. The kitchen has substantial damage. Let me show you. Please be careful."

"Chief, my daughter Melanie and our bartender Antonio should be arriving soon. Can they join us when they get here?"

"That's fine, sir."

"Lieutenant Packer, this is Chief Stone. Please let the police aide know Melanie Bellasari and a worker, Antonio, have approval to come on the scene," he radioed.

"10-4, chief."

Mario held a dampened handkerchief to his face. He struggled to breathe normally and keep his emphysema in check. The kitchen was a bare framework. His senses overwhelmed him. Viewing the charred exposed beams. Smelling the stench of burnt wood. Dodging sloshes of water from the holes in the roof. All this served as a messenger of doom. He continued to walk with Chief Stone to survey the damage.

"Mr. Bellasari."

"Please chief, call me Mario."

"Mario, we find indications the fire was started intentionally. Can you think of anyone who might want to shut down your business?"

"No, nobody. What makes you think this was arson?"

"Firefighters are trained to understand something called the *Fire Triangle*. We learn it's composed of oxygen, a fuel source, and heat. We found kerosene in several different places. Also, notice the hole in your roof? We didn't make it. Whoever started this fire did so with kerosene and then cut the hole in the roof to spread the fire faster. There's also a ladder leaning against the outside wall of the kitchen. The ladder is not ours. When one or more factors in the *Fire Triangle* are tampered with, we suspect arson."

"Damn it, Chief. I can't believe that's even possible."

Melanie stepped cautiously around the fallen debris. She hugged him. "Papa, everything will be fine."

This is Chief Stone, Melanie. He tells me the fire is most likely the work of an arsonist."

"I'm sorry to meet you under such circumstances."

"Yes, but I'm pleased to meet you as well, chief." She looked at her father. "Arson-- Papa, why would anyone want to hurt us or our business?"

"I have no idea, Melanie."

"Wait Papa. I didn't tell you this, but about two week ago Antonio escorted an intoxicated customer from the building. He didn't leave in a friendly manner. The guy did ramble on, saying he would not forget this--and we wouldn't either. I didn't want to upset you."

Chief Stone spoke up. "I'm sure the police will want to speak with both of you, As of now, this is a crime scene."

"Sure, anything they need, we'll be glad to cooperate. I want to help in any way to catch whoever did this."

"Papa, Antonio didn't answer when I called. I left a voicemail to call you or me. I told him it was an emergency."

"Thanks, dear."

"Two local news station vans were arriving as I pulled up, Papa. I'm sure all the employees will be calling you."

"Mario turned to the chief. "The bar section didn't sustain any damage. Will I be able to open for drinks?"

"I would think so. I'll give you the number for the Code Enforcement Department. Once the smell of smoke is completely gone you can call them. A building Inspector will stop by and make a decision. No one will be allowed near the kitchen though. I think the two of you should move out of here soon. This is still a danger zone."

"Thanks, Chief," Melanie responded.

"I'll be leaving a truck here with six firefighters for at least five hours. The fire is out but I want to be sure nothing flares up again."

"Makes me happy I bought those extra raffles tickets at the fireman's banquet."

"I'm pleased you're handling this well, sir."

"I have no choice, Chief Stone. The fire has already happened. I can't change that. I can choose how I react. I need to set an example for my employees."

Chief Stone nodded and moved on to give instructions to his team. He moved outside the building to address the gathered media.

Mario cleared his throat. "I'm sure the smoke didn't help my emphysema."

"You shouldn't have stayed in the damaged area so long, Papa."

"I know," he said. He reached inside his pocket for his cell phone.

"Who you calling, Papa?"

Sam answered the call before he could reply. After a moment he put his hand over his mouthpiece. "It's Sam."

"Sam, this is Mario. Are you watching the news? He listened for a moment. "Yes, I know it's seven-thirty in the morning. There's been a fire at the tavern. The kitchen is severely damaged. Don't worry about your job. I know you were just hired, but I'll take care of you."

Mario listened and responded. "Thanks for your offer to help. In fact, we do need you here. The Fire Department is leaving a fire truck at the scene for a while. I'd like you to go to the market. Buy a bunch of picnic stuff, whatever you think hungry firemen would appreciate. Figure on ten to twelve people, including us. I'll reimburse you when you get here. Do you know if Lucky is off today?"

Mario's called waiting tone beeped. He saw Antonio's name appear.

"Sam, do me a favor. Let me take Antonio's call. Would you call Lucky? I'd like her help too if she's available. Talk to you later, Sam."

He clicked on the call waiting button.

"Hey, Antonio," he paused to listen. "Oh, so you have the news on." He heard Antonio yawn. "You do have a class this morning, right?' Mario paused again. "No, everything is under control now. Go to your class and call me when it's over." He listened again. "Of course I'm sure. The Fire Department is here. If any of the employees should call you, just let them know their job is protected."

❧

The bridge at Oakland Park Boulevard was up. Two luxury yachts sailed through the opening. Lucky and Sam sat listening to the car radio. "No one was injured in an early morning fire at the acclaimed High Hopes Tavern. The kitchen sustained most of the damage and flames could be seen a mile away. The fire is now under control; however, firemen remain at the scene. We'll have more on this breaking news at noon."

❧

The traffic around the tavern dragged. Gawkers inched their way toward a single open lane, slowing down to catch a glimpse of the smoldering building.

Sam alternated her foot between the gas pedal and the brake. "We're almost there."

As they approached the High Hopes Tavern, clusters of news teams were wrapping up their operations.

A few seconds later, Sam grabbed the first available parking spot, a distance from the commotion. "We're here."

Each of them grabbed armloads of grocery bags and stumbled toward two folding tables.

Mario stood beside his car. "Let me help you ladies. Melanie should be back any minute now. I sent her to buy an ice chest and ice.

He hugged Lucky and Sam. "Later, I want to hear all about your cruise."

"I'd certainly do another one again," Sam replied.

"Later, we'll show you the pictures we took. For now, what else can we do to help?"

Here comes Melanie now. "It's almost 10:45 in the morning. You can begin to serve sandwiches around noon. Help yourselves as well."

"We'll take care of everything, Mario. You do whatever else you need to do."

"Oh, and I'll reimburse you both for your time."

"The hell you will. This is what friends are all about."

"Let's grab a cup of coffee at Starbucks since we're free for a little while." Sam suggested. "You guys want to join us?"

"No. It's better for us to remain here."

Lucky and Sam sipped lattes and reminisced the recent fun-filled times aboard the Emerald Princess.

"I don't think the timing's right to ask Mario if I can take a vacation in six months, is it," Sam chuckled.

"Hardly."

"So what's the story with Karl? Have you seen him since we're back?"

"Yes, twice. He extended his stay and is leaving the day after tomorrow. I think he's annoyed because we haven't gone farther faster."

"You haven't? "Why are you so inhibited when it comes to sex?"

"I think I'm more concerned about him being from Georgia than anything else. To me, Sam, romance isn't a lot different than real estate. It's all about location, location, location. And here's a news flash, Sam. Long distance relationships just don't work. And I'm not leaving Fort Lauderdale."

"And what about you? Have you called your father yet?"

"No, I promised myself I would call him tonight. Hmm, we really should begin to head back."

"I'm ready."

Several tired firefighters lined up at the lunch table.

They had stripped off their protective fire jackets unveiling sweat drenched T-shirts, embossed with their distinctive logo.

Roast beef, corned beef, or ham and cheese," Lucky asked the first firefighter in line.

"Roast beef, please, ma'm."

"Here you go." Lucky pointed. "The condiments are on the table."

The second firefighter stepped up. "I'll take a corned beef sandwich and your phone number."

"That's an old line," Lucky said with a growing smile on her face.

"Did it work?"

"I'm just helping out here today. I work the front desk at the Crystal Palms Hotel, day shift, if that's any help."

"Thanks for the hint. My name is Kevin. Kevin Preston."

"I'm Lucky Larkin."

"Will Lucky be having a sandwich?"

"Sure, after we take care of you guys."

"I'll be sitting right over on the wooden walkway beside the Intracoastal. Care to join me?"

"Well, a girl likes to dine where she feels protected. I'll be there in a few minutes."

Sam unwrapped a sandwich, snapped open a can of Diet Coke and leaned toward Lucky. "Am I hearing things, or did that stud just try to pick you up?"

"He didn't just try, Sam. He succeeded. And, obviously he *lives* here."

"I'm sure that alone fires up your imagination."

❧

Chief Stone received a call mid- afternoon from the ranking officer at the scene.

"Yes, you can leave in half an hour," the chief barked. "If Mr. Bellasari is still nearby, would you hand him the phone?"

A moment passed. "Mario, Chief Stone here. The police have lifted some identifiable fingerprints from the ladder outside your building. Of course, we expected to find yours. But they also found another set of prints they were able to ID. Do you know a Robbie Alston?"

CHAPTER 24

SAM...IT'S ME, GARY!

Sam collapsed onto the couch and took inventory of what now lay on her lap and all around her. *How the hell did primitive women polish their claws without all this crap?* She placed a small towel on the coffee table and organized a nail file, polish remover, nail polish, and clippers next to a large box of cotton balls and her cell phone. *At least I can put my phone on the speaker and do something productive with my hands while I listen to his hypocritical nonsense.* Sam took a deep breath and dialed her father's number. She listened with mixed emotions. *Hey, if it goes directly to voicemail, at least I've done my duty.* When her father answered, she picked up the polish remover and began working on her nails.

"May I please speak with The Reverend Burnside?"

The familiar voice on the other side asked. "May I tell him who's calling, please?"

"Your daughter, Dad. I didn't think you'd remember my voice. You called me?"

"Samantha, I'm so sorry. How are you, dear?"

"Dad, or should I call you Reverend... stop the bull. We've not spoken in years. Remember you told me, I would never amount to *anything* because I didn't follow your religious beliefs? I call now and you talk like everything is fine between us, and I'm dear again?"

"Samantha, I was wrong. I allowed the people in my church to become more important than my own daughter. I'm so sorry. My focus is different now. I've got some encouraging news for you."

"Let me guess. You changed your will and I'm the beneficiary again?"

"I never removed you from my will, Samantha. Give me a moment please. I'd like to give you some good news."

"Don't tell me... you're now serving seconds at communion."

He ignored her sarcasm. "No, the police in Georgia recently arrested a suspect in your brother's murder."

The Reverend Burnside waited while Samantha finished sobbing. She cleared her voice. "You're right: that's the best possible news. Did this just happen?"

"No, they arrested him a couple of weeks ago. I called to fill you in, but your boss told me you were on a cruise."

"I'm sorry, Dad. I apologize for not calling before now."

"Yes, my dear. I waited a long time for your call."

"Dad, would you have been eager to return a phone

call to someone whose last words to you were, 'You're headed for Hell'? Somehow those words still hurt. I wasn't eager to call you. Now, I'm glad I did."

"The trial will not begin for a month, Samantha. I do want to keep in touch."

"Where in Georgia did they catch this guy?"

"In a small town called Sugar Hill. The detective who caught him, called me. His name is Gary Branchfield."

"I'd like to call him and thank him. I'm sure he gave you his number."

"Yes, of course. It's his direct number."

Speaking with her dad again, and learning of an arrest in her brothers' murder, was overpowering. Her hand shook as she jotted down the number.

"Let me hang up, I want to call the detective right now."

"Okay, we'll talk again later."

She couldn't wait to tell Lucky and Mario the news, but dialed the number for the detective first.

Gary answered.

"Detective Branchfield, my father, The Reverend Frank Burnside, tells me you're the detective who arrested a suspect in the murder of my brother, Charlie Burnside."

She listened and then responded to his question. "Yes, he did work in an auto repair shop in South Carolina. She dropped her jaw. Her eyes widened. "Is this for real...you're Gary from the cruise?" Sam had never focused on his last name. She reached into her purse and uncrumpled the piece of paper he had given her before leaving the ship. Gary Branchfield 770-555-3245. " I never believed in coincidences before, but this is a biggie."

She tapped on a table while listening. "So you didn't say anything on the cruise until you could be sure the guy you arrested was the suspect in my brothers' murder. I never said anything about the murder on the cruise."

"What do you mean Lucky did?" She listened in disbelief as he explained.

"You're telling me Lucky told Karl I'm not a fan of the police. Since you're a detective she found it pleasing that we got along so well. Then she told you about my brother, and the circumstances seemed to match the guy you arrested. "Why didn't you all bring this up to me, Gary?"

She continued listening intently.

"I appreciate that you wanted to verify the details, and didn't want to have me thinking about this on the cruise. It's also thoughtful that you preferred for me to get the news from my dad. I guess I understand why everything should be kept a secret."

Sam continued talking to Gary when the incoming call signal clicked. She pressed, *ignore*.

"My father told me the District Attorney in South Carolina is requesting extradition? Will you be coming to the trail?"

"Yes, I will be testifying."

She frowned.

"I didn't think it would be possible for us to stay in the same room. I agree, we don't want to jeopardize the case."

His comment about staying in the same room amused her.

"I doubt if I'll stay with my father, we'll see, Gary."

Sam could hear the phones at the Police station ringing in the background. "Yes, Gary, I'm sure I can call you anytime. Thanks so much. I wish you all had told me on the ship, but I guess I understand. Okay, we'll talk again soon."

Sam closed her cell phone in disbelief. She sailed with, and kissed the guy who captured her brother's murder suspect. Gary, a flame she thought burned out, suddenly reignited. She re-dialed her dad's number.

"Hello Dad. It's Samantha. Yes, I spoke with Detective Branchfield. You're not going to believe this. Lucky and I spent many hours with two detectives on the cruise. It turns out Gary Branchfield is one of those two detectives."

Her mind scrambled between the excitement of the

arrest and uncertainty toward her father.

"I'm not sure if I will stay at your house. The only promise I will make is to keep in touch. I don't know how I feel about us yet. Parents shouldn't have to bury a son or daughter like you and mom did. It's unnatural. Dad, because I didn't follow your religious beliefs, you chose to bury me. My phone call is proof I'm still alive."

Chapter 25

A CHANGING TIDE

Clarice and Daniel sat poolside, enjoying the hearty breakfast he had prepared. He leaned over to kiss her forehead as he poured her another cup of coffee.

"I was thinking, Daniel, we haven't seen Lucky and Sam since they returned from the cruise. Shall we see if they're available for dinner tonight? We can go to the Peacock's Feather."

"A superb idea. What do you think about asking Mario

and Melanie to join us as well?"

"Sounds good-- as long as you allow me to treat, Daniel. I am grateful for the comfort of your home the last few days and would enjoy an opportunity to play hostess."

"My comfort level is elevated as well. The evening will be better if our friends are available. I'd like to ask you a favor though."

"Anything."

"I'd like you to go to the beach with me today. Let me share something with you."

"Yes, however, like generations of Southern ladies before me, I choose not to linger too long in the sun.

"I understand. Let's leave here around noon. Is that okay with you?"

"Perfect. I'll go call our guests. With luck they're available to join us this evening."

When she returned, he had already placed the last of the plates and silverware into a custom-designed cabinet.

"Everyone is available for dinner this evening." She said. "I told them we'd meet at High Hopes at 7:00 for cocktails and then head for the Peacock's Feather for dinner. I want to support Mario's bar as much as I can while the kitchen is being repaired."

"He treats us so well, Clarice, we owe him that."

"You got that right."

Daniel lifted his eyebrow at Clarice. She recognized his signature gesture and promptly corrected herself. "You *have* that right."

"I know most people like to indulge far too much in the vernacular. I spent too many years teaching English at Harvard to accept anything but correct usage. It's just the principle I believe in."

"Principles, Daniel, they can be such an inconvenience. However, you are correct, Professor Kent," she said with a nod.

Clarice turned on the radio as Daniel backed his car out of the garage. The broadcaster announced, "Welcome to another beautiful day in South Florida. It's a great day for the beach if you don't have to be at work.

She tilted her head against the soft leather head rest. "I just love living here, Daniel. The balmy temperatures all year round are so healthy."

The ride to the beach was short. Daniel directed her attention to a vacant parking space ahead. "Look, we're even lucky enough to find a parking spot on Ocean Boulevard."

"So where are we going?" Clarice asked.

"Methinks milady doth object to a bit of surprise."

"You love to be mysterious, don't you?"

"Only with an appreciative audience."

They swung hands as they nearly skipped along in the sand. With their outer hands they twirled their sandals. They giggled and whispered as they occasionally hopped a few feet up the beach to evade an oncoming wave.

Clarice pointed upward. "Look at the flock of seagulls. They're so swift and graceful, gliding through the air." They walked past a jet-ski rental sign that trembled in the air. A minute later, Daniel made an abrupt stop.

"This is the spot," he said somberly.

"I'm afraid I don't understand what you mean by 'the spot'."

"This is the area where the lifeguard placed me on the sand after he pulled me from the ocean."

"Oh, I'm beginning to understand."

"This spot on the beach means a lot to me. I could have died here. Instead, the lifeguard and paramedics saved my life. Lucky Larkin restored my faith in people. I was a lonely man. When Lucky came to see me in the hospital, she didn't even know who I was. After her visit I began to enjoy life. I met people at the High Hopes Tavern. More important, I met you."

Daniel knelt on one knee, reached into his shorts and took a small Beverly's Jewelers' box from his pocket. He lifted the lid with a flourish to reveal an elegant diamond ring.

"Tomorrow is promised to no one, Clarice. I want to live every day in the future with you. I want to share my life and love with you, in peace and harmony. Clarice Thompson, will you marry me?"

"She knelt in the sand to face him. Yes, Daniel Dooley Kent, I would be pleased to share your life."

"Shall we advise our friends at dinner this evening?"

"They would be pleased, I'm sure. What shall we do until dinner?"

Clarice giggled, "Are you suggesting we be naughty? Again?"

CHAPTER 26

THE TRUTH

Lucky glanced at her watch as she entered the tavern: 7:15 P.M. "Hey, Antonio," she called, blowing him a kiss.

"Hey, sweetheart. How ya doin'? Your usual?"

"Please. I'm doing okay, you sexy hunk. Is Sam here yet?"

"I'm sensing mental telepathy. She's coming through the door now."

Lucky glanced around the bar as Sam approach.

"Aren't you tanned and relaxed." Antonio called out.

"Thanks for noticing."

Lucky held out her arms, and greeted Sam with a hug and a kiss on each cheek and asked, "What's new, dear?"

"Not much."

"What's happening with the trial, any further news from Gary?"

"No, just what I told you after he called the first time, but hey, he may tell *you* first," she said with a hint of irony.

"You're not still upset with me, are you?"

"Nah, y'all did what you believed was right. At least a suspect is in custody."

Antonio looked toward the entrance. "Daniel's coming through the door. Is he part of your dinner group?"

"Yes, Mario and Melanie should be joining us as well. And, of course, Clarice."

Daniel greeted them. "Good evening, ladies, ready for a drink?"

"No thanks, we're all set."

"Here come Melanie and Mario, Daniel said. "They're joining us, you know."

Sam spoke up. "Yes, and I'm thrilled. I've never really socialized with Melanie. I'm sure she's a lot of fun."

"I expect my darlin' to show any minute. She was at my home earlier today, but left to prepare for the evening. You know how she is about being on time."

Minutes later Clarice opened the doors, and strolled confidently toward them. She approached her stool at the amen corner.

"Miss Clarice, shall I get started on your usual?"

"I would, or Grey Goose stock might plummet and I find I'm not capable of such barbarism."

"This is going to be somewhat strange," said Sam. "I've never dined where I worked."

"It will be different for us as well," Clarice added. "I think we're all so accustomed to High Hopes."

"Hey," Mario piped up. "I like to support all local

restaurants. I may even steal an idea or two tonight."

"It will certainly be an interesting night," Daniel added. "I'm sure you're excited to share the highlights of your cruise."

A while later Antonio's eyes focused on their empty glasses. He walked to their seats. "Another one, guys?"

"No, we're going to the Peacock's Feature for dinner at 8:30. We'll try one of *their* adult beverages and see how you stack up, Antonio."

"Ouch," Clarice.

"I'm confident you're the best," she said.

"I'm looking forward to the evening," Mario said. "I believe it's been a year or more since I've dined at the Peacock's Feather. I enjoy the friendly competition between restaurants. The owner and I respect each other."

※

They were immediately greeted and seated at a choice table. The Maitre d' whispered to Darren he would be serving VIP guests.

As he distributed the menus, Clarice pointed out, "Don't be alarmed your menu doesn't include prices. It is my pleasure to host this evening and that part of the menu is irrelevant. Darren may also try to entice you with the specials for the evening. I've always enjoyed his recommendations when dining here."

"Good evening, I'm Darren and I'll be your server this evening. May I start everyone off with a cocktail or a glass of wine?"

Sam's eyes followed him as he headed to the bar to fill their drink orders. She didn't recognize him from when she worked there.

Daniel started the conversation. "The suspense is killing us, girls. Tell us all about your cruise."

Sam spoke up. It was my first cruise. I suspected it would be impressive but I couldn't believe all the gourmet food and lavish show-style entertainment. Lucky dug into her purse and passed around some photos taken during the cruise.

"Did either of you meet the man of your dreams?" Clarice asked.

"Interesting you should ask. We met two young detectives, Karl and Gary, from Sugar Hill, Georgia. Sam has some other news for you, but I'll let her tell you."

"You're not getting married, are you?"

"No, not yet, Daniel. This is really something straight out of the movies. A suspect has been arrested in my brothers' murder. But, here's the kicker. Gary is the detective who arrested him."

"How weird is that?" Melanie said.

"Actually," Lucky said, "We were on a beach tour. While Gary and Sam were in the water, Karl, the detective I was attracted to, told me that Gary had arrested a murder suspect just before leaving for the cruise. The more we spoke about it, the more it appeared he might be the man who killed Sam's brother."

"The three of them didn't tell me anything about this on the cruise," Sam added. "At first I was pissed."

Lucky placed her hand on Sam's shoulder. "We didn't tell Sam because Gary wanted to be sure the guy he arrested was, in fact, related to her brother's case."

"The arrest is cause for celebration!" Daniel said. They raised their glasses. "May your beloved brother receive the justice he deserves."

Mario added. "I want to give you all some interesting news as well."

Clarice set her martini down, "Give us the lowdown, Mario. What's up?"

"Newspaper articles are reporting the tavern fire to be a case of arson. Well, Robbie Alston is a prime suspect. The police think he'll confess soon. Please keep this to yourselves."

Daniel looked shocked, "Robbie Alston, really?"

"Well," Clarice said, "I liked him, but sometimes

suspected he had a loose interpretation of honest behavior."

"Daniel, don't you also want to share some news with our friends?" she asked, waving her fingers."

"I most certainly do. Earlier today, I asked Clarice to marry me and she accepted. I plan to make an honest woman out of her on Valentine's Day."

Mario began a sustained round of applause from the table. "Congratulations and best wishes to you both. Do you plan a large family?"

"Each of you at this table are all the family we need," Clarice began. "P.S., I don't think Fort Lauderdale is quite ready for that level of miracle. Not that we won't try, of course."

Daniel rearranged the cutlery on his linen napkin. "On a more serious note, I should explain. Lucky, I thank *you*. Today, I took Clarice to the spot on the beach where I escaped death. I also told her while the lifeguard and paramedics saved me, *you*, restored my faith in people. I needed to change some aspects of my life. Your visit made me feel better about myself, and I decided it was important to enjoy every day after."

She acknowledged the compliment with a nod.

Lucky looked away from the rest of them. She held both hands to her face and began to cry quietly. Clarice drew her close and hugged her.

"What's the matter, Lucky?"

Her crying became more intense. She stood up and hurried toward the ladies' room. Clarice followed her and handed her a tissue.

"I'm sorry, Clarice. Daniel's surprise wedding announcement caught me off guard emotionally."

"Why?"

"I continue to wrestle with my desire to be married, yet draw back at romantic opportunities. I need to share an inner secret with everyone tonight, but I don't want to ruin everybody's joyful occasion."

"Do you care to provide me with a little insight?"

"Yes, in one word, Clarice. Rape."

Clarice looked horrified. "My word, Lucky, we are family. You will not ruin our evening if you share your secret and can erase horrible memories. Come on, Lucky, we're here for you.

They returned to the table. Lucky sat, while Clarice stood behind her resting her hands on Lucky's shoulders.

"My friends, Lucky has something to say. I've assured her it's okay to tell us what's on her mind." Clarice sat down.

Lucky sniffled and wiped her eye. "I need to make a confession and exhibit honest behavior. I've been untruthful to all of you. I must share a secret I've held in far too long."

"Go ahead, we're here for you," Melanie assured her.

"Thank you, Melanie. My family is long past," she began, "except for each of you. You're my family. All along I've told you I left my flight attendant job because I was tired of the endless travel hassles. Being told by passengers I was lying to them about the reason our flight was delayed. Tired of being cooped up in a plane for hours on end, and other false reasons. Now I'll tell you the real reason I stopped flying."

"Continue, my dear." Clarice said.

"I want to someday do what Clarice and Daniel just did. Tell people I'm getting married. My reason for leaving the airline has haunted me and kept me constantly on guard. I've resisted romantic advances because of it."

She stopped speaking and took a deep breath. "I left the airline because I was raped while on a layover."

Silence hovered around the table.

Lucky began to speak again. "We had just landed at JFK from Rome, and because of a snowstorm all flights were cancelled for the rest of the evening. We were forced to remain in New York for the night. Since we had no advanced reservations, the hotel couldn't honor our contract requirement of rooms on the first floor."

Lucky' crying simmered. Sam placed her hand on her shoulder. "It's okay, tell us as much as you're comfortable sharing."

"The earliest we could possibly leave was the next afternoon. I changed out of my uniform and went to join my co-workers for a cocktail at the lobby bar. When I returned to my room and began to undress, I heard a noise coming from the bathroom. I screamed and ran to the door. A man wearing a mask chased me. He put his hand over my mouth, threw me to my bed, and thrust himself upon me. He tore off my clothes and raped me, and left me on the bed in a state of shock."

"Oh my Lord," Mario said shaking his head.

"Lucky's face revealed her struggle with the recollection, her attempt to steel herself from the pain of the memory but determined to unburden herself of some of the long suppressed agony. "It was like an out-of-body experience. I had to disengage. If I acknowledged the assault, the humiliation, the stench of his breath, and the horrible grunting sounds he made, I would be participating. So my mind escaped my body and watched with the detachment of a hunter casually looking on as his kill bled to death. Everything was slow motion, exaggerating the assault on my senses as well as my body."

"Did the police arrest a suspect yet?" Melanie asked.

"Yes, fortunately he was running down the hall as our Captain and First Officer were coming up from the bar. The crew shares room numbers with each other for safety reasons. Captain Williams heard uncontrollable crying sounds as they walked by my room. He knocked on my door to see if I was alright. I struggled to let them in, then collapsed on the floor. The next I remember I woke up in the hospital with a female detective waiting to speak to me."

"I can only imagine how such a travesty would change you," Daniel said.

"I wish I could say that was the worst part. The detective showed me a mug shot of the alleged rapist. I stared in disbelief as I looked at a photo of Billy, my first live-in boyfriend. In his written confession, he stated, during the time we dated I had mentioned the names of the hotels the airline contracted for crew layovers. He flew to New York and told the hotel guest relations agent I was his fiancée. He would be joining me as a surprise for my birthday. He watched her dial my room and noted the number. I didn't answer my phone but Billy had a knack for picking locks.

The others sat in numb silence, barely breathing -- afraid to react and not knowing how. Lucky continued her toneless account, speaking even more slowly.

"The me I used to be was gone. Disappeared into the pain. In those few dreadful moments, the one who laughed easily and loved carelessly evaporated into the air with my sobs of pain and disgrace. A once sweet girl was replaced by a cold detached creature who angrily held her turf for a long time, determined not to let the simpler me return. It was a long time before a pale replica of my former self returned briefly from time to time. She is growing, regaining some of her composure, but always fearful, hesitant to stand her ground."

"That was long ago, Lucky." Clarice whispered. "Now you're surrounded by people who care about you and want to protect you from those memories with their love and concern."

Lucky permitted herself a smile. "And I'm grateful. I want to be able to care again. To trust. Without fear. With some...genuine hope."

Clarice wiped a tear from her eye. "Don't let the past steal your future, Lucky. The middle ground -- the present -- is always the most promising."

"I apologize if I ruined our evening, but it was time I shared the truth."

Mario reassured her. "Lucky, it's like you said, we're all

family. And families are there for each other."

"I thank you all."

They recovered from the shock of the news and completed the rituals of ordering their meals.

As they passed the menus back to the waiter, Mario continued. "How about a tavern repair update for a change of pace?

"Ready when you are, darlin'."

"The repairs to the kitchen are ahead of schedule and we should re-open just before Christmas."

"That will be a holiday treat for sure." Daniel said. "We'll all be there for the debut of the new kitchen."

Daniel continued. "Tonight, we shared some good news and some that is difficult to understand why some things happen. All of us are in a better state of mind because of what we shared. My good friends, our evening is a success because we shared."

"My birthday is in December, two months away," Lucky said calmly. "I've made a promise to myself to be over this by then, if not before. As I move further from what happened to me, I'm learning more about life. I can't control what someone else did to me, but I certainly have some control over where I let their actions lead me."

"You're correct," Clarice said. "We always have choices: we can stall at a dead end or we can devise an escape route. Why make a U-turn to your past when you can continue you're journey to a destination you choose."

Lucky smiled. "I refuse to be held hostage by my past any longer."

Sam leaned to give Lucky a big hug. "Isn't there a firefighter who could help you with that?"

CHAPTER 27

CLARICE AND DANIEL, THIS IS KEVIN PRESTON

"Hello, beautiful."

Lucky raised her eyes from her work at the guest reception counter to see Kevin, the firefighter from the High Hopes Tavern fire. "I can't say I'm surprised you're here since I did tell you where I work. What a pleasure, Kevin."

"How could I forget your delicious sandwiches and

your killer smile?"

"Flattery just might get you a cocktail after work, handsome."

"Let me think for a minute. You're attractive, you make a superb sandwich, and you're also a mindreader. Hmm, rather than simply a cocktail, can we upgrade to dinner?"

She raised her hands up and down as if she was tipping the scales of justice. "Let me think for a minute, shall I go to dinner with a fascinating guy, or do the laundry? What time can you be at my place?"

"How's 7:00?"

"Yes, I'm out o' here at 5:00.

She reached for a piece of hotel stationery and with a quiver of excitement, jotted down her address and phone number.

"How shall I dress?"

"Fancy. Only an elegant restaurant will do."

"You're such a charmer. I'll catch you later."

After Kevin turned to leave he pulled his smart phone out of his pocket. *I better call the Capital Grille and make a reservation.*

⁂

Lucky awoke from a brief nap, and selected a Diana Krall CD as she prepared for his arrival.

He'll be here in an hour, she thought.

After a soothing bath, she pulled together her favorite classy outfit; a basic black dress, a string of pearls and sensible heels. She was putting the finishing touches on her makeup when the doorbell rang.

She opened her door to find a nervous Kevin with his face framed by an armload of roses.

She took the flowers from him. "Oh, Kevin how thoughtful. I'm impressed. You're right on-time." Make yourself comfortable while I put these in water. She returned, sniffing the roses while setting the vase on the coffee table in front of him.

"You keep dressing better every time, Lucky. It makes me wonder what's next."

"What's next, young man, is dinner. I'm starved. How 'bout you?"

"Is a quick tour of your apartment out of the question? I've driven by these apartments many times and wondered what the units were like inside."

Her living room was a tribute to her travels around the world. She pointed out a replica of a Durrow High Cross from County Offaly in Ireland. There was an encased 11th Century Celtic Goddess figure, *Sheela Na Gig*, on one of her walls. Framed travel magazine covers featuring several world capitals decorated the others. A pair of ballet slippers she had purchased in Italy highlighted an end table.

"What a combination. An extraordinarily attractive woman who lives in a tastefully decorated apartment."

"Thank you, Kevin. Shall we go?" she patted his back.

"Yes, we should leave. Our reservations are for 8:00."

Lucky set the security alarm and locked the door behind her. Kevin took her hand and led the way to his late-model BMW convertible. He closed her door after she was seated. She stroked the rich leather and glanced at the multitude of upgrades in the interior. She sensed an air of sophistication in everything about him, which she found appealing.

"I love the elegance of this car, Kevin."

"Yeah, it drives like a dream. I was living with my dad at the time because of his health issues. Without rent to pay I was able to save enough to afford my favorite car."

"How is your father doing now?"

"Sad to say, he passed away seven months ago."

"I'm so sorry for your loss."

"Thanks. I loved him and miss him dearly. A real man's-man, ya know. I'd like to hear about your family too."

"You lookin' for a short story? Let's share more at

dinner."

She was at ease with Kevin, which was a new experience for her. She leaned back and let her hair blow. She enjoyed every moment of the brief ride and the air of freedom provided in the convertible.

Kevin pulled up to the valet station. "The Capital Grille? Excellent choice; I haven't been here in years."

"I'll settle for nothing but the best for you, Lucky."

He greeted the hostess. "Good evening. I made reservations for two at 8:00. The name is Preston."

"Yes, Mr. Preston. You're table will be ready in a few minutes. Would you care to enjoy a cocktail at the bar first?"

"No need to twist my arm, and you, Lucky?"

"I like your way of thinking, Kevin."

"I'll come and get you when your table is ready. Do you prefer inside or outside dining?"

"I'd prefer something intimate," Kevin suggested.

"Yes, I agree," Lucky added.

He thanked the hostess and guided Lucky to the bar.

They were greeted by a young Asian bartender. "Welcome to the Capital Grille. What may I serve you this evening?"

"I'd like a glass of Sterling Chardonnay," Lucky responded. Kevin reached into his wallet for a crisp fifty dollar bill." Dewars and water with a twist for me, please."

"Couldn't be easier," the bartender said with a smile.

Kevin leaned over and gave her a peck on the cheek.

The bartender approached. "Here you go folks. Enjoy!"

Lucky and Kevin picked up their glasses and toasted each other with their eyes.

Lucky faked an accent. "Do I detect a wee bit of Ireland?"

"Good guess, Lucky. Sometimes when I'm not working I enjoy a little Scotch in me. It's an effective way to hose down the aftereffects of a fire."

"How long are you with the fire department?"

"Ten years in December. I started when I was twenty-two just around my birthday."

"You're birthday is in December?"

"Yes, the twenty-ninth. I'm a true Capricorn. People say I'm shy, but strong and ambitious... my mom was nearly always right."

"You can get away with such an ego because we share the same zodiac sign. Mine is December twenty-seventh," Lucky said. "Does that mean we don't have any secrets from each other?"

The host interrupted them. "Mr. Preston, you're table is available. Follow me please,"

The hostess seated Lucky and Kevin at a table and handed each a menu. "Your waiter will be Colin."

They glanced at the dinner selections. Kevin stroked her hand, "All I want to look at is you. I enjoyed the ride to the restaurant. I'm captivated by the sight of a full moon on the ocean. It almost makes you think you could walk to Europe."

"I've flown over that walkway many times as a flight attendant. I never get tired of such magnificence."

"My dream is to see Ireland some day. My parents were born there but moved to the states almost forty years ago. We lived in New Jersey for a brief time before moving to Fort Lauderdale."

"You seem like a goal-oriented guy. I'm betting your wish to visit Europe will come true."

"Hopefully, we'll see. Kevin took a sip of his Scotch. So, how long were you a flight attendant?"

"Almost fifteen years."

"Why did you ever give up such a glamorous job?"

"Honey, the glamour days of flying are long gone. I'll share with you another time more reasons why I stopped flying."

He moved his chair closer to her, and lifted her hands to kiss both palms.

"The fact you're considering another time encourages

me. You took my breath away when I met you at the fire."

"And you, my dear, Kevin, were hotter to me than the fire itself."

They continued to chat seductively until Colin returned. "May I refill your beverages?"

Kevin raised an eyebrow in Lucky's direction. She nodded her approval.

"Another Sterling Chardonnay and a Dewars and water with a twist. We'll be ready to order when you get back, Colin."

"My pleasure, sir... ma'am."

"Tell me more about this handsome man sitting across from me."

"Well, I'm six foot, with red hair and I would dare to say, a firm build."

Lucky eyed him playfully. "Tell me something not evident on your driver's license. Any sisters or brothers, ever married, any arrest for terrorism?"

"I have no brothers or sisters. You already know my father died recently. Caring for him was a priority, so I never married. I still live in his house. My mother passed away four years ago. My father missed her so much he didn't take care of himself. I tried to persuade him to get back into living a full life, but he was too depressed. On a much brighter note, I just won my Division's, *Firefighter of the Month* award.

"Firefighting is a dangerous occupation. What made you choose that line of work?"

"A snow storm."

"Okay, you've got my attention. Please explain."

"I was a member of the Safety Patrol for my school. My assignment was to assist, Wanda, a policewoman and seven other Safety Patrol members. She directed traffic. We assisted students as they crossed the street at a busy intersection by the school. Are you bored yet, Lucky?"

"No, but I can't envision Wanda Sykes as a policewoman."

"I get it. Wanda, Wanda Sykes. At least you're paying attention. I was so proud to wear the white belt across my chest. The shiny badge was like jewelry to me. My goal was to wear the Lieutenant's badge by the 8th grade. For a kid, this was a big deal. One morning, as I left for school, snowflakes began to fall. The snow stuck to the ground and the winds kicked up. At 10:30, the School Board instructed the Principal to close the school for the day. The roads became treacherous in a hurry and made driving dangerous. The storm prevented Wanda from returning to direct traffic."

Colin returned with the drinks. "We'll order now. We both will have The Sliced Filet Mignon with Cipollini Onions and wild mushrooms, and a side of au gratin potatoes."

"Excellent choice, both come well recommended."

"Thank you, Colin. To finish my story, the other safety patrol members went home. Cars occasionally skidded to a stop when the light turned red. My fear of a child being injured took over. I decided to remain behind to direct traffic and help the children cross the street. Without my knowledge, someone from the principal's office watched from the school window. The next year, I leapfrogged the Lieutenant's badge and proudly wore the badge of Captain. From then on, I was destined to select a, *service to others*, type career."

Lucky lifted her arm and held it toward him. "Kevin, you're story gave me goose bumps. You must have been adorable. I'm proud of you, honey."

"It's your turn, Lucky. Tell me about yourself."

"Both my parents passed away. My father died seven years ago and my mother three years ago. They didn't take well to my being a flight attendant. Fears of a crash, you know. I've travelled the world, and enjoyed every place I visited. To me, my friends are my family and I cherish them all.

"Were you ever married?"

"No, I've dated a few guys and even lived with a couple, at separate times of course," she said with a quick laugh. "One turned out to be a cocaine addict, and one died early."

"I'm so sorry, Lucky."

"My girlfriend and I were on a cruise, about three weeks ago, and I met Karl, a detective from Georgia. He wants me to come to Georgia to visit him next month. I just don't know if I would ever want to move to another state."

"You know *my* vote, Lucky."

Colin set a tray with their dinners next to them. Lucky's eyes widened as he set the plate in front of her. He then placed a separate bowl- shaped dish with a side of au gratin potatoes beside the Filet Mignon. He then served Kevin.

"Bon Appetite, may I get you anything else?"

"Anything else for you, Lucky?" She turned her head. "No, I'm more than fine with this."

"I think we're good, Colin. Thank you."

They talked and laughed as they enjoyed their meal.

"Would you care to go for a nightcap after dinner?"

"I wouldn't mind at all; in fact, I'd love it." "You may not believe this Lucky but I can be shy at times, yet I am extremely comfortable with you."

"Shy, you? I don't think so. Who asked who out for dinner tonight?"

"Yeah, you're right. I forgot."

They enjoyed the luxury of the Capital Grille and the professional staff. It's a place where guest don't simply have dinner. They dine.

"Where are we off to afterward?"

She leaned over the table, and kissed him on the cheek. "The place where it all started…the High Hopes Tavern."

After dinner, they drove the scenic route along the ocean to the tavern. Lucky was especially vivacious as the couple walked through the door of the tavern. Not bothered by the ongoing kitchen repairs, the bar had a full complement of loyal customers.

"I want you to meet two special friends."

She led Kevin to the amen corner, where Clarice and Daniel sat sipping their cocktails, clearly enjoying each other's company.

"Good evening, Lucky," Clarice said, her eyes sweeping Kevin. "Who might this handsome gentleman be?"

"Clarice and Daniel, I'd like you to meet Kevin Preston. Kevin, this is Clarice Thompson and Daniel Dooley Kent. They're two of my favorite people."

Kevin extended his hand. "It's my pleasure to meet you both."

"Well, now I finally understand the meaning of the term 'Mr. Right,'" Clarice said with a smile.

"Thank you, Clarice. How very kind of you."

"Are you sticking to the Dewars and water, Kevin," Lucky asked?

"Yes, but only one more."

"Clarice and Daniel, are you ready for a refill?"

"Oh, why not."

Lucky introduced her date to Antonio as he sat the drinks on the bar. "It's a pleasure to meet you Kevin."

"Same here, Antonio."

"Daniel," said Clarice, "Show Kevin around the place. Somehow, I sense he has a burning desire to come back often."

Kevin and Lucky exchanged glances and burst out laughing. She took a tissue from her purse to wipe her tearing eyes.

Clarice began to join in the laughter but stopped to ask, "What's so funny?"

"I met Kevin here when the kitchen burned. He was one of the firefighters who responded. Your *burning* desire comment tickled both of us."

"I had no idea. That *is* funny."

Daniel's instinct told him Clarice wanted to talk with Lucky alone. "Grab your drink, Kevin. I'll show you around. We'll be right back, ladies."

"So, what do you think, Clarice?"

"Lucky for you darlin', he's not just another bit o' eye candy. He definitely crosses the road from, Mr. Right Now, to Mr. Right. As my fisherman daddy used to say, "He's a fine catch." Or, if he didn't say that, he should have. You know, of course, most old Southern quotations are actually original remarks. We're just too modest to take credit for obvious wisdom."

Lucky laughed and patted her on the shoulder. "I am very comfortable with him, Clarice. Before meeting Kevin, I sometimes reminded myself that I've dated a lot of guys, yet received no sustained comfort...so why should I feel the next will be any better. Yet with Kevin, the feeling is different, one I can't explain right now."

"You don't need to explain it. He really *is* a looker. You may want to consider moving your December commitment to yourself up a month or two."

"I've certainly been thinking about that. Six years of my life were ripped away, stolen." She struggled to hold back the anger, the lingering need for revenge. "You see, Clarice, being a victim of rape didn't erase my desire for commitment, but it did instill a fear of intimacy."

"And that fear will evaporate soon."

"Somehow, I agree, Clarice. On the way here, he asked me to go to the Hard Rock Casino tomorrow night, and a movie the next. Three dates in three nights," she said lifting her eyebrows, "that alone is a change for me."

"Change is good, Lucky"

"And I'm fully aware it's needed, Clarice. I think of how many times I tried to please others, sacrificing my own desires...hoping to be loved. And in many cases, for persons who are not as worthy, or were less intelligent, or ethical, than I. I'm tired of living alone and hugging my pillow at night. My loneliness surfaces when I notice a wedding band on another girl's finger. I am happy for her, but I wonder, *when will it be my turn?* Why have I been so fortunate in many other ways in my life, but not fortunate in the one that means the most to me?"

"Well Kevin certainly appears to be a person of good character."

"I like this place," Kevin said returning with Daniel. "I'm sure the patio next to the Intracoastal can be very romantic"

"Yes, Kevin, it is. Clarice and I plan to be married on the patio next Valentines' Day. Of course, you both will be invited."

"Invited? Hell, Daniel, I want Lucky to be my maid of honor," Clarice added. "If you recall, you and I met because she brought you out of your shell."

"That's true. And isn't it interesting that Lucky and I met when I almost drown, and Kevin and Lucky met when this place caught fire? I guess it's true that sometimes out of tragedy, goodness survives."

CHAPTER 28

BETRAYED

"Hey, Lucky, it's Karl. I'm in my car driving and you're on my speaker. Can you hear me okay?"

"Oh, hi Karl," she responded. "Yes, I can hear you fine. I need to discuss some things with you as well."

"What's the matter, somethin' wrong?"

"That depends, Karl"

"OK, what's on your mind?"

"I've decided I won't be coming to visit you next

month. Karl, I enjoy living in Fort Lauderdale. I don't think I'll ever move, and a long-distance relationship wouldn't interest me. I've met a man here, and I am fond of him."

"In a way I'm relieved. I contemplated whether or not you should visit. I've been meaning to call you before now, but couldn't get up the nerve."

"Why?"

"I was ashamed."

"Of what?

Karl hesitated. "Spit it out, Karl?"

There was another moment of silence. She could her him clearing his throat, as if he was searching for the best way to say what was on his mind. She waited a short time longer before taking command of the call.

"Karl, I'm waiting."

"Sam and I shared an intimate evening when I stayed in Fort Lauderdale."

"You what, when?"

"We had sex one evening when you weren't available. I tried to entice you, but you never appeared interested in me sexually. You bristled every time I touched you."

This time the long pause came from her end. "You son of a bitch, Karl," she blurted out, "I wanted to have sex with you, but couldn't do it emotionally. I am healing from being raped, Karl. I didn't want to share my horrible experience with you yet."

"I had no idea, Lucky. What a devastating crime."

"Karl, I can't believe this. Why Sam?"

"I asked you, Lucky and you said, no. I asked Sam and she said yes. Now I understand why you said no to my advances. Your past is haunting you and I'm so sorry."

"I never mentioned to Sam whether or not we had sex. How could she do this to me?"

"I can't answer that. She called me one evening and asked if I wanted company."

Her lips began quivering. She gasped for breath as tears

trickled down her cheek.

"Has Gary been told of this encounter? I thought the two of them were getting closer."

"Yes, he's aware. Lucky, I can't change what happened. I can tell you how sorry I am."

"How is he taking all of this?"

"He knows it won't happen again. He's still infatuated with Sam."

"I can't believe Sam would do this to me. I feel so betrayed."

"I hope this won't hurt your friendship with Sam."

"Hurt our friendship? Oh no, Karl. Your encounter erased my friendship with Sam."

She glanced at her watch, her hands shaking from what she had learned. She needed to leave for work.

"Karl, I think it would be better if we don't communicate for a while."

"As much as it hurts, you're probably right, Lucky."

Lucky slammed the cover of her cell phone. She paced the floor, furious with Sam.

Should I confront her now, or later, she thought, pacing, pacing, pacing. Her stomach had developed a nervous knot from what Karl told her. "Why, why did she do this to me?" Lucky said out loud.

Still upset, she called Sam's cell phone. *You have reached Samantha Burnside. I am not available to take your call, but if you leave your name, phone number, and a brief message, I'll return your call as soon as possible. Thank you.*

"Samantha Burnside, this is Lucky. I need to speak with you as soon as you get this message," she said before flipping her cell phone shut.

She hopped into her car and headed for work. Her mood was far from conducive to delivering excellent customer service. She decided to call in late and make a detour. *I need to tell Clarice about this. I need to let off some steam*, she thought. "Calm down," she kept repeating to herself. She was still shaking as she knocked on Clarice's door.

"Good morning, Clarice, I'm sorry to bother you, but I know you're an early riser."

"Come in, Lucky, come in. It's 8:30 in the morning. What's the matter?"

"I need to share a secret with you about Sam. It's about betrayal."

"I'll get you a cup of coffee and you'll have my full attention. My intuition tells me I won't be laughing."

"If I wasn't headed for work later, I'd insist on a Bloody Mary, she said loosening up. Remember I told you Sam and I met two detectives on the cruise?"

"Yes, one was Gary and one was Karl, if I recall correctly."

"You're right. Sam was aware of my attraction to Karl. She also encouraged me to get together with him after the cruise while he vacationed in Fort Lauderdale for a few days."

"Yes, go on, dear."

"Karl called me this morning and told me he was intimate with Sam while he vacationed here after the cruise. I always wondered why she was so interested in the name of the hotel he stayed at here. Now, a lot falls into place."

"Had you been intimate with Karl?"

"No, but what I did or did not do with Karl remained between him and me. She still went and had sex with him."

"Well, to be honest with you Lucky, I've had some reservations about her. Y' know, honey, being Southern isn't just a matter of geography. No, it's more a matter of attitude and perspective. A girl can put a Confederate decal on the back of her pickup, but that don't mean she can milk a cow or hoe a row o' beans."

"She's had some tough times, but I find what she did disgraceful."

"I agree. For a Southern girl, she's not your usual migratory creature."

"That's evident now."

Clarice took a sip of coffee. "Darlin', it takes two to tango, but Sam's the one who put the quarter in the jukebox and pushed the button for that song to dance to. Oh, wait, am I the only one who knows what a jukebox is? I tell ya', getting' old ain't for the faint of heart."

Despite not being in a fun mood, Lucky managed a light laugh.

"I can't image Sam and me being friends any longer. I'm so pleased with Kevin, but the point is, she did what she did before my first date with Kevin."

"A person's frame of mind tends to color everything. Perhaps in time you will be friends again."

"That's difficult to imagine, Clarice. I just needed to vent my frustrations. You're a wise woman. Thanks for listening."

"Wisdom begins with wonder, according to Socrates. I wonder about many things. It's the key to being wonder*ful*."

"You're such a Southern belle. I better run."

"Are you sure you're alright, my dear?"

"I'll be fine. You're a peach for listening to my woes."

"That comes with being a *genuine* Southern belle."

Lucky scampered to her car and headed for the hotel. Her brief visit with Clarice absolved some of her rage…at least temporarily.

The familiar rhythm of her cell phone echoed loud as she strolled into the lobby of the hotel.

"You just caught me in time," she said excitedly. "I was just about to turn my cell phone off since guests will be at my counter any minute now How are you, Kevin?"

Cradling her phone, she placed her purse in the desk reserved for the front desk personnel.

"I'm always happy when you're doing well, honey. Yes, we're still on for tonight. Boy, if I ever needed a diversion, tonight's the night. It's been a rough morning, but nothing I can't handle, and certainly nothing for you to worry your handsome head about. What time will you pick me up tonight?"

Her hearing was impaired by the sound of bells signaling an incoming fire alarm call.

"8:00 is fine. I'll catch you later, Kevin. Be safe."

Lucky had just flipped her cell phone closed when her ring tone immediately alerted her to another incoming call. She opened the phone again. The name, "Sam," appeared.

"Sam, I'm at work right now. I don't have the time, nor do I choose to speak to you. But I would like to know, how was Karl in bed?" she asked, pressing the power button off and slamming the cover closed.

She gave herself one final look in the mirror, composed herself, and walked toward the front desk to greet her first guests of the day. The call from Kevin had doused her anger and reignited her composure.

CHAPTER 29

WE'VE GOT A DEAL

Melanie sat next to her papa in a rescue truck holding his hand tightly. As the siren warbled, vehicles pulled to the side of the road, allowing the truck to navigate through the red lights. They were headed north on Federal Highway.

"Papa, you're going to be okay. You passed out and were having problems breathing so I called 911. We're headed for Holy Cross Hospital."

Mario, breathing through an oxygen mask, lifted his fingers and gave her the high sign. He tried to tell her something, but was interrupted by the EMT.

"Try not to talk, sir. We'll be at the hospital shortly."

"You told me your father suffers from emphysema. Has he told you what prescriptions he takes?" asked the young EMT.

"He carries a list of his medications in his wallet. Let

me check."

"He's smart for doing so, ma'am."

"Please call me Melanie, Sir. Here, I've found it. He takes these. I'm not aware of any other medications but these."

Mario had regained color to his face as the rescue truck pulled into the Emergency Room parking entrance. The EMT's quickly reviewed his vital statistics with the attending ER doctor, who directed them to an available room for further tests.

"Gentlemen, you're the best. My dad owns the High Hopes Tavern. Stop in for one on us."

"We may do that, Melanie."

She had answered additional medical questions about her father and now sat in the ER waiting area reading an outdated magazine.

Before long, the attending physician approached her. "We're going to keep him at least one night, Ms. Bellasari. Perhaps even a little longer. Has your father been around any smoky conditions recently?"

"Yes, he has. He owns the High Hopes Tavern. The kitchen was set on fire recently. He surveyed the damaged area with the fire chief for a while."

"I remember, it was on the news. They think it was arson, right?"

"It appears that way."

"Mr. Bellasari will be going to room 207," an assistant informed the physician."

"You can go with him, Ms. Bellasari. Please don't stay too long. You can come back later if you want."

"Thanks, doctor."

Mario sat up in his bed. "I'd be lying if I didn't tell you that was quite a scare, Melanie. I guess walking around in the burnt kitchen with smoke still lingering in the air wasn't a wise choice."

"It was rather ill advised, Papa."

"Well, we can't change the past."

"The doctor asked me to keep this visit short. You need your rest. I'm going to leave now, but I'll be back early tonight. Can I bring you anything?"

Mario laughed slightly. "Yeah, I keep a bottle of Chivas in my apartment. Empty a bottle of mouthwash and replace it with the Chivas. Now that's my idea of gargling."

"Too funny! Now I know your gonna recover."

She could sense he wanted to rest. She leaned over and kissed him on the forehead. As she reached the door, she turned back toward him. He had already closed his eyes and turned his head to sleep. "Be well, Papa," she said in a low, caring voice.

She sat in the hospital parking lot, shifting through her purse to find her car keys as the calypso music call tone began. Incoming call from, *Antonio*, appeared on her phone. She started her car and pressed the hands-free speaker for her phone.

"Hi Antonio, what's up?" She held her hand over one ear as another rescue truck with blaring sirens whooshed by toward the ER.

"You've got some interesting news for us?

"I tried calling his number but he didn't answer. I also left a voicemail which he hasn't answered either," he continued.

"My papa is in the hospital, Antonio. We were in the office and he began to have difficulty breathing. I called 911 and the rescue truck brought him to Holy Cross."

"Geez, Melanie. Why didn't you call me?"

"This just happened a little while ago. I'm leaving the hospital now. I've been told they'll keep him a least one night, maybe longer. The doctor wants to do some more tests."

"Can I visit him?"

"Sure. I'm going back tonight. Are you off?"

"Yes, and I will go with you. I'd like to share some news with both of you at the same time."

"Can you meet me at the tavern at 6:00?" She asked.

"Sure, we can drive together. Don't tell your father I'm coming if you speak to him between now and then. I want to surprise him."

"Okay, see you then."

She clicked her cell phone off and continued out of the parking lot, heading for her design class. *I think I know what the good news is, but I'll wait to hear it from him*, she thought.

After her class, she stopped by the tavern to check on the repair work. "You're right on schedule," Melanie said to a contractor. She walked around inspecting other work, then headed home for a quick nap before returning to meet Antonio.

It was close to 6:00 when she left her condo and drove to the tavern. Despite her papa being in the hospital, she entered the tavern in an excellent mood.

"You're looking quite GQ tonight, Antonio."

"You're not too shabby yourself, young lady. Come on, I'll drive. We can stop back here for a drink after we visit Mario."

"I think I know what you want to share with papa and me. I'll be elated if I'm right.

"Melanie, my dear. I applaud your effort to guess, but sorry, no previews. We're almost at the hospital and you'll hear the news soon enough."

"You want to be a Mystery Man? I might just give you a nickname. How does, 'Mystery Man Antonio,' sound?"

They arrived at the hospital to find Mario dozing. He immediately woke up when Melanie touched his shoulder.

"Antonio, what a surprise," he reached to shake his hand.

"I wanted to come and visit when Melanie told me what happened."

"I'm doing well. The doctors are doing some tests. I should be out by Thursday afternoon. Giving up this gown might be hard to do. I'll miss the lack of modesty."

Antonio snickered. "Maybe I'll print a little sign to stick on your butt," "'Beware of crack addict.'"

They all laughed. "The gown is certainly not a Hilfiger design." Melanie said with a clap of her hands.

"How *is* my beautiful daughter this evening?"

She gave him a hug and a kiss. "I'm doing okay, Papa."

"I did listen to your voicemail, Antonio, but as you can tell, I couldn't return your call. My aging body had other plans for the day."

"I'm just glad you're doing well. I called to set up a meeting with the two of you. This isn't exactly what I had in mind for a place to talk," he added. "I can't wait to tell you any longer."

"What's up, son?"

"Dwight and I discussed your offer to invest in High Hopes Tavern. I've got excellent news. With a significant amount of effort, and countless overtime hours, Dwight's firm landed a huge architectural contact. His firm believes his efforts were extraordinary and played a major role in being awarded the contract. They extended his contract with an extremely lucrative bonus."

"That's terrific news, Antonio."

"Dwight wants to help me make your offer possible. Of course, we would own it jointly. He would be a silent partner."

"Yes, of course, Antonio. I think it's time to begin the acquisition process. The years are creeping up on me. We'll contact the attorney after I get out of here."

Melanie perked up. "I was right. I figured that's what you wanted to tell us, I'm so delighted for all of us."

"Well then, if I'm Mystery Man Antonio, you must be Clair."

"Clair?" she questioned."

"Yes… clairvoyant."

"It is taking enormous will power for my eyes not to roll to the back of my head."

"Moving on, I'll share some confidential news now." Mario said. "I got a call today from the police. It turns out Robbie Alston confessed to setting the fire at the restaurant."

Antonio showed his surprise. "I had my bet on the nitwit I threw out a few days before the fire. Robbie Alston, you're kidding!"

"In a way, I wish I were."

"Did they say why?"

Mario motioned for them to come closer. Melanie moved to sit on the edge of his bed. Antonio pulled a chair from the corner of the room and placed it close to Mario and sat down.

"Yes. I heard he was sobbing and remorseful when he confessed. He told the police he is an only child. Robbie's father was an alcoholic and beat him. He is still alive, but his mother died when Robbie was twelve. He moved out on his own when he was eighteen."

"That somewhat explains his demeanor when he worked with us. You're still going to press charges, right? After all, he almost destroyed our livelihood, Mario."

"No, Antonio, I'm not."

"Papa, you're crazy. You've got to press charges."

Mario continued. "The defense attorney, asked me to consider not pressing charges. Robbie wants to straighten out his life by joining the Army. If I press charges, and the jury finds him guilty, he will be a convicted felon. Felons must obtain a waiver to enter the service. When the charges are recent, waivers are usually denied. He can enter the service if I don't press charges."

"Papa, I feel bad for him, but it doesn't change the fact that we suffered damage to the tavern and loss of income. We're paying employees for doing minimal work while the kitchen is being repaired. We're losing business, and they're losing tips. "We're all losers."

"Listen to me. What he did was awful. I was devastated when I heard he confessed. Melanie, your grandpa and grandma were immigrants to this country. They both loved America, and the opportunities they enjoyed here. When I was in my late teens, I wanted to join the Marines. But health problems prevented me from serving."

Mario held one finger to his mouth shushing Melanie for trying to add a thought.

"I'm sorry, go on, Papa."

"Robbie will be twenty-eight in May. I'll be sixty-nine next month. He has his life ahead of him. How can I think about destroying this young man's life by not giving him the opportunity to serve and become a useful member of society? I'm doing it for me as well. If I allow him to serve, indirectly I am serving. This is a land of opportunity. I want to give him his chance."

"Papa, I don't agree, but it's your decision. I will support whatever you decide."

"Mario, you're a class act and a real inspiration," added Antonio.

"Listen guys, I'm feeling sleepy. Go and enjoy yourselves."

"I'll be by again tomorrow, Papa. I love you."

"And I do too, Mario."

"Wow," Antonio said driving down A1A. "Your papa is one hell of a man. I've always admired him. His reason for not pressing charges is so incredibly unselfish."

"That's my papa," she said, resigned. "Antonio, buying the tavern is going to be an expensive proposition. Are you sure you and Dwight can do this?"

"I wouldn't announce it if we couldn't. Dwight and I tossed around the pros and cons for hours."

"How soon will you two be able to invest some money?"

"In two weeks, but why do you ask?"

"I've got a little money stashed away in savings. Not much, but some. What if we remodeled High Hopes Tavern so when you do take over, the tavern has a fresh look? The kitchen is being repaired, but an interior remodeling would allow my papa to witness the decorating skills I'm acquiring. And the exterior is in need of a fresh coat of paint."

"Talk to me, Melanie. What type of remodeling are you thinking of doing?"

"I don't want to change the overall theme. People like the High Hopes Tavern the way it is. But, the bar stools need to be replaced soon. I thought of placing different linens on the tables, new carpeting, repainting the interior, and a little larger dance floor. We could also use an enhanced sound system. A balloon payment of twenty-five thousand dollars is also due soon."

"Being the Interior Decorator you are, I'm sure it would look nautically elegant," he laughed. "I like the idea."

"I'll begin to get some estimates."

"I'm in," Melanie. "We may need to close down for two weeks or so, don't you think?"

"Yes, maybe even a bit longer. I will make sure Papa gets the rest he needs and keep him away from the place. I want this to be a big surprise for him."

"You were reading my mind, Melanie."

"You said I was Clairvoyant. I envision it as the best of both worlds. You will take over the place in due time, and I will use my creative design skills to illustrate my interest in the tavern."

"I think we're on to something, Melanie."

The hospital intercom blurted, "Code blue in room 207, code blue in room 207."

Mario had suffered a relapse of his breathing problems. Within seconds, two nurses and a doctor were tending to him, eventually restoring a normal breathing pattern.

Clarice sat at his bedside in the Intensive Care Unit at Holy Cross. "All those tubes. You could be a bionic man." He looked so shriveled, even in the narrow hospital bed with the sheets tucked neatly under his chin, held down by trails of tubes attached to his body.

"Since when does the fair damsel come to the super

hero?" With considerable effort, he shifted himself to face her and struggled to offer a hint of a smile.

"Since she wanted to make sure he isn't fakin' all this just to get some attention from a damsel in distress." She smiled down at him and squeezed his hand.

"You don't look distressed to me. In fact, you look pretty good to an old guy. Didn't I check your ID a few weeks ago?"

"Hmm. Now I'm not sure whether to ask the doctors to check your brain or your eyes."

"Hey, all my body parts are working, okay? Perhaps it's your memory we should be checking." They both chuckled.

"Actually, my own memory has been working overtime," he continued. "Nothing much else to do but lie here and worry about dying. So I've been thinking about the good old days instead. But, hey, life shouldn't be seen through a rear view mirror. Too much of that isn't good."

"You're right, Mario. It's time to focus straight ahead into the future. Besides, aren't the best memories the ones you haven't made yet? I have a good feeling about you. You're a strong man with family and friends who need you. More good old days are just around the corner.

You'll see."

Chapter 30

DOLLARS AND LOTS OF CHANGE…ALL IN ONE NIGHT

Lucky stood next to Kevin as she counted her winnings. "One forty-eight, forty-nine, fifty, fifty-one, a hundred and fifty-one bucks. Not bad for an evening. This is a new high for me."

"My pockets are lined with additional *Andrew Jacksons* too honey. The Hard Rock Casino did me justice tonight."

"How much did you win?"

"Enough to buy us a superb dinner next week."

The traffic light switched to amber. Kevin slowed to a stop. He pressed the accessory lowering the convertible top.

"Want to take a drive by the beach?"

"I don't see why not. Later, we can swing by High Hopes for a drink. I'm buying since I'm wealthy now."

Lucky turned the radio volume up a notch, leaned back, and placed her hand on his knee. He punched the speed up a bit and within seconds entered I-595 and headed east toward the beach.

"Yeah, let's stop for a drink at the tavern after we drive by the beach. You can buy the popcorn at the movie tomorrow night. I'll get the drinks tonight. Deal?"

"Deal," she said leaning over to peck him on the cheek.

"Did you have a particular movie in mind?"

"Nah...do you?"

"No, we'll figure it out tomorrow night."

"I was just thinking, Lucky, after tomorrow night I'm back to work for four days. Not seeing each other will be hard."

"Do ya think? Work is what brings the money in, honey. I'm sure we'll call each other."

He parked the car. "Come on, Lucky, let's take a walk on the beach."

"You're so romantic."

He walked around to the passenger side and opened her door. "Thank you, kind sir."

The evening was cool and refreshing. Two sea gulls paraded on the sand, pecking to grab a few morsels of food.

"Ya know, Lucky, it's been a long time since I dated anyone. My father was my hero. I devoted my life to caring for him once he became ill. Rarely could I eke out an hour or two for myself. My evening out usually consisted of bowling with buddies for a few hours."

"I'm sure he's aware you're with me now. I spend most

of *my* time either at home or at High Hopes when I'm not working. I enjoy being with people. She turned slightly serious. "Kevin, I do need to share something with you."

"What is it, dear?"

She paused for a minute and clasped his hand tighter. Taking a deep breath, she continued.

"I need to tell you the real reason I quit being a flight attendant." She took a deep breath.

"Go ahead, my dear."

"Kevin, I was raped in my hotel room while on a layover. There was a period when I didn't think I would ever want to be with a man again. Sharing the details is difficult for me, so I'd rather let it go for now. I believe in being honest and needed to tell you."

"How awful, Lucky. I'm so sorry. As far as I'm concerned, this doesn't change anything between us. I'm comfortable with you and I believe in you."

"I'm gratified. Your kindness is appreciated and I'm fortunate to be with you. I'm relieved you're not upset."

"Why should I be? I won't allow myself to worry about things I can't change."

"I'm so blessed, Kevin."

He slipped his arm protectively around her waist turning her toward his parked car a few yards away.

"I love this car," she said.

"Care to drive?"

"I've been waiting for you to ask."

He tossed her the keys. "Careful now, this is my other baby."

"What do you say we have a drink at my place instead of the tavern? I've got Dewars."

"Okay by me."

Lucky paid careful attention to the speedometer and used her signals to turn, an endearing and perhaps surprising act in Florida. She pulled into the Visitors parking spot at her complex, and handed him his keys. "Like you said, Kevin, she drives like a dream."

"Told ya, didn't I?"

"Here ya go. Dewars and water in a tall glass," she said handing him his drink. "She poured herself a generous glass of wine and raised it. "Thanks for a lucky evening. No pun intended," she laughed. "I enjoyed the casino."

He settled down on the couch as she turned on the multi-speaker sound system.

"Do you have a favorite artist or type of music? Should we listen to earsplitting or soft and romantic?" She asked.

Lucky blushed, recalling it had been quite a while since she said anything to a man even remotely close to a suggestion of romance.

"I like a wide variety of music, but my preference is a soft piano and sax combination. Whatever you choose is fine with me."

Lucky selected a CD of soft piano music. Kevin remembered her traumatic past and deliberately sat at the end of the couch to avoid any trace of impropriety.

"Come, sit next to me. Like I said, I am at ease with you."

He slid over and placed her hand in his, giving it a slight squeeze. "Same here, Lucky."

"I was deliberately honest with you earlier tonight. One shouldn't assume, but I get the idea I won't find a smoking gun in your past."

"You're right. For the record, I don't even own a gun," he laughed.

"Neither do I. I suppose I should buy one for protection, but I've learned to take precautions. Within a year I probably will move anyway."

"You're staying in Fort Lauderdale, right?" he asked with a hint of panic.

"I wouldn't live anywhere else. A lawsuit is pending against the hotel where I was raped. My attorney tells me they want to settle out of court. If I agree to their offer, I could be depositing a sizable check into my now meager savings account. I may want to purchase something more upscale."

"You deserve the restitution."

"Another drink, Kevin?" She asked lifting his empty glass.

"No thanks. I better get going. You have to work tomorrow, right?"

"Nope, I'm off. I took a comp day."

He placed his hands behind his neck and leaned back on the couch, stretching his arms. She felt an amorous sensation running through her body. His stretching movement cemented her decision. Lucky took a deep, calming breath and knew in her heart as she led Kevin to the bedroom that this would be the experience that finally erased all other memories.

CHAPTER 31

LUCKY…IT'S CLARICE CALLING

As she slowly awakened, Lucky reached to the other side of the bed. She was startled awake by the emptiness. The covers were turned back. The impression of his head remained in the pillow. No Kevin. She gasped and looked around the room. The fear of abandonment ricocheted through her body.

Quickly discarded clothes were piled at the foot of the bed. His were still mingled with hers. Where was he? As her breathing became almost normal again, she heard the scrape of a chair on the balcony, followed by a grunt. She pulled a robe around her naked body and crept to the open door to the balcony.

Kevin smiled and winked at her. "I stubbed my toe on the balcony door. I was coming to see if you were awake and would join me to watch the sunrise." Her heart filled with long forgotten sentiments as he pulled her to his side to witness the first shimmering of a Fort Lauderdale sunrise. It foretold a new beginning and high hopes.

"Happy *early* birthday," she whispered to herself.

They viewed the spectacle of a brilliant sunrise and returned to the bedroom for a cuddle and snooze before breakfast.

She awoke to feel his muscular arm around her. The leftover fragrance from his tropical sunscreen mixed with his manly scent, and a ripple of a snore, again reminded her how long it had been since a man's touch pleased her.

The unset alarm clock flipped from nine ten to nine eleven as Lucky tied her bathrobe and tip-toed to the kitchen to answer her cell phone. "Why didn't I turn this off last night?" she muttered to herself.

"Good morning, Clarice." Lucky opened the refrigerator and took out the coffee container. " No, you didn't wake me."

Lucky respected and admired Clarice Thompson. She always enjoyed calls from her, but today was different. Kevin had shown some awakening signs and she was ready to provide him some morning oral gratification.

Lucky set the coffee maker to begin the welcoming drip in thirty minutes. She walked to her bedroom, talking in a low volume with Clarice. She sat down next to him and started to lightly rub his chest. She streaked the bits of hair surrounding each nipple. He smiled, but kept his eyes closed.

"I'm sorry Sam's calling you about our differences and she's upset because I've not returned her calls. She should move back to South Carolina if she is considering a move." Lucky paused. "I know she wants to speak with me, and you did relay the message. I'll tell her you did what she asked when I call her."

Lucky rolled her eyes. *Why did Clarice call now?* She thought focusing her eyes on the energetic bulge beneath the sheets. She recalled from the night before that his hose was quite substantial.

"Yes, Clarice you did what Sam asked. Thank you. I think she's nothing short of being a fraud after what she did to me. It's a subtle reminder when you decide to travel in life with someone you need to assess how much baggage they have. You're absolutely correct, Clarice. There's no question she has scars she can't cover with any number of ruffles."

Kevin opened his eyes and pecked her on the neck. Lucky's emotions ran wild. She felt as if she was in a race between being able to pounce on Kevin before he got up, and politely ending the conversation without even a hint to Clarice that he lay right next to her.

"Clarice, I don't mean to cut our call short but I have to go." Lucky rolled her eyes. "Yes, I'll give some thought to giving Sam a call. I understand she and I have been friends for a long time. I'll call you later today, Clarice. Hugs."

Emerging victorious, she mounted Kevin and began kissing him all over his face, neck, and nipples before ending up in the place that would start his morning off just right.

It was around 10:15 when Lucky's cell phone rang again. She reached across Kevin's chest and answered the call, kissing a nipple as she listened.

She cupped her hand over the phone and lifted it up just past her ear. "Terry called in sick. They want me to come in to work until 3:00."

She returned her attention to the caller. "Did Terry tell you what's wrong with her?

Kevin whispered, "It's okay with me if you want to work. I've got to cut the grass and wash my car anyway. We're still on for tonight, right?"

"Absolutely."

"Okay, Marlene. I'll be in soon." She flipped the phone closed and kissed him again.

"I guess I won't be dazzling you with my culinary skills, Lucky. I was prepared to make you a sumptuous breakfast before leaving. I'll just take a quick shower so you can get ready for work.

I think we should shower together, I'm on this kick to save water," she chuckled.

"A commendable idea. Remember, I'm a firefighter." He began to seductively remove his underwear. "Saving water is a mandate."

⁂

Kevin completed the last lap of cutting his grass by mid-afternoon. He paused for a moment to appreciate the smell of his fresh cut lawn. Sweat trickled down his bare chest. His leg began to tingle from the vibration of his cell phone tucked in the pocket of his shorts. Kevin admired the appearance of his house and lawn as he wiped his eyes and lifted the phone cover.

"Hey, Lucky, what's up? He picked up the last small pile of brush. "You called just to listen to my voice? You're so sweet, my dear. He smiled, and listened to every word. "Naw, I'll drive. We can put the top down."

Kevin held the cell phone to his ear with his shoulder as he stuffed the brush in a baggy and headed toward the house.

"I'll pick you up at 7:00, okay? Talk to you later, beautiful lady."

He said goodbye but couldn't help think, *Lucky has been halfway around the world. I hope I'm good enough for her.*

Later in the evening, he looked across at her as they waited for dinner to be served at their favorite table in the tavern corner. He was quiet for a moment, as his brow furrowed. He struggled for how to express the fear in his heart.

"I'm not sure we're much of a match. You're such a refined lady, and well, I'm a little rough around the edges. I'm working class and you're *first* class. How's that gonna work?"

Lucky reached over to stroke his cheek, pausing to fight back the mist in her eyes. "If I could change anything I wanted about you, you know what it would be?"

A cloud of concern darkened his eyes. He cleared his throat. "Okay, what would you change?"

"Absolutely nothing," she replied. "You're everything I need in a man. Everything I want." She smiled and added, "Actually, maybe a bit more."

CHAPTER 32

A LESSON FOR THE PREACHER

Sam was anxious as she left Fort Lauderdale and headed to Charleston. She was nearly oblivious to the splendid scenery unfolding outside her car window because of the relentless tug at her attention to rehearse the words for the first confrontation with her estranged father. There was a terrifying potential for a miscarriage of her intensions.

She was determined to drive straight through to

Charleston, but surrendered to her Southern roots and stopped at a Cracker Barrel Restaurant for both breakfast and lunch. 566 miles after she left Fort Lauderdale, Sam was back in Charleston. She pulled into the driveway of the home she grew up in. She sat for a minute, flirting with the idea of first checking into the motel, and returning in the morning to join her father.

He was pleasant enough, even somewhat conciliatory when we spoke on the phone, she thought. *What's the worst that can happen?*

She got out of her car and hesitated, taking a look at the house, sparkling in a fresh coat of paint. She stooped to pick up the evening paper from the porch, paused a minute, and nervously pressed the doorbell.

He greeted her with a smile. "Samantha, Come in, come in!"

She stepped inside and looked around the familiar scene. Sam recognized the enticing aroma coming from the kitchen. Her father was cooking his famous spaghetti sauce. "Not too many changes, Reverend."

"I prefer *father* or *dad*, but the choice is yours."

"Okay, Dad, but we do need to talk about the past at some point."

"I find no better time than the present, Samantha. Where's your luggage though?"

"I'm not staying here, Dad. I've got a reservation at La Quinta downtown, close to the courthouse."

"Aren't you staying for the trial?"

"Yes, and I may try to find work here in Charleston. Mario assured me I can always go back to work at the High Hopes Tavern. I want to take my time before making any decision. Too much hurt still lingers inside me, Dad."

"The trial doesn't start for another few weeks. The hotel will cost you a bundle," he said in a concerned tone. "That's what you want to do, stay at a hotel? He pointed to the couch. Samantha, please sit down." She moved toward the couch while her father slowly lowered himself into his favorite wingback chair.

"You're moving a little slower. Tell me the truth, how are you doing these days?"

"Not too bad, Samantha. I need to watch what I eat, but then again, who doesn't? One day a news report tells you red meat is okay to eat, a few weeks later, it's not. I take a pill for my blood pressure, nothing else. Overall, I'm doing well."

"That's excellent news, Dad."

"Samantha, I hope you might change your mind and stay here with me. But first, I need to listen to what you want to share. I realize you're still bitter with me."

She sat on the couch and folded her legs under herself to get comfortable for the conversation. He reached for his pipe and tobacco.

"I see you're still smoking."

"Pipe smoking is my only vice, dear. Tell me now, what's on your mind."

"Dad, I'll keep my comments direct but simple. I never felt loved here."

"I understand, Samantha, and I was wrong.

"Dad, I have friends with more degrees than a rectal thermometer, but lack common sense. It would be a serious mistake on your part to think because I didn't graduate college, and I'm a waitress that I'm not successful. During the tourist season, I would say I bring home as much being a waitress as you do preaching."

"You're probably right."

"I often think about what more I could have accomplished with some proper guidance from you and mom. As a child, you demonstrated nothing but animosity and ridicule toward me. You coerced mom to act the same. I also ask myself, how much of our problems were my doing as well. Life isn't easy, but the goal for parents should be to make life easier for their children. To provide for them and make them happy. You failed me in that regard."

Tears began to well up in his eyes. He reached for a tissue from the box beside his chair and wiped his eyes. He sobbed and blew his nose. "I can't deny anything you said. How can I ever repair the damage, Samantha?"

"Most preachers are honest people. You may want to consider the subject of *forgiveness* in one of your upcoming sermons. Be honest with your congregation. I welcome the idea for you to share our story with them. People who give birth to a child should understand it was their choice. Along *with* such a decision comes the responsibility to nourish, teach, provide for, and -- most of all -- love your child.

Samantha stood up, walked to his side and wiped away the remaining tears.

A sermon on giving and receiving forgiveness would give me a reason to acknowledge you as my father and to call you Dad again. Something I never thought I would want to do."

"Samantha, I love you. It's not because Charlie and your mother are gone and I don't want to die alone. It's because what you expressed was a lesson about love. Preachers need to be good learners as well. I learned something tonight."

Her father stood up more briskly than he had sat down, and held her lovingly. He kissed her on the cheek. "You might be the best waitress in Fort Lauderdale, but perhaps you should consider being a teacher."

"Nah, not for me. Plus the pay sucks. Oops...I mean..." she said reaching for her ringing cell phone.

"It's okay, Samantha. The word is not new to me." He smiled.

"How ya doin, Gary?" she asked excitedly. She paused to hear his response.

"I'm doing well. I came to Charleston early for the trial. When are you coming this way?" She whispered as her dad began to leave the room. "I understand it may be impossible because of the trial, but I want to share some special time with you."

She slowly walked around the room.

"He's asked me to stay here, but I'm not sure yet if I want to. I made a reservation at the La Quinta downtown to start tonight." Sam sat down and placed her toes on the edge of the coffee table. "You're staying at the same hotel? When will you arrive?"

Sam appeared somewhat confused, yet excited as he continued.

"Gary, am I correct? You asked me to cancel my room when you arrive, and stay in yours? I thought you said we couldn't be together since it might jeopardize the case. I don't want to hurt any chances of this guy being convicted."

She paused.

"The attorney has told my dad the case against him looks solid. Sounds like you agree."

Sam stood up and began to pace around the room. "We must be discreet though, and I also need to tell you something when we do meet."

Her jaw dropped and her eyes widened. "Karl already told you and you're okay with what happened? "What a relief, Gary. Lucky won't answer my voicemail or e-mail messages. She's furious with me, and our friendship may be beyond repair."

She began to weep, slowing her speech.

"I know I need to give her time, Gary. I know you weren't pleased when Karl told you about our encounter in Fort Lauderdale, but you didn't overreact. I understand from Clarice that Lucky is dating a firefighter named Kevin. Rumor is this could develop into a serious relationship."

Her father returned to the living room. He sat down and picked up the newspaper.

"Yes, I guess I'm thrilled for her. I'm also happy you're more interested in *us*. Gotta run now, Gary. I'll call you later tonight."

She blew him a double-kiss "Okay honey, later."

"I spoke to Gary, the detective. He will be here soon for the trial," she said walking into the kitchen.

"I thought you mentioned his name while speaking to him. I'm grateful to Gary. It will be my privilege to finally meet him. Will you stay with him while he's in town?"

"Maybe, some of the time, Dad," she answered, puzzled by his about-face.

"He's welcome to stay here with you if you would like, it's your choice."

"My, you *have* changed. Staying here would be much better for Gary and me. I'll ask him what he thinks."

Samantha held on to the railing, jumping two steps at a time up the stairs to her old bedroom. She closed the door behind her, and walked to the window. "One relationship repaired and one to go."

CHAPTER 33

THE INSPECTOR IS HERE TO SEE YOU...

Daniel and Kevin sat on the High Hopes patio sharing their views on week eight of the NFL season. Their opinions were aligned regarding the Commissioners hard-line stand on helmet-to-helmet hits. Inside, posted signs advised customers the High Hopes Tavern would be closed from November 15th to December 20th for a facelift.

Clarice and Lucky enjoyed their usual adult beverages.

"Lucky, I'm curious. "What's the *real* attraction to Kevin?"

"Easy to answer. He believes in me so strongly, which makes me believe in myself and elevates my confidence. It's precious. That makes him indispensable to my happiness. I'm just relived that I recognized it in time to keep him close to me."

"I'm pleased for you, and *I'm* glad to have met Daniel. I'm a gal who can be perfectly happy twirling alone in her own living room to the strains of a favorite old tune. Maybe a cocktail in one hand, head tilted back, eyes closed. I can do that. But true dancing has to be a symbiotic relationship -- whether with a single other person or a group on a dance floor...or even a stage. Dance, to be complete, must be complementary."

Clarice continued," For me, 'cause I'm an old fashioned Southern girl', dancing is best within the arms of a man. Dance is a metaphor for life; the shared intimacy expresses the boldest essence of existence. At our core we all have primitive instincts. I even love the smell of a man. The caress of his lips against my skin quickens my pulse and guides my body to synchronize with the tempo of the music. I must be careful with my reminiscences or I may need to refresh my drink sooner rather than later.

Lucky spoke up. "You're right, though. I can't help feeling that sometimes you tango; sometimes you waltz. Perhaps only our bodies recognize the rhythm and may not even know its name. The dances could be as opposite as an adagio or a samba, even suggestive of a gang scene from "West Side Story."

The best technique for becoming one with dance is to simply surrender. Let your emotional and physical selves converge to guide the movements. I'm ready to dance, and I may have found the right man to start the beat. This might well be the steamiest explanation of dance ever.

"Enough of the schmaltz," Clarice said moving closer to Lucky. The parade of karaoke singers in the next room made talking to each other difficult as the amateurs screeched to reach a high note of their favorite, but in many cases, mutilated number.

"What bar doesn't have karaoke these days?" Clarice continued, holding one finger in each ear. I find it somewhat annoying at times, but many people like it, and some even do it well."

"What's the alternative?" Lucky asked.

"I wish I had an answer to your question." They both shrugged and took a sip of their drinks.

"Lucky my dear, I've never asked you, what brought you to Fort Lauderdale?"

"I was fortunate enough to be assigned to Miami as my base when I was a flight attendant. A friend of mine lived in Fort Lauderdale, and I moved here to share an apartment since it was an easy commute to Miami. I liked the weather, the beach, and the thought of not shoveling snow. What about you?"

"The lure for me was the chance to be on stage in dinner theatre. The hotels on Miami Beach attracted the likes of Frank Sinatra, Dean Martin, and Sammy Davis, Jr. Jackie Gleason's weekly TV show was filmed in Miami Beach and a popular show, *Surfside Six* was filmed there on location."

"*Surfside Six*? Never heard of it."

"I didn't think so. It was a weekly program about a Miami Beach detective agency. It took place on a houseboat, docked across the street from the Fountainbleau Hotel."

"Oh, interesting. What finally got you twenty miles north?"

"I was enjoying a leisurely drive through Fort Lauderdale when I came upon an exquisite home for sale in the Harbor Beach section. My divorce with Calvin was amicable and enriching. I scooped up the place up and moved."

"His loss I'm sure."

"Lucky, I have an idea."

"About what?"

"The alternative to karaoke."

"Huh?"

"A spinoff of what we both just said. Everyone who comes to High Hopes Tavern is either a visitor to Fort

Lauderdale or a resident. Each has a story about why they're here," Clarice continued. "Some have transferred here, while some were born here and don't plan to leave. One night every week, people could gather and share their Fort Lauderdale stories."

"Now that sounds rather boring to me. How many of those Grey Goose martinis have you had? "Why would anyone want to do that?"

"Lucky, this could become a High Hopes Tavern tradition. Daniel and I are just two of many other older people who like this tavern. Kevin and you represent the younger generation. If everyone could share their Fort Lauderdale story, the line between the young and old would disappear. Of course, no one would be obligated to speak." Daniel and I recently discussed this concept with Mario.

"Hmm, the idea is sounding better, Clarice."

"We could ask Mario to begin this program right after the reopening. You do know he's not aware of any of the facelift plans, don't you?"

"No, I didn't."

"Melanie wants him to recuperate. Coming to the bar will not help so she's asked him to stay away for a while. She wants to surprise him by redecorating the place. I ask myself, though, is it fair that this place gets a makeover before I do? Shouldn't it be based on need? This place is comfortable, lived in. If *I* were a building, I'd be *condemned*. Of course, we both appear more beautiful after an alcohol buzz and dim lighting."

"You're marvelous just as you are. How will Melanie get the money to pay for all this?"

"A new investor may be in the picture."

Lucky's cell phone rang. "What a coincidence." Lucky said. "It's Mario calling."

"Must be fate, darling'. Please allow me to speak with him once you're finished."

"Hello, stranger. How's your day going? Clarice and I

came here to enjoy a cocktail." Lucky sipped her chardonnay.

"I'm told you're home recuperating. Take your time. Don't rush the healing process."

She paused to listen.

"No, I haven't spoken to Sam in a while. I understand she went back to South Carolina." Lucky's desire to talk about Sam was minimal at best. "Here's Clarice, she wants to speak to you. It's rather loud in here, but she has a stage trained voice."

"Mario, darlin', from what I overheard, you're doing well."

Clarice held the phone away and lip-synced to Antonio that Mario was on the line.

"Terrific. Mario," she continued. "Remember our chat about customers entertaining each other? Clarice refreshed the concept for an evening of, "why we live here." Then she listened as Mario explained the suggestion from the two artistic waiters.

"I'm so pleased you're still comfortable with the idea, Mario."

She motioned to Antonio that she would like him to refresh her cocktail.

"I agree. Both ideas will bring more people to the tavern. We'll name the show *Lauding Lauderdale*."

"You just rest, darlin'. We'll take care of everything here."

A week later, the tavern closed to begin the renovations. Melanie called to check in with her father every day since she was nervous about his health. The work was on schedule. They never discussed anything going on at the tavern.

"That looks great," she said to a painter as she patted his back. "Excellent work," she told another.

"The new glassware is due in today, Melanie, so I'll be here for a while. Why don't you go home and relax?"

"Are you kiddin'? I designed this make over and I want

to be sure it's what you and I agreed to down to the last detail. I can't wait until we can share this with Mario."

"I know, Melanie. It's only four days until Saturday's big event."

"Yeah, and surprisingly my nerves are still functioning properly. Did my papa call you about *Lauding Lauderdale*?"

"It's an amusing idea, and the timing is right for a tavern sporting a makeover."

The last few days went by so fast Melanie thought each day had only ten hours rather than twenty-four. Between several trips to Home Depot and the Restaurant Supply Store, she was worn out.

Step-by-step, a handyman carefully climbed a ladder with the last of the new mariner - themed art pieces to be hung. Another whistled while he polished the new ship's wheel separating the two main dining rooms.

"What's taking so long?" Antonio asked as he and Melanie sat nervously sipping iced tea.

"It's hard to tell, Antonio. I hope nothing is wrong. You know these Building and Code Inspectors like to display their power," she said with a tinge of sarcasm.

Her eyes remained focused on the art piece as the handyman stepped down the ladder. She smiled at him, "This is the perfect spot for that piece, thank you."
"You're welcome, ma'am."

A few seconds later, the inspector motioned for them to follow him.

Melanie gestured to Antonio and lip-synched. "My stomach is in a knot now."

"What could possibly be the problem?" Antonio whispered.

The inspector entered the kitchen, stopped and leaned against the new stainless steel food preparation table. Melanie was trembling, and prepared for the worst. The fear of not being able to open on-time consumed too much space in her brain.

"I have to tell you," he began, "I have inspected

thousands of restaurants in my thirty years of doing this job, but this is, by far, the most outstanding redesign I've ever experienced. You have surpassed the code requirements. Every aspect is flawless. Congratulations."

Melanie exhaled a sigh of relief. She turned to Antonio and high-fived him.

"Thank you, sir," Melanie said, resisting the urge to jump up and down. "You had us worried for a minute."

"You're good to go," he said handing Antonio the required certificates. The inspector reached the front door, followed closely by Melanie and Antonio. "High Hopes Tavern is a class act," he said. "I'll be sure to bring my wife here. She'll love it."

"You've already given us the green light, so I guess it can't be considered a bribe if your first dinner is on us," Antonio suggested.

"That's quite generous of you, but I can't accept your offer. Good day," he said.

They closed the door, high-fived each other again and scoped the entire tavern. "It's absolutely spectacular," Antonio said. "Your interior decorator skills will make you rich someday, Melanie."

"I hope so."

"High Hopes Tavern, this is Antonio. How may I be of service?" Antonio greeted the caller. He smiled and gave another worker the high sign.

"My pleasure, sir. What time do you wish to dine and under what name? Six for dinner at 8:30," he scribbled on the calendar. He looked at Melanie. How far away from a 5 star rating at Zagat can we be?" *I can't wait to tell Dwight to get ready to dance to the tune of ka-ching.*

CHAPTER 34

THE GRAND REOPENING

The sun had long disappeared for the evening when Melanie and Antonio sat at a little Mexican restaurant dining on burritos, refried beans, and guacamole. She called her father from the table. "Papa, are you feeling up to coming to the tavern tomorrow?"

"Of course, my dear. I feel pretty good. Besides, it's time we announced the good news about the change in ownership. You *did* send out the grand reopening postcards to those on the mailing list."

"Oh, I completely forgot." She laughed and paused. "Of course I did. I'll pick you up at 2:30."

"Pick me up? No, I'll drive myself, Melanie. I certainly remember the way, dear."

"I insist. I don't want you to drive yet."

"Oh...alright. You're so stubborn. I wonder where you get that?"

"Thanks, Papa. Be ready to go at 2:30. We open promptly at 4:00."

Shortly after 2:00 Melanie used her key to let herself into Mario's condo. The shower was running.

"Papa, it's me. Don't be alarmed, I let myself in." She shouted.

"Okay, my dear. I'll be ready on-time. I've got beer and soda in the refrigerator if you want."

"No thanks, Papa."

Melanie sat down on the couch. She glanced at her watch in anticipation, growing more excited.

Mario sprinkled cologne on his face as he came into the room. "I told you I'd be ready."

"You're as handsome as ever, Papa, always the dashing gentleman."

They drove along A1A before making a left for the short drive west to the tavern. The weather was balmy, the blue sky, cloudless, adding delight to the countless visitors escaping the trappings of the cold season up north. They shared chitchat about the Dolphins' loss the previous Sunday.

Antonio waited with Clarice, Daniel, and Lucky, the only non-staff invited before the opening time, "Here they come,"

Melanie grabbed his hand and led him toward the front door.

"Ah, Melanie, you had the outside painted while I was away. The color complements the tropical palms and shrubs. I approve."

Antonio peered through the window. As they approached the door, he opened it to the applause of the favorite few gathered.

Mario's jaw dropped, his eyes widened. "Oh my, oh my," he repeated. "This is an amazing transformation."

"Papa, I hope you like it. I always told you I didn't' want to own High Hopes Tavern. But I do *understand* what it means to you, *and me*. My heart was just in a different direction. Under Antonio, your dream will live on. The design is my tribute to your legacy."

Mario's shoulders heaved as he sobbed, occasionally drying his eyes. Melanie held his arm as they all walked from room to room, viewing the simplistic, yet elegant changes created in her mind, and so well crafted by the workmen. Clarice, overwhelmed by Mario's emotions, took a handkerchief from her purse. She dabbed her eye before a lone tear could ruin her lavish makeup.

"Melanie," he cried, "I love you." He turned to the others. "And I love all of you too. This is truly impressive. You upgraded High Hopes Tavern without diminishing the original charm."

"That's what you paid my schooling for, Papa," she said squeezing his hand.

Daniel's curiosity got the better of him. "Melanie, what did you mean when you said," 'Under Antonio, your dream will live on?'"

"Tonight," Mario stopped and put a hand over his mouth. After he regained his composure, he removed his hand and continued, "We will announce Antonio Castalanos as the new owner of High Hopes Tavern. I'm almost sixty-nine and I want time to relax. Antonio will be graduated from culinary school in three weeks, and I offered him the opportunity to purchase the tavern."

Clarice led the applause. "This is truly cause for a celebration."

"Clarice, you think a change in the weather is a reason to enjoy a cocktail," Mario piped in.

"Careful, Mario, I may ask the new owner to remove you from his establishment."

At 3:30, regular customers as well as newcomers began to sit on the benches outside the famed tavern, waiting in the warmth of the Fort Lauderdale sun for the big event. The press release had paid off. Two of the local television stations sent the same news crew who covered the fire to report on the event.

"A half-hour to opening ladies and gentlemen," Antonio reminded the staff in a friendly tone. "Let's pick it up a notch or two. TV news crews are set up outside."

Every table was adorned with freshly pressed table cloths. There were also live flowers, and a, "We thank you for your patience, welcome back," coupon that offered the first drink on the house. Thirty minutes later, Antonio, Melanie, and Mario clasped their hands together on the key. They took a deep, collective breath, and turned the key in unison to open the door for business.

"We're home," one of the regulars called out. "I couldn't wait to get back."

"This place is like a second home, except I don't have to clean up. Check out that nautical artwork," another shouted. Mario pulled Antonio and Melanie aside to address the waiting news crew.

"The usual, Miss Clarice and Daniel?" Pete asked.

"Hey, Pete. I'm still sipping those Grey Goose martinis, darlin', and my first one was history ten minutes ago."

The place was jammed. The trio was underway with light jazz.

Lucky glanced at her cell phone and noticed an incoming call. She stepped outside the building so she could hear Kevin.

"Hi, honey," she responded while sliding her gold charm along her necklace. "Kevin, you will love what they've done.

"Perfect. I'll call you when I get home. Oh, Kevin, they're starting a new weekly event, *Lauding Lauderdale*. People get to talk about why they came here, or why they stayed. Won't that be fun?"

"Love you too," Slightly startled she closed her cell phone and thought to herself, she couldn't recall Kevin ever saying he loved her. It was a pleasant surprise, especially since he used the, "L" word first.

Lucky arrived home later than she expected, but she still called Kevin. They spoke for nearly an hour before agreeing it was time to turn in for the evening.

She was beginning to feel that a head on the other pillow could become more than a dream.

CHAPTER 35

LAUDING LAUDERDALE

The foursome arrived at 7:30 the next evening and sat with Clarice in the *amen corner*. The trio caught everybody's attention with a drum roll followed by a stroke on the cymbal. "May I have your attention please?" With Melanie by his side, he began to speak.

"Thank you. For those of you new to High Hopes Tavern, I'm Mario Bellasari. I bought this tavern from the original owners. I've known some of you for many years, and in some cases, your parents came here before you. Over the years, we've served both a younger as well as more mature crowd, representing a variety of cultures and ethnic groups.

As our friendships grew we participated in each other's lives. There were good times and not so good times. I also watched many of my employees advance their careers here at High Hopes Tavern. Earlier this evening I announced to the staff, and I am pleased to now share with you, that Antonio Castalanos, a bartender here for many years, is the new owner of the High Hopes Tavern."

At first, the reaction was mixed. The newcomers applauded. The regular customers slowly joined in. Some of them looked bewildered. Did Mario's selling signify deteriorating health?

Dwight had arrived shortly before the event and stood by himself, avoiding any of the spotlight. Antonio stepped up to the microphone.

"Ladies and Gentlemen, I won't keep you. I just want to express what an honor it has been to work here. Mario has always treated his staff like family. I plan to carry on that tradition and hope you'll join us here frequently. Enjoy the evening. Please join us tomorrow at 8:00 for our very first *Lauding Lauderdale* event where you'll be the stars. Stop by tomorrow evening and see what it's all about. My exceptional staff and I thank you and look forward to many years of serving you."

"I'm fine, feeling great," Mario told numerous customers as he headed toward the bar. Many, fighting back a tear, patted him on the back, while others shook his hand and congratulated him on his future relaxation time. "I'll have a drink now, Pete."

He poured Mario's drink. "That will be eight dollars, sir. Gotta charge you. You're a customer now." Mario reached into this pocket for his money. "You know I'm just teasin' your ass, Mario."

"You had me there for a minute, Pete."

Mario walked over to join Clarice and her group. "How did I do?"

"Splendid, darlin'," Clarice responded. "It's good the place will stay in the family -- and he's the best kind of family y'know -- the one you *choose*."

"Well said," Clarice.

The accomplice to Mario's nostalgia was his final Chivas and water of the evening. He sat on his couch reminiscing about the time he bought the tavern, as well as the people who passed through the doors since. He always knew that Melanie was gifted. But what she did to the tavern was beyond anything he might have imagined.

Shortly after midnight Mario retreated to his bedroom. The grand reopening was a huge success, but he looked forward to the new *Lauding Lauderdale* event, now just hours away.

The patio decorations were a hodgepodge of Fort Lauderdale travel posters. Three small innocuous fake frogs, battery-operated to croak intermittently, sat besides three potted palm trees intertwined with festive lighting.

"I see people gathering on the patio, Clarice. Let's begin to make our way toward the show." Daniel suggested.

"My darlin,' I wouldn't miss this. I know why I'm here. I want to listen and learn why others enjoy the magnificence of Fort Lauderdale as well. Perhaps I'll say a word or two."

More people gravitated toward the patio to mingle before *Lauding Lauderdale* started. A microphone, speakers and a strategically placed bar stool marked where the speakers would perform.

Clarice and Daniel nudge their way to where Lucky and Kevin stood.

"Good evening, Lucky, Kevin," Clarice said, "I'm so anxious for the festivities to begin."

"We are as well." Lucky pointed, "An open table for four, let's grab it."

Mario and Melanie were still talking to guests when Antonio, who appeared a bit nervous, stepped to the microphone.

"Good evening and welcome to the first ever, *Lauding Lauderdale*. I know some of you don't like to speak in front of a crowd. Let me assure you that this is an evening to share why you're here in Fort Lauderdale. It's your choice to speak or not. However, to entice you, everyone who participates will receive a free drink of your choice--that includes top shelf liquors. Who would like to be the very first?"

A tall slender man, dressed in shorts, a tropical shirt, and sandals approached. Antonio handed him the microphone. His hair was white and well-groomed.

"My name is Sander Topperfield. In 1978, my wife and I came to Fort Lauderdale on vacation. We fell in love with the weather. We lived in New England most of our lives, but the winters became unbearable. After a splendid two-week vacation here, we went back home, put our place on the market, and moved. My wife passed away three years ago. My son and his wife want me to return to New England and live with them. I've told them they have their own lives to live. Besides, I love it here and have no intentions of returning to the snow country.

As the crowd applauded, a young African American man approached and took the mike.

"Good evening everyone, I'm Carlton Best, and I'm thirty-seven years old. My parents and I moved here when I was only four. I graduated from Fort Lauderdale High School and Nova Southeastern University. I can truly say I am enamored by this city. My business is yacht sales, and Fort Lauderdale is the *Yachting Capital of the World*. Many of my sales are finalized over dinner, and this city offers some top of the line restaurants, including the famous High Hopes Tavern. Fort Lauderdale is truly one beautiful place to live. If you're in the market for a yacht, and have a million or so to drop, see me after the show."

As they did for Sander, a round of polite applause followed Carlton's brief remarks. A cavalcade of people, both younger and seniors formed a line waiting to speak. Antonio looked at Mario and Melanie and gave them the thumbs up.

Around 9:30 Clarice rose to speak. As is her style, she was dressed impeccably. Lucky sat between Kevin and Daniel at the table. As Clarice lifted the microphone, Lucky took Kevin's hand in hers.

"Good evening everyone. My name is Clarice Thompson. As you can tell from mah accent, I hail from the South, originally. I lived in Savannah, Georgia where I attended college. My former husband and I performed in the dinner theatre on Miami Beach. This was before he had the bad manners to leave me for a younger lady."

She paused to sip her martini, which allowed time to let the laughter subside.

"I moved to Fort Lauderdale shortly after that. The city offers so much to everyone, young and old. I enjoy the golf courses, casinos, and race tracks. Our beach is magnificent, offering so many water activities. However, my new friends, let's not forget the cultural aspects. Visitors and residents can enjoy concerts at the Broward Center for the Performing Arts, countless museums, and an International Film Festival. And my darlin's, even when you're not lookin' for love, it may find you. It happened to me."

Clarice set the mike down to a sustained round of applause. More customers rose to speak. The waiting line grew longer.

Mario and Melanie joined the table. "What a wonderful testimonial, Clarice."

"To paint a masterpiece is easy when you have such an enchanting model, Mario."

Daniel reached for Clarice's hand. "What a successful

beginning to *Lauding Lauderdale.*"

The lights from a passing sailboat and the patio décor provided a great photo op.

"Sir," Mario asked a guest, "Would you take a photo of us, please?"

"My pleasure," he responded. "Smile folks, one, two, three."

"Wouldn't this be the perfect setting for our wedding reception, Clarice?"

"What a fabulous idea, Daniel."

Kevin put his arm around Lucky, pulling her close to him. "I couldn't agree more, Daniel," he said. "What a perfect setting for a wedding reception."

Kevin nodded to Daniel who pulled a small jewelry box from his trousers and handed it to him. Clarice, Mario, and Melanie gathered around as Kevin dropped on one knee. "Lucky Larkin, in front of our family of friends, I ask you, will you marry me?"

Lucky kissed his forehead. "It would be my honor."

CHAPTER 36

CALL HER FIRST

Clarice sat at an antique roll-top desk in the corner of her study. She believed in the personal touch and addressed each invitation by hand. Daniel sat in her living room, smoking his Meerschaum pipe. The room design was worthy of a Turkish sultan, but suitable for a contemporary Southern lady. He sat captivated by a nature story on the Discovery Channel. She addressed a few more invitations, then turned off the light and joined him.

"I'm finished for tonight, Dear. I'll complete the rest of the invitations tomorrow. Calligraphy is an art form and addressing the invitations takes time if each is to be perfect. And I consider myself a perfectionist."

"How many people are you inviting?"

"It will be small gathering, Daniel. However, I can assure you our wedding will be a memorable occasion."

"Without a doubt."

Daniel put his pipe in the ashtray and put his arm around her. "Did I tell you I received a call from my real estate agent? He's pretty sure he has a renter for my house."

"No, you didn't. I'm sure you're pleased. If you rent your house, it would be one less headache and one less expense."

Her house phone rang, which caught her by surprise. "I'll get it," she said. Clarice walked toward her study. She stopped momentarily to glance at the dark-wood Seth Thomas grandfather clock, a family treasure, passed down by her mother.

Who could this be? Clarice thought. *Nobody calls after 9:00 P.M.* She entered the study and picked up the receiver.

"Hello, Lucky," she said. "No trouble at all, we're still up." She sat down in a two seat leather couch and propped her feet.

"Well share it with Miss Clarice, my dear."

"You've selected April 18th for your wedding? I'm so excited for you and Kevin. Your dream of a sincere and lasting relationship is coming true. Kevin's love has allowed you to conquer the fear you held so long."

Through the opened door, Clarice heard the shuffling of slippers. Daniel headed toward her bedroom with a book tucked under his arm.

"Daniel and I sensed the growth of a true commitment between you and Kevin," she continued. "I tell ya, darlin', some people marry for money, others for love. I've always believed if you're only into men with money, that's not love, it's a business deal!"

Clarice listened for a moment. "I'd like to share this news with Daniel so let's talk again tomorrow."

After another moment, "Of course, I'll help you plan the wedding. It's not too early to begin. April will be here in a flash." She stood up from the couch. "Call me tomorrow." Yes, you too. Good night now."

Daniel was sound asleep when Clarice got into bed

next to him. The occasional snore provided a sense of security that someone was by her side. Lucky's new happiness added to the comfort Clarice felt.

❧

Early the next morning, the rich aroma of freshly brewed coffee drew Daniel to the kitchen. "What did Lucky call for last evening?" Daniel asked, reaching for the coffee pot.

"I thought of waking you, but you looked so peaceful sleeping. They've selected April 18th for their wedding."

"Lucky must be ecstatic. We all enjoy the happy things in life. She made a wise choice to accept his proposal. Kevin is an honorable man," Daniel said.

"Did Lucky give any particular reason why they've selected April for the wedding? It seems frightfully soon, don't you think?"

"When you're in love, you're in love. Why wait?" She also alluded to being inspired by our selecting Valentine's Day for our wedding. They wanted to follow in our footsteps shortly after our special day."

❧

Lucky spotted Clarice and Daniel through the crowd. "I'm so pleased the two of you are here. Kevin is on his way home from work and will join me later. He would like to treat us all to dinner."

Daniel leaned forward. "What a nice gesture. We accept, Lucky."

"Lucky spoke to Clarice, "I need a favor once we're seated and comfortable."

"Oh," she responded, looking suspicious.

The name for each of the two newly decorated dining rooms hung over their entrances. Written using nautical rope, the name appeared on the portion of a boat oar that dipped under the water. Lucky requested Phillip seat them in, *The Conch Shell Room*, since, other than the patio, it provided the most picturesque view of the Intracoastal. They spoke for a while before Lucky spotted Kevin.

"Ah, here comes my man now."

"Hello everybody, sorry I took so long. Traffic was bumper-to-bumper tonight."

Kevin took Lucky by both hands and kissed her on the forehead. "How's my little slice of heaven this evening?"

"I couldn't be any better, my love!"

"Your usual, Kevin?" Daniel asked, motioning to Antonio. "The owner will be serving you this evening."

"Thank you both. He turned toward Clarice. You are as elegant as usual.

"Awwww, Kevin, you are just the sweetest thang!"

"Thank you, ma'am."

Clarice tapped on her watch, as Phillip neared the bar. *The Grande Dame*, being the perfectionist she is, expects an on time dining hour. "Miss Clarice, we're running a bit behind tonight. I apologize; however, your table is ready." The gentlemen took their ladies by the arm, and followed Phillip.

"Lucky called us with the good news, Kevin," Clarice began after being seated. "Congratulations. The weather in April is perfect for a wedding."

"Daniel and I are both fortunate men, Miss Clarice. We both got lucky!"

"Were you attempting a pun, Kevin?" Lucky asked, affectionately punching his arm.

Raul, their favorite waiter returned to the table with a fresh round of beverages. Clarice noted the larger size of the glassware Antonio purchased.

"I'm pleased with the new glasses, Raul. I certainly hope those extra few sips will permit me to maintain my dignified persona."

"I trust it will, Miss Clarice. On a personal note, I enjoy serving you, ma'am."

"You are a pro at working the crowd, young man," Daniel said.

"Clarice, since we're all seated and comfortable…"

"Yes, you want to ask a favor. I'm listening."

"I would be honored if you would be my *Maid of Honor.*"

Kevin felt Daniel nudge him. "Come my friend. Let's adjourn to the patio. I think some lady talk is coming on." Daniel stood up.

Clarice waited until they were out of earshot, and safely on the patio. She lifted her martini, took a sip, and looked directly at Lucky.

"I would be honored to serve. However, I must ask, why not Sam? You didn't phone her yet, did you?"

"Not yet. Please, don't be upset with me. I'm still not comfortable speaking with her.

"Lucky, I agree with the Indian philosopher, Krishnamurti who said, "to observe without evaluating is the highest form of intelligence. I try to make a practice of watching what's going on around me. That's easy. The hard part is to resist making a judgment. I don't pretend I always succeed. But I try, darlin', I try. *Honest I do*! Oh, my, don't let me burst into song. I couldn't possibly remember all the words."

"You are a true Southern belle, Miss Clarice. I will call her. It may be I rushed to judgment, or maybe I was too stubborn. I need to work on repairing what was otherwise a close and memorable relationship."

"You're right on both your decision and your observation."

"Observation, Clarice?"

"Yes, your observation that I am a true Southern belle. However, and don't let Daniel in on this, I do sway sometimes when Raul walks by. I've fantasized about burying my face in his sublimely perfect chest and yodeling until he whimpers. I nearly collapsed into a forlorn heap. He is one hot young man."

"Sam also thinks the world of Raul."

Darlin', I'm way too old for him, and truly love Daniel,

but fantasies don't age. Sometimes when I'm alone I think of him and frantically paw through the wine shelves in hopes of finding a few drops of absinthe with which to drown my despair. Nothing else will do. Then I think, I may have to settle for matte tea. Ain't life a bitch?"

Anyway, he is otherwise terminally adorable. I picture him as a tasteful nude, draped over a fainting couch, staring into the camera, but really at me, asking with his eyes to be ravished.

He's tall and thin with long slender fingers. Suitable for playing the violin is, of course, all I meant by that allusion."

"I'll be sure to keep your fantasies between us, Clarice. You're in love with Daniel, and I'm in love with Kevin. How lucky I am to have found him, you know, especially since I'm just a front desk agent at a high end hotel."

"Lucky, darlin', you're not *just* anything. No one is *just* anything. Be proud of who you are and what you do. I always find a kind word for everyone, regardless of their position in life.

"I sometimes wish I was still flying, Clarice. To visit parts of the world I haven't seen. But Kevin might not be in my life if I were still flying. I'd rather be with him and work as a front desk agent.

"Herr Freud was correct," Clarice began, "as he so often was, when he declared that, 'the more we try to deny who we are, the more we become what we fear.' I've thought of that more 'n once when I was swirling my tiny ice cubes in a small bath of Grey Goose. I believe Freud called it, 'return of the repressed.' That's far too abstract for me, but then I was never one to consider too carefully the option of being repressed."

"Here come our future husbands now.," Lucky said. "It's time to change the topic so we don't scare the men away again. I will call Sam later," she reminded Clarice.

"She is your best friend, Lucky. Ask her to be your Maid of Honor. If, and I doubt that she will say no, but if she does, I'd be honored to serve."

Daniel stepped toward the ladies. "I'm starving, can we order our dinner now?"

"I'm ready,. Are you, Kevin?"

"Yes. I've been waiting for the steak and lobster all day."

Raul passed their table carrying a large tray of entrees. "I'll be right back to take your order, my friends. Just give me a second or two."

It was after 11:00 when Lucky walked through the door of her apartment. Kevin was due back at work at 7:00 in the morning so he and Lucky decided to stay in their own places for the evening.

Should I call her now, it's after 11:00, Lucky paced the floor of her living room deep in thought. "I'm off tomorrow, I'll call her then." she said out loud.

Lucky went to bed after the late news, but tossed and turned, unable to sleep. Her mind raced with thoughts of both the good times and bad times she had shared with Sam. She turned the TV back on to the *easy listening* channel, hoping the soothing music would lull her to sleep.

☙

"Mornin', sleepy head," Kevin said. "It sounds like I woke you."

Clearly audible stretching sounds followed by a yawn confirmed his assumption.

"You didn't sleep well? Go back to sleep and I'll call you later. Kisses and hugs, I love you."

She told him she loved him too, closed her cell phone and cuddled with her pillow.

"Lucky peered at the alarm clock. It was 10:30 when she reached for her cell phone and dialed Sam's number.

"Hello, Sam?"

A nonchalant response followed.

"I know you've left several messages for me for over a month. I apologize.

Lucky asked about her father. She shared how pleased she was to hear he was doing well before telling her why she called.

"Sam, when you had sex with Karl, I felt betrayed. I was enraged and thought the only way you escaped vengeance was because I really don't believe in it. I was only looking for my turn at a relationship that will last after trying over and over again to make everyone else happy. But, Sam, I need my happiness as well. I thought Karl was the answer to my happiness.

Lucky slid two pieces of whole wheat bread into the toaster while she absorbed Sam's side of what happened with Karl.

"I know now Karl *approached you*. He told me about his sexual needs and, according to him, I wasn't measuring up. When I was young Sam, I allowed several men access to my heart. Way too many of them were devious. I just turned cold after I was raped. I cringed and retreated when someone tried to touch me. Then I met Kevin."

Lucky's tone switched from serious to cheerful.

"I understand Clarice told you I'm getting married in April."

Sam commended on her persistence to find a special someone.

"Thanks, Sam. I know in my heart I was wrong for not calling you. Each of us suffered for it, and I can't tell you why I didn't call. But who can measure the amount of pain in someone's heart?"

Lucky turned as the toast popped up. She placed her cell phone on the table and clicked the speaker on, then reached for a knife and butter.

"We were both hurt, Lucky. I miss you and I know you missed me."

"I needed to call you, Sam. Being angry or upset with each other doesn't erase the memories of the better times. There are many people in your life you can never repay for how they've helped you. I think of the teachers and relatives who are now passed, but who left an indelible lesson behind. Your friendship adds an extraordinary depth to my life. *That's* what I choose to remember.

"I wish I could reach through the phone and hug you, Sam. I would be honored if you would serve as my maid of honor. Any plans yet for April 18th?"

The sound of Sam choking back tears was clear over the cell phone speaker. "I have plans now. I'll be by your side to be a part of your wedding ceremony."

Lucky continued, "I'll invite Gary. How is he?"

"He's good, but he left for Georgia immediately after his testimony. I guess his interest dwindled. I will always be grateful to him for capturing my brother's killer. You are welcome to invite him, but we're no longer an item."

"Oh?"

"Yeah, it was fun while it lasted, but you know how it is. I fell for him quickly, perhaps too quickly. Sociopaths know which buttons to push. They know how far to take you and then they eat you alive. They'll call, say charming things to make you feel so special and then pull the plug after they get what they want. All of a sudden, you're not their dream person any longer."

"I'm sorry, Sam."

"No need to be sorry. Regret is a wasted emotion."

"Are you at your father's home?"

"Yes, we've patched things up. The trial should end later this week. Unless the defense produces a surprise witness we're unaware of, things are pointing toward a conviction."

"That's good news. I'm glad to hear that. Now for the sad news."

Sam poured herself a second cup of coffee then returned to the kitchen table.

"And the sad news is?"

"I read in the Sun-Sentinel that Ralph Becker passed away. He was eighty-four years old."

"You mean Florence's husband from the cruise?"

"Yes. I spoke with her yesterday. You're not going to believe this. She told me the ol' codger, as she referred to him, died of a heart attack in a hotel room while having sex with a younger lady."

"He was eighty-four and still having sex?"

"Yup, according to Florence. She's doing fine though."

"Lucky, I've gotta run. My father needs me. Call me later if you can."

They blew each other a kiss through the phone and hung up.

Sam entered the living room. "Dad, that was Lucky. She's getting married in April and asked me to be her maid of honor."

"I prayed for you both, my dear. I know you were very upset with your falling out, and I'm glad everything is settled."

Lucky and Sam kept in touch daily, but temperatures in the fifties in January, and an invitation to Clarice and Daniel's February wedding, had Sam driving back to the warmth of South Florida earlier than expected. She was eager to see Lucky again and to help prepare for her wedding.

Sam jerked a hand in the air to make a fist. She pumped it in a jubilant gesture as she passed the "Welcome to Florida" sign. Within hours she had reached Fort Lauderdale.

She called Lucky with her phone plugged into the car's speaker system. "Lucky, I'm back in town. Are you at work?"

"Yes, stop by the hotel for a quick hello."

"I'll be there as fast as I can without making friends with another cop."

Sam purposely did not insert a CD, or even play the radio as she drove down A1A. Although she had not been out of Fort Lauderdale long, she slowed the car as she drove by the beach. The salty ocean air and the guys playing volleyball in skimpy bathing trunks brought back pleasant memories. She was comforted by the conviction of her brother's murderer and knowing her father was getting along well.

Lucky sat on a bench outside the hotel as Sam pulled up. "I didn't expect to find you here. But, oh, it's so great to see you."

Sam got out of her car. They hugged each other and cried like a pair teenagers. "I am so glad to be back where we belong, Lucky."

"When you told me you were on the way, I asked for the rest of the day off. We were slow today, so it was okay. Where are you staying, Sam?"

"At my old place. I continued to pay for it while I was out of town. Follow me, Lucky. I'm sure you want to talk about the wedding."

"Hell, it's only four months away. I need to give you all the details."

"How is Kevin doing?"

"He's as scrumptious as ever. Thanks for asking. He's glad you're back and looking forward to seeing you. How about joining us for dinner tonight at the High Hopes? I can't wait until you see what a wonderful job of remodeling Melanie did."

"Sure, I'd like to. Perhaps Clarice and Daniel will join us."

"Yes, they will. I asked them to come tonight. I know Clarice. She probably has everything set for her wedding, but I'd like to offer my assistance if she needs it."

❧

Time passed quickly. It was sunny, but cooler than normal on Valentine's Day morning. Clarice had already called Antonio to be sure the patio had been decorated according to her specifications.

She and Daniel decided not to dress extravagantly for their wedding. He would wear a black suit, a marked departure from his normal attire. She would wear a simple, yet elegant, white dress with white shoes. Of course, a fashionable hat was a must. Clarice had asked Lucky to drop by the morning of the wedding for coffee and Danish.

Lucky enjoyed the pool area at Clarice's home, especially the wicker lounge chairs around the patio. They sipped coffee and enjoyed the cooler temperature. "Are you nervous, Clarice?"

"Darlin', this is my second time around. If I recall from the first time, all I'm required to do is say, "I do." I can handle that even without being primed by a martini.

"Well, I'm *already* getting nervous, Clarice, and my special day is still months away."

Another thirty minutes passed. "I better head home, Clarice. I need to shower and get ready for your big day."

Clarice looked at her watch. "My word, darlin', it's later than I thought. You know how I am about punctuality."

The parking lot at the small, but quaintly decorated church was full. Inside, guests sat in quiet anticipation and spoke with soft voices. A few occasionally looked back to see if the bride had arrived. The pastor, with a black suit and traditional white collar, faced the crowd. Daniel stood a few feet away, with a solemn smile suiting the occasion.

"It's 12:55. Where is she," Sam asked?

"Any minute now, Sam. She's like clockwork."

At exactly 1:00 by her watch, Clarice Thompson stood at the back of the church. The pastor signaled to the organist in the balcony. Clarice took her first step up the aisle on the first note of the wedding march.

Twenty minutes later the pastor placed one hand on Clarice's shoulder and one on Daniel's.

"By the power vested in me by the State of Florida, I now pronounce you husband and wife. You may kiss the bride."

Lucky tightened her grip on Kevin's arm. She looked at him, moving her eyes back and forth, gazing into his eyes before kissing him. "We're next, Kevin."

"Yes, we're next--but second to none." He replied.

Chapter 37

AN ELDERLY CUSTOMER

"Who is *that*?" Hushed voices speculated.

They stared intently as the frail elderly lady walked with the aid of a cane to a stool at the end of the bar. Her disheveled hair was white with dashes of gray, framing a severely wrinkled face. She wore long white gloves, a blue sequined dress, and matching blue shoes. A white necklace dangled almost to the bottom of her bosom. She carried an unmarked box about the size of a medium pizza.

Antonio approached her. "May I help you, ma'am?"

"Yes, you can, sonny. I'll take a shot of Wild Turkey and a Bud Light."

"Comin' right up, ma'am."

"Are you Mario Bellasari?"

"No ma'am," he said pointing. "That's him at the end of the bar."

"Sonny, as you can tell I'm older than Mr. Bellasari. Would you ask him to come over here for a minute? I need to speak to him."

"Yes ma'am, I will."

"How much for the shot and beer?"

"Seven fifty, ma'am."

She sifted through her pocket book and laid a crisp ten dollar bill on the bar. "Keep the change, sonny."

"Thank you, ma'am. I'm Antonio, the owner of High Hopes. I'll be back with Mario in a moment."

"Thanks, Antonio. You're a fine looking young man. Any chance you'd like to make an old lady happy?"

Antonio blushed. "I'm already taken ma'am. But thank you for your kind offer."

He walked over to Mario and whispered in his ear. They both walked to where the lady sat. After he introduced Mario, Antonio walked around the bar eyeing his customers' drinks to be sure no one required a refill.

"May I help you, ma'am. I understand you asked to speak to me."

"Good evening, Mr. Bellasari," she said, extending her hand. "My name is Margaret Alston-Ridge. This is an interesting place you've got here."

"Please, call me Mario. Mr. Bellasari, rest his soul, was my father. I prefer Mario. I sold High Hopes recently. Antonio is now the owner."

"He did tell me he is the owner. Remember I'm an old lady with memory issues," she said, her voice cracking.

"What can I do for you, Margaret?"

"First, agree that if I need to call you Mario, you'll call

me Peggy."

"Agreed, Peggy, so what's on your mind?"

With one gulp, she downed the whisky and then took several swigs of her beer. Despite her frail appearance, it was clear she still maintained a zest for a shot and beer.

She motioned to Antonio. "My drink appears to have vanished. I'll need a refresher."

He refilled her shot glass and placed another cold one in front of her. "These are powerful. You seem to handle them well, though."

"My mother, God rest her soul, always said, 'practice makes perfect.'"

"Please, Antonio, put Peggy's refresher on my tab."

"Thank you, Mario," she said sliding another ten dollar bill back into her pocketbook.

"I'm sure you can't forget my grandson, Robbie Alston. He worked here for a short time."

"Peggy, when you said your last name, I thought a connection might exist. We all remember him well."

"I am fully aware of what happened here, Mario. What he did was dreadful, to say the least."

"Yes, Robbie did a terrible thing. My compassionate side told me to give him the second chance everybody deserves. He sent me a letter of thanks after he completed boot camp, but nothing since."

Peggy leaned down to pick up the box resting at her feet. She caressed it for the last time.

"There won't be any further letters, Mario," she said solemnly, handing him the box. "He wanted you to have this."

Mario slowly opened the box. His face turned ashen.

"No, please no, Peggy," he said placing his hand on a traditionally folded American Flag.

"Yes, Mario. It breaks my heart to tell you Robbie was killed in Afghanistan a month and a half ago. His Jeep was ambushed. Robbie and his buddies were killed instantly."

He put his arms around Peggy. His shoulders heaved as

he cried hard and loud. Antonio hurried to his side to see what was wrong. The regulars in the bar watched with concern.

"I'll be okay, Antonio. "Peggy just gave me some devastating news."

"He wanted you to have this flag. This flag draped his coffin on the journey home from Afghanistan." She removed an envelope from her pocketbook and handed it to him. "I received this envelope from Robbie. He asked me to give it to you in person, along with the flag."

"Do I dare open the letter now, Peggy?"

"It's sealed. I have no idea what he wrote, but perhaps later would be better."

"I must be on my way. I'd like to stop back in again."

He wiped another tear from his eye. "We would enjoy the honor of many return visits."

Peggy walked out of the tavern as slowly as she walked in, giving Mario a final salute as she reached the door.

"You sure you're okay, Mario. Should I call Melanie to drive you home?"

"No thanks, I'll be fine. I'd rather tell you later what just happened."

It was time. Mario sat on his bed. He used a kitchen knife to open the envelope simply marked, "To Mario." He was impressed by Robbie's penmanship. He took a deep breath, and began to read.

Dear Mario -- I asked my grandmother to give you this letter if anything happened to me. You changed my life more than you probably realize. I don't know who that crazy kid was who thought setting a fire would somehow solve a problem. Some people think all the military does is make us into killers. If we pay attention and we learn, we have a chance to become men and women. I can't be there to shake your hand, so I want you to accept this flag as my appreciation for the second chance you and the U.S. Army gave me. My father was not a role model to me, but you were.

Love,
Robbie

Mario dropped the letter on the floor and fell back on his bed. He finally fell into a fitful sleep.

CHAPTER 38

A DREAM FULFILLED

A mixture of white puffy clouds floated against clear blue skies to create the perfect beginning for April 18th. The local TV stations were in synch forecasting no rain, but in South Florida no weather guarantees are given. Lucky sat on her bed with her hands cupped together giving thanks and letting her mother and father know her big day had arrived. She gave thanks for her bountiful blessings, and especially mentioned the gift of Kevin's love, and that of all her friends.

Sam spent the night on a futon in Lucky's guest room. She awakened early and busily made pancakes and sausage for breakfast. Lucky tied her bathrobe, put her slippers on, and shuffled toward the kitchen, not yet surrendering to the excitement of her wedding day.

"Sam. I can't thank you and Clarice enough for all your help the last few weeks."

"This is the day you've dreamed of for so long, Lucky. I'm glad I could help. If I ever decide to settle down, I'm sure you'll return the favor. Will two pancakes be enough, Lucky?"

"Make it three. I may not eat again until the reception tonight."

While devouring the pancakes, they gossiped, laughed, and shared pleasant memories before deciding Sam would shower first.

Lucky returned to her bedroom where a half-packed suitcase rested on her bed. April is still tourist season in Fort Lauderdale, and time off is hard to get, so the newlyweds opted for a four day honeymoon in Orlando. She carefully folded jeans, shorts and T-shirts and added them to the suitcase. A garment bag with her evening dresses waited on a door hook. She gave their hotel confirmation one last glance, and put it in the outer side pocket of her luggage.

Kevin had taken Lucky to the *Islands of Adventure Theme Park* at *Universal Studios* before. When it came to riding the roller coasters, they shared something in common. They both enjoyed the first row of the rides, especially those that went the fastest, looped and turned the most.

Lucky took a shower and then sat in her favorite bedroom chair as Sam combed her hair. Her eyes moistened.

"Wipe the tear from your face, Lucky. Today is a joyous occasion and I'm getting ready to apply your makeup."

"This chair has what I hope are prophetic memories. I was reflecting on its sentimental value. It was a gift from my mother who sat in it as she groomed herself on her big day."

"Your mom groomed herself? You're fortunate a lovely assistant is available to help you."

"Oh? I hope the lovely assistant shows up soon or you'll be done, Sam."

"Be thankful today is your wedding day, or you'd be wearing lipstick all over your cheek, sweetie."

The two laughed and hugged before Lucky slipped into her wedding dress, a Vera Wang Twill Gazar Mermaid gown.

"You're a gem, Sam."

"Your gown is stunning."

Lucky reviewed her checklist to be sure she had everything. "I guess we're all set."

"Yes, and we better be, the limo just pulled up. I'm more nervous now than I was ten minutes ago." Her hands were moist as she opened her apartment door.

"Good afternoon, William. You remember Sam don't you? When I booked the limousine, I specifically requested you to be the driver."

"I appreciate your thoughtfulness, ma'am. Congratulations on your special day."

"Thank you, William," she said, handing him her suitcase. "This should do it."

She glanced around the room once more before closing the door for the last time as simply Nancy Larkin.

※

Clarice and Daniel sat in the second pew of the church. "Kevin is a handsome man," she whispered to Daniel.

"You have me in the same category as well, I hope," he said with a slight laugh. He placed her hand in his. "Love is grand, isn't it?"

"Couldn't be bettah darlin', couldn't be bettah."

Lucky looked splendid in her wedding gown. She stood in back of Sam at the entrance to the church, waiting for the wedding march. A minute later the organist began to play.

"Fulfilling a dream is minutes away, Lucky. I'm proud to stand next to you."

"Don't make me cry now, Sam."

Lucky proceeded down the aisle constantly looking left to right. She nodded to the guests on both sides as she passed. Kevin beamed as he stood and waited for his bride. He extended his hand as she neared.

The minister began the service with the traditional remarks extolling the institution of marriage. Kevin and Lucky then shared their sentiments of love and devotion toward each other. He placed an elegant diamond ring on Lucky's finger. She followed, placing a simple but meaningful wedding band on his. Minutes later, they officially became Mr. and Mrs. Kevin Preston.

The newlyweds embraced in the limousine as it neared the High Hopes Tavern. Outside, an excited crowd of invited guests and regular customers waited. They stepped out amid applause and cheers. They smiled and waved to acknowledge the cheerful crowd. Melanie had designed and created a gift for the couple. An eight foot archway of stephanotis, lilies, and baby's breath to decorate the entrance to the patio. The flowers' sweet fragrance permeated the air, adding to the festive atmosphere of the reception soon to begin.

"A glass of Sterling for the lovely, Mrs. Preston," Kevin asked?

"Yes, I would love one."

The couple had selected a bountiful buffet of shrimp, oysters on the half shell, baby lobster tails, tenderloin tips, and a variety of other mouthwatering delicacies for their reception. Antonio scheduled extra wait staff to serve the lavish buffet. A three tiered wedding cake with vanilla on the inside and a Kahlua flavored chocolate icing outside rested securely on a separate table nearby. Pete and Andy, a new bartender, tended the open bar with orders to pour guests whatever brand they wanted.

"Ladies and Gentlemen, my name is Smitty. As Kevin's best man, I'd like to propose a toast to the newlyweds. Since I got an early start on the cocktails, I'll keep my comments brief."

Clarice, Daniel, and a handful of others departed the dance floor as Mario approached the microphone.

"May I have your attention for a few minutes," he said.

"Do you think you still own the place?" Antonio taunted with laughter.

Mario giggled, "No, but I'm still better looking than the guy who does."

He gestured to quiet the applause and laughter.

"I'll be brief. I want to congratulate Lucky and Kevin and wish you both many years of happiness." The guests tapped forks against their water glasses. They applauded as Lucky and Kevin kissed on the lips and then looked toward Mario. He continued.

"I owned this establishment for many years. Often, I've been asked how I selected the name High Hopes Tavern. Generally my answer was simple. Today is a fitting day to provide a bit more detail for my selection."

"Brevity, Papa," Melanie chided.

"Lucky is the perfect example behind the name. One day she told me being a flight attendant provided her the opportunity to travel worldwide. However, her dream of a loving relationship eluded her. Like other people who frequent this tavern she hoped one night to meet a soul mate. Many people sit alone, telling themselves the person across the bar is getting better looking as the evening slips away. They listen in pain to a song that stirs memories of a lost love, or worse yet, living their life never at all experiencing the marvel it brings. For many people, when they fly solo in life a lot of hurt and loneliness boards with them. Despair sets in and they accept loneliness. Lucky dared to hope and was rewarded for her effort."

Mario caught Melanie as she lifted her eyebrow sending him a message. Similar to a parking meter, his time at the podium would soon expire.

"Yes, my friends, everyone can hope for the change they're searching for. Not necessarily through sitting in a tavern all day, drinking, but through the friendships and sense of family one can develop here. When Lucky met Kevin, he sparked a flame."

"Bad choice of words doncha think, Mario?" Kevin laughed." If I recall correctly, I was actually extinguishing a few flames at the time."

"Yeah, real bad play on words," he frowned. "I just didn't want to serve up a good drink and fine food. My goal was to serve up an ample portion of hope, for those who were hungry for it. Now, it's time for Lucky and Kevin Preston to dance to their favorite number."

"Thank you, Mario, for everything," Lucky said with a hug.

Lucky and Kevin arrived early at the tavern before her invited guests. She had left all of the arrangements for a special evening with friends up to Antonio. She sat at the corner of the bar with Kevin, watching the restaurant come alive.

"I'm excited, honey. At this moment, I'm recalling the time I went to my first Broadway musical. I sat reading my Playbill, watching as new arrivals filled the seats. I remember the excitement of the orchestra members tuning their instruments. Within minutes the trebles flirted with the basses. The curtain rose. The theatre would soon churn with song and dance." I felt a sense of exhilaration that could be sliced and passed out at a picnic.

On the patio, people gathered to witness the last rays of the sun. Boats lined up to wait for the draw bridge to open. Lucky turned to the TV where, several months before she had cheered for the Dolphins.

Her thoughts continued to drift as she recalled the first time she walked into High Hopes Tavern. She thought about all the changes in the lives all around her. She met and married Kevin. Mario had sold the restaurant to Antonio. Clarice married Daniel. Melanie graduated with honors and received her Bachelors in Interior Design. Sam was still Sam, comfortable with her life, and not in a hurry to marry.

Their guests arrived and enjoyed cocktails before heading for their tables in the Conch Shell Room. Once seated, Lucky rose to speak. Raul and two other waiters each popped a champagne bottle cork and served a glass to each.

"I'd like to propose a toast. To my loving Kevin," she said with a nod. She turned toward her guests. "To you, my dear friends. She patted her stomach. And to baby Preston developing inside me." Yes, my friends, I'm pregnant."

Clarice turned toward Kevin and Lucky. "Congratulations to you both. In my view, darlin', a new baby is a gesture of God's optimism."

Lucky continued. "I'm too grown up to believe we can always expect 'happily ever after' endings in our lives." She paused a moment. "I might be persuaded to believe in 'happy *right now*."

Mario stood up and raised his glass. "Here's to friendship, to love, and to a world where high hopes always triumph."

ABOUT THE AUTHOR

Ken Nunn

When asked how he felt qualified to write a novel mostly from the perspective of women, Ken had a ready response. "I was a feminist long before it was fashionable and have spoken up for every aspect of equal rights as long as I can remember. I've always been interested in women's views and worked throughout my airline career with talented, distinguished women at Eastern Airlines and later at Amadeus North America, Inc., a world leader travel technology company. You get thoroughly indoctrinated in the gospel of women's rights in 35 years.

"I also sought the advice of women while writing this novel. I'll leave it to the readers to tell me if I've captured the feminine essence with my characters."

Born and raised in New Jersey, Ken was transferred to Miami in 1981 with Eastern Airlines. Fort Lauderdale is home and his love for that city and travel inspired him to write his debut novel, High Hopes Tavern

Made in the USA
Las Vegas, NV
31 October 2020